TOMBSTONE, 1881

The Symbiont Time Travel Adventures Series

Book Two

———◆———

T.L.B. Wood

Cover and Book design by eBook Prep
www.ebookprep.com

ePublishing Works!
978-1-61417-836-1
February, 2016

DEDICATION

For Amy and Bobbi

CHAPTER 1

———————◆———————

I startled awake and stared, momentarily disoriented, into the darkness that surrounded me. It was only a second later that I recognized the familiar surroundings of my bedroom and felt the rapid beating of my heart begin to slow. I was cold, but that was not unusual for one of my kind—the result of a very slow metabolism. Taking a deep breath, I slowly let the air escape my lungs and with it went the tension in my body. The tortured dreams of my companion, Kipp, had buffeted me all through the night, and I lacked the will to block his thoughts from my mind.

I hazarded a quick peek over my shoulder; Kipp lay still, for the most part, except for a tiny twitching of his shoulder which had just recently undergone orthopedic surgery. Normally he would be awakened by my thoughts, but the medication he received for pain the previous evening had deepened his slumber.

With as little disturbance to the bed as possible, I slid out from beneath the sheets and bit back an exclamation when my bare feet hit the worn wooden planks of the floor. It was mid January and cold in this part of North Carolina. Local weather predictions called for snow by the weekend. Sliding my feet into some worn house shoes, I padded softly from the room, pulling the door almost shut in my wake.

Yawning, I found the familiar path to the kitchen and welcomed the soft glow of the overhead light. I'd frequently traveled in time to places with no electricity or running water; of the two, I found water—especially hot water—to be most missed.

This room, like all in my house, was small but oddly cozy. With my interest in things old, the shelves were filled with aged bottles and bits and pieces of junk that I'd found at antique stores and yard sales. The idea I was surrounded by the past was comforting, and I liked to think, as I stared at an amber colored bottle, that someone years ago had held the piece of glass or had placed a flower bouquet in it. Philo liked to think of me as practical, but I suspect I had more than a little of the wistful romantic in my soul.

While the coffee was brewing, I walked to the living room and checked the fireplace. Fortunately, I had visited it during the middle of the night for stoking, and there were a number of hot embers glowing from the ashes. I placed a couple of pieces of red oak on the grate and left them to make up their minds whether or not to succumb to the lurking fire.

Back in the kitchen, I inhaled deeply and almost salivated at the scent of the coffee. During my times of deprivation, I'd been called upon to drink many noxious brews and to be home, safe, with a cup of strong, black coffee seemed to me to be the most treasured pleasure of all. I sat at the scarred kitchen table and stared out the back window which overlooked an untended garden in the rear. Of course, this time of year, the ground was frozen, and I had little worry about when I would get time to cut the grass or pull weeds. With delight I spied a cardinal who was paying a visit to my solitary bird feeder. At least I had presence of mind to fill it with sunflower seed, and he attacked the bounty with greed. His bright red color was a nice contrast to the grey outside. But it was early, I thought to myself. This could be one of those cold, crisp days with a sky that is a bright, endless blue.

I propped my feet up on an adjacent chair and allowed

my mind to wander. With care, I did a gentle, sweeping canvas of the bedroom; Kipp was still asleep. But in the next moment, I could feel a wave go through his mind as he began to cycle into another relentless session of nightmares. Sitting there, I debated over whether to wake him or allow him to process all the mental debris with which he struggled. Both Juno and Philo had counseled me to let Kipp deal with his issues in his own good time. But it was hard. I mean, when you love someone, you don't want to see him in pain.

The fact I suffered, too, was of little concern. Yes, I was a telepath—a very talented one, or at least I'd been told—and Kipp's dreams buffeted my psyche as much as his...maybe more. But I knew I had the discipline to shut out his thoughts. Why I chose not to, I wondered, as I took another sip of coffee.

The thought hit me that I chose to remain connected and active with Kipp's mind because we had made a commitment to one another. And in my book, one does not run away and hide simply because there are rough roads to traverse. Kipp was my bonded partner, and I would be with him, at least mentally, as long as he needed me. The phone rang shrilly, and I rushed to grab it before the sound made its way to Kipp.

"Hello," I said, but the comment was not a question on my part. I recognized the vibrations from a distance and realized the caller was Philo. Distance caused our telepathic accuracy to suffer...with the exception of Kipp...and I only knew the caller because of an impression I formed.

"How are you this morning?" Philo's deep voice crossed the miles. He, too, lived in the general vicinity of Research Triangle Park but not in my neighborhood.

"Okay," I answered, walked over to pour more coffee. "Enjoying some hot coffee," I added. "Kipp is still asleep."

Philo was quiet for a moment. "I guess that's to be expected. The physical therapy each day is pretty taxing, and he is receiving pain medications pretty regularly." He paused before asking, "And his dreams?"

I didn't want to get into that, since I'd never appreciated a whiner. And to make comments about the dreams brought the inherent understanding that I was negatively affected. Since I knew I could handle the mental load, I hesitated to comment.

"I know you, Petra," Philo said. "You won't complain, but the reason I ask is to see if Kipp needs help. I recognize you are a complete hardhead, and that you are beyond needing anyone's assistance."

His voice dropped off while I mentally counted to ten. Either he was baiting me into losing my temper and revealing some tidbit for which he fished, or else he really meant what he said. That latter thought seemed a little sad to me.

"Kipp's dreams are tortured and alarming," I answered, taking a deep breath. "They don't seem to be dissipating as I had hoped."

"I was afraid of that," he answered. "When I saw you the other day when he was finishing therapy, I could feel the drain on you."

"I'm fine," I began, before he rudely cut me off.

"Yes, yes, yes; you're always just fantastic. But beyond that, I think Juno and I will drop by today and spend some time with you both." Unexpectedly, he hung up, not giving me an opportunity to argue or decline his arrogant plan to intrude into my life.

Angry now, I slammed my coffee cup on the counter so hard that the ceramic edge chipped off and skittered down the length of the tile. I guess I was fortunate I didn't break the tile since it was old and probably not in production any longer. In my irritation, I failed to sense Kipp, who had padded quietly into the room behind me.

"Don't you think you need to take it easy on the crockery?" he asked, his thoughts flowing with the ease of our bond into my agitated mind.

"What are you doing up?" I asked, dodging his question. Of course, lying and evasion was out of the question. Kipp could read every corner of my mind, and I never denied him access, even to the dark areas where I hid my thoughts of shame and remorse. He loved me, universally, and I he, so there was no need for artifice.

"I had another bad dream," he commented in his honest manner. "So I decided to watch you drink coffee, instead."

I took a bowl, filled it with fresh water, and placed it on the floor.

"Join me," I invited, resuming my seat.

Kipp limped forward, favoring the side of his body that had suffered injury, and bent his head down to the bowl. He began to lap thirstily, and the sound was soothing to me; it was the sound of life. There had been a time, and in the not too distant past, when I thought Kipp would die. His strength and resolve served him well, and he was here with me, even if he still carried the mental and physical scars of our recent historical venture.

He stopped drinking and turned his massive head in my direction. The upright ears seemed even more erect, and he tilted his head slightly to the left as he gazed at me. His auburn coat gleamed, despite the slightly less robust form of his body. The slanted amber eyes, ringed with dark fur, blinked at me.

"I love you, Petra," his thoughts came to me.

I rose and went to where he stood and sat down on the cold floor. Kipp managed to lie down next to me, after a minor struggle to get his reconstructed joints to work. He allowed his head to drop into my lap, and his eyes closed as I gently scratched through the fur on his head.

"I love you, too, Kipp," I said.

I lived among humans and could easily be mistaken for one of their kind. To their ignorant eyes, Kipp was my dog...a faithful companion. For reasons of history, symbionts, as a rule, kept their nature concealed from humans. Here I was, sitting on my kitchen floor, holding Kipp. I was over 400 years of age; Kipp, at half my age, was a novice, but yet he typically was my superior in terms of judgment and reasoning...a fact he was about to demonstrate once again.

"I think it is a good idea for Juno and Philo to try and help me," he commented.

I allowed my hand to gently caress the bare areas on his shoulder and leg where the fur had been shaved for surgery. The shaved areas felt prickly and unpleasant to my palm. Looking down, I saw tiny bits of orange colored fuzz trying to take hold and flourish with new hair growth. I felt sad in the knowledge that I was unable to help Kipp with his mental struggle. As his bonded symbiont, I felt I should have been able to perform that duty for my partner. Kipp twisted his head and opened his amber eyes to gaze at me.

"Petra, consider the fact you are too close to be objective." He turned his head slightly so that I would scratch the base of his left ear. "Ah, that feels good," he groaned. "I think the opinions of others, especially a fellow lupine like Juno, will be of help."

It was with some shame that I realized I was probably being selfish in my need to be the primary healing factor for Kipp. Well, symbionts were subject to just as many foibles as were humans. Except for the amazing Kipp, who was, indeed, unique. Kipp, for his part, followed my shameful thoughts down into the deep recesses of mind where I hoped to corral the more distasteful aspects of my flawed nature. I felt his curious fascination as the thought dropped into a mental box, and I shut the door behind it. Kipp managed to stretch and yawn.

"I may need some help getting up," he commented. "It's hard for me to get a purchase on these slick floors."

After gently displacing his head, I stood and managed to grab him beneath his belly and lift so that he could get his feet underneath him. Kipp was large and even though he'd lost weight since the accident, it was a struggle for both of us.

"I may have to rig up a block and tackle," I commented with humor.

He wanted to know what that was, so I filled my mind with pictures of them and then added humorous pictures of us struggling in various funny scenarios. Kipp's tongue lolled out with a good humored lupine version of a laugh.

"Well, if you don't quit baby sitting me and sitting around all day eating cookies and ice cream, I'm gonna need a block and tackle to get you off the sofa," he commented.

"Gee, Kipp, that's kinda rough," I replied, feeling stung. My hands fell down to my usually trim hips, and I realized that I'd not had on a pair of jeans for weeks and had reverted to baggy sweat pants with elastic waist bands.

"Don't worry, Petra. I'll love you even when you can't get through the door. But, I'm better now, so it's time you get out and exercise. Why don't you go to the fitness center at Technicorps? I have to go for water therapy, and you really don't have to sit and stare at me."

He walked to the door and waited for me to open it, since crunching down to use the dog door was too much of a strain. Wrapping myself in my bathrobe, I followed him outside and watched as the condensation of my breath billowed into little white jets in the frigid air. From across the yard, Kipp's thoughts came to me.

"We will be getting back to work, eventually, so you need to think of yourself as being in training. At least, that's what I think of my recovery." He discretely disappeared behind a hedge to take care of his morning constitutional.

I confess, I'd not allowed myself to think of work since I'd not known when or if Kipp would be able to time shift. Since the mere effort of time traveling was so massive and all encompassing, I knew he would not be able to manage for the foreseeable future. Yes, he was amazing and unique, but even Kipp was, well, a symbiont and not immortal.

Leaving him to his devices, since his fur coat was much warmer than my thin bathrobe, I reentered my small kitchen and poured another cup of coffee. With mug in hand, I wandered down the narrow hallway towards the back of the house. Entering my bedroom, I allowed the robe to fall to the floor and opened the closet door to reveal a full length mirror. I pulled my t-shirt up and my sweatpants down. To my dismay, my hips had grown in the time I became nursemaid to an ailing Kipp. I could feel

Kipp's sense of wry amusement in my head and he allowed himself to share in the moment.

"Go away!" I commanded. Even symbionts had a right to some privacy, I thought with extreme irritation at my companion.

In disgust, I reassembled my baggy clothes and returned to the kitchen. As I reclaimed my chair, I thought, with dismay, that I'd really allowed my discipline, fragile as it already might be, to slip. Kipp was right: even if we never travelled together again, there was no need to compromise my health by not observing some decent practices. With a renewed sense of focus, I promised myself that when Philo and Juno left after their visit today, I'd go for a jog-walk for at least two miles. That seemed to be a reasonable place to begin. Kipp's approval drifted in from the cold outside.

To work off my sloth and ill temper, I wandered through the house, picking up dirty clothes which had been thrown on the floor. Realizing I had a full load, I stuffed everything in my hands in the washing machine and started the cycle. I'd never been one to sort laundry, feeling that to be a poor use of time. Pleased with the effort, I managed to wash a sink full of dirty dishes and wipe down the counters. A slight buzzing in my head told me that Philo and Juno were not too far distant, and with that thought in mind, I started a fresh pot of coffee. Kipp limped in, nudging the slightly ajar back door open with his muzzle. He looked around with a grunt of satisfaction.

"Things look better already," he commented.

"You could be a little more help," I answered, staring him down.

"I'm not sure how," he said, whining slightly.

"Don't let the fact you lack opposable thumbs be a hindrance." I was scolding, but only in a mock way. With a mild dart of surprise, I realized that the goal directed activity had energized me. Feeling a little frisky, I dug in the cabinet and found a scented candle which I lit and carried into the small living room. Kipp limped after me and, after circling slowly, lay down with care on the small woolen rug.

I disappeared momentarily to change into sweat pants that were minus a large hole where my left cheek was located; a clean sweatshirt completed the new look. As I brushed my teeth, I glanced up at my reflection. The few extra pounds had actually added some color to my cheeks; with the prominent nose I inherited from my mother, a little more rounded face nicely balanced out the large central feature. My dark hair fell over my shoulders, and I pulled the mass off my neck and twisted it into a coil which I clipped to the crown of my head with an octopus clip. Overall, I felt noble for the extra effort I'd made.

The tingling in my mind increased; Philo must be pulling up outside. I'd finished...and just in time. If I ever bothered to spend any significant amount of time on my appearance, I might have to rethink my entire approach to life.

CHAPTER 2

Philo Marshall, a friend of many years acquaintance, didn't bother to knock. By the time I entered the living room, he was standing in front of the fireplace, holding his hands out to warm in what had developed into a pleasantly brisk fire. He turned at my approach and smiled broadly.

"Morning," he commented in his typically brief manner.

Juno met Kipp in the middle of the room, after Kipp slowly rose from his comfortable spot in front of the fire. Juno touched noses with Kipp as do lupine symbionts as a friendly hello. I could feel his gentle attachment to her and an almost overwhelming sense of protectiveness. Juno had served as his major lupine role model after he was launched, unexpectedly, from 70,000 years in the past to the present day continental United States. To say there was culture shock would be an understatement. I, of course, as his partner could help with the transition, but even more so could one of his kind.

Juno had, in her sweet natured and perceptive way, taken a young Kipp under her wing. I knew she had discovered amazing depths to him and was intelligent enough to keep many aspects of his nature under wraps. In fact, she and Philo—and maybe Fitzhugh—were the only ones to recognize Kipp's truly unique character. Time and genetic degradation had taken a toll upon our species, but Kipp was refreshingly and alarmingly pure. I freely confess he was not only more skilled than was I, but also he was simply better in terms of heart and character.

Kipp, consummate gentleman that he was, led the ancient Juno over to the wool rug in front of the fireplace and waited until she could maneuver her arthritic body into a comfortable huddle on the floor. He followed her down and ended with his head lightly resting on her flank. As I watched, I read his thoughts and realized a tiny pang of longing for his long deceased mother. Juno recognized it, too, and moved her grey face closer to his.

Philo and I had the vocal cords to communicate with spoken language. I was fluent in seven languages and had a smattering of several others...the benefit of having lived over 400 years. While we chose to speak English to one another, Kipp and Juno could follow our thoughts and were murmuring to each other in their unique lupine language. The reverse was also true: I understood their whimpers and barks but could not speak them myself. None of the spoken words were necessary, since our telepathic communications were all entangled, but it helped to stay fluent in language since it was a necessary part of the work of traveling symbionts.

I sat on the sofa and Philo sat next to me. For a few minutes he made comments about the weather; this, of course, was a delaying tactic. It is almost impossible for one symbiont to fool another. The room was becoming toasty warm, and I glanced at the large double window on the front wall of the room. The panes were frosted as the cold air outside battled with the warmth on the glass that radiated from within my little house. It painted a cozy picture, and I glanced down at Kipp and Juno. The elder lupine's eyes had drifted shut but she was not asleep.

"I thought we might go to town," Philo began, crossing his long legs. "Kipp and Juno need time together, and we will only be in their way if we hang around."

I clearly remembered a time when I would have felt alarm sirens blare in my head at the thought I should relinquish Kipp to anyone other than myself. And truth be told, Kipp felt the same way. But he had learned to trust Juno and others in this brave new world, and I needed to allow him to expand his relationships.

However, it was cold outside, and I felt lazy and was honestly in no mood to go on a snipe hunt in order to allow alone time for Kipp and Juno. I felt I had the mental discipline to stay out of their moment and would prefer to be in my bedroom reading a book. Of course, I didn't have to say this to Philo, since he was reading my thoughts.

"Come on," he said, in what he obviously thought was a beguiling tone. "It'll be fun. And you can look for some new running shoes."

For all my current bout of ill temper, I was usually fairly even keeled and almost shocked myself when I replied, "I don't need to be managed."

Philo's smile froze on his face.

"If Kipp and Juno need to be alone, that's fine. But I don't need you talking to me like I'm a three year old, and we're going to get ice cream or something." I felt really heated and stopped myself with effort. Kipp's head rose from Juno's flank and his concern for me radiated across the room.

"Petra, what's wrong?" he asked, his amber eyes taking on an almost human like expression of concern.

"Nothing, Kipp," I replied, trying to soften my tone. With that, I rose and walked to the small hallway closet and pulled out my jacket. "Okay, Philo. You wanted to go, so let's go." Not waiting, I walked outside and inhaled deeply as I tried to retrain my focus. Deliberately, I shut out the thoughts of my friends and walked down the uneven sidewalk to where Philo's ancient Honda Civic rested at the curb. He'd not locked it, so I hopped inside and waited.

The driver's side door opened and Philo sat down behind the steering wheel. He started to look at me but resisted the urge. He, too, was blocking his thoughts from me. In contemporary symbiont fashion, we politely did not intrude unless invited. Kipp was the only one I allowed unfettered access to my thoughts, and I only did that because I wanted him to remain in what for him was a natural symbiotic state.

Philo didn't speak. He turned the key; the engine coughed, alarmingly, in a petulant fit of minor rebellion. Finally, he encouraged the Civic to life by pumping the gas pedal and the wheels spun into action. He almost skidded away from the curb in his typically fast, abrupt manner of driving. As we disappeared down the street, I felt Kipp touch my mind one more time.

"It's okay, Kipp," I reassured him. "I'm just out of sorts, but not with you...never with you. Enjoy Juno, and when you see me again, I'll be in a better mood." He gave me a mental head nod in return.

We approached the outskirts of Durham, and Philo exited the interstate and veered in the direction of the mall. Philo turned on the radio, and we listened to some crackly 70's station as he located a place to park.

"I'm hungry," he commented and walked ahead to the food court. I felt his pleasure as he spied a Manchu Wok and lined up to order.

"Do you want anything?" he asked, looking over his shoulder at me. I shook my head in the negative.

I staked out a table since the place was filling up, even though the mall had just opened. Perhaps the cold weather had caused everyone's appetite to soar. Philo brought his tray to the small table, and I almost sighed at the aroma of the piled up vegetables and lo mein noodles. Philo was, like most humanoid symbionts, a vegetarian by choice and carnivore by necessity. I'd found through my travels back in time that I was compelled to eat whatever was made available...and that included many types of meat, fowl and fish, as well as some other things I'd rather forget.

"Are you sure you don't want some," he asked, his dark eyes peering over the table at me. "I brought an extra egg roll," he added, pointing at it with the fork.

"No, I'm on a diet," I replied, shrugging my shoulders.

"Why? You don't look fat to me," he commented, staring

at me for longer than necessary to draw such a conclusion.

"My jeans are too tight. Haven't you noticed I only wear sweat pants at the present?" I was starting to feel irritated at him. He was supposed to be able to read my mind and here I was having to explain myself to him. It was tedious and stupid. He sighed and put the fork down. Sitting back, he crossed his arms and stared at me again.

"I know you want to help Kipp," he began, after taking a deep breath.

I didn't respond since there was no need. Kipp was my number one concern now and in the future. As my bonded symbiont, his welfare was primary.

"These bad dreams that are disturbing Kipp are being initiated by you, Petra," he commented, holding up his hand when he saw the expression on my face. "Let me finish. Juno has been working with Kipp during his recovery, and she believes that your issues with losing your baby and then Tula are driving your current state in response to almost losing Kipp. It's all unconscious on your part, but due to Kipp's amazing depth of connection with you, he feels it, even if he can't put it all into perspective." Philo took a deep breath, his food all but forgotten. "In other words, all that psychic energy makes him feel bad, and he experiences it in his dreams."

I felt my face flush hot and tears welled up behind my hazel eyes.

"You can't think I would ever hurt Kipp," I said, struggling with what Philo and Juno obviously believed to be the truth. "I would let him go before I'd harm him in any way, Philo."

He nodded his head.

"I know you would, Petra. But I don't think you need to be so hard on yourself. Kipp is not a child, and what he's experiencing just furthers the bond between the two of you. But you know, as a bonded symbiont, it behooves you to be honest within yourself so that there is clarity in your relationship with Kipp."

I stared back at him. Philo was one person I knew I could

trust and was the closest relationship I had, outside of Kipp.

"And you know what I mean, Petra. All those dark cubbyholes of your mind are places where excess garbage resides. And if you and Kipp have to put your lives on the line again, as happened in Far Point Colony, there can't be any lingering mysteries."

I knew he was telling me the harsh reality that only can come at the hands of a best friend. He looked at the expression on my face and rose. As I watched, he dumped his uneaten meal into the trash and walked over to the coffee bar and ordered. After a short wait, he returned and nodded at me.

"Let's go," he said, handing me a large black coffee. Obviously he heard my comment about my hips and was respectful.

I trailed him back outside and a moment later we were in the Civic. Philo turned the dial on the heater to the maximum heat, and a moment later we swayed off, in the direction of the interstate.

"I think we'll take a little loop in the country," he commented.

We drove along after that, as he headed north. When we reached the Butner-Creedmore exit, he left the interstate and turned left towards Butner. He obviously planned a large loop, not a little one. The heater was beginning to burn my feet, and he turned it down a notch.

"One thing about little cars," he commented, "they put out the heat."

It fell quiet again, and I mentally ticked off the things I needed to do. My own car was woefully neglected. Typically, I walked the two miles to the Technicorps building where our symbiont community worked and planned. Sometimes, I biked. But with Kipp's injuries, I had resorted to driving. The tires on my car were bald and I was about 20,000 miles past a needed oil change. I knew I couldn't avoid the obvious any longer.

"I'll admit, when Kipp was injured, I thought he was going to die." There, I said it.

"Tell me about it," he commanded, swerving the car around a mourning dove that refused to yield the right of way on the lonely county road.

"You know all about it, Philo," I said, my voice taking on a slight whine. "I was debriefed more times that I can count."

"Tell me about it."

I took a deep breath and turned my head so that I watched the passing country vista. It was winter and the trees were bare, skeletal, with bark darkened by the cold. The hilly terrain of the piedmont was covered with dead, faded grass.

"It's like in slow motion, the way it replays in my mind. I was being dragged off by Sir Edward, who was completely demented. Kipp only knew I was in danger. I kept, in my mind, calling out to him—no, make that ordering him—to stop his run to defend me. At the last minute Edward swung out with a club and caught Kipp in the shoulder. I felt the pain of the blow shudder through me as Kipp fell away in the brush. He was helpless, and I was unable to protect him but knew I would die trying."

I took another deep breath, my shoulders rising and falling with effort.

"Thank God for Perdy. If she'd not arrived and shot Edward, Kipp would be dead and I'd have not made it home."

I hazarded a glance at Philo, who continued to stare ahead at the winding road. Shrugging my shoulders, I added, "That's about it."

He took his eyes from the road and stared at me, hard. It was all I could do to not grab the steering wheel before we ended up sideways in a ditch or halfway across someone's rutted, fallow field.

"So, that's about it," he commented, finally taking his eyes off of me and glancing at the road. A quick jerk of the steering wheel yanked the small car back into the correct lane. We were approaching the small town of Butner. I knew, from having made this journey before, that Philo intended a loop through Butner to pick up a back road that would wind through the piedmont's sloping hills to eventually deposit us in Durham. I hoped he'd not forgotten that I was in need of running shoes.

"Only you would condense something so complex into a few, neat, concise words," he commented, his voice tight and controlled. "If you can bother to think outside your safe, little box, you might consider the fact that the reason Kipp is having such difficulty with his sleep cycles, has more to do with you and less with him."

"What do you mean?" I asked, irritated at his tone of voice but curious, as was typical of my species. Our boundless curiosity had led many of us widely astray over the centuries.

"You are struggling with what happened in your mind and your subconscious. After having lost Tula, it would be understandable that the fear of losing Kipp would be grossly disturbing to your psyche."

Tula...my dear Tula. Yes, Philo was correct in that I still had much grief over her death and felt personally responsible. She died trying to defend me...and that was the comparison to be made here. Kipp, too, was almost killed in trying to defend me. A symbiotic bond between members of my species was such a complicated matter that it defies logical explanation. I loved Kipp, just as I loved Tula, but in a different way. Tula was my first bonded partner and would always have a special place in my memories.

"So, since the wheels in your brain are finally turning, have you reached any conclusions?" Philo asked. This time, he kept his eyes on the road.

"Both Tula and Kipp were put in danger because of my choices," I stated frankly. "Maybe I'm everything I've been accused of being....reckless, brash, impulsive." I reached over and turned up the heater setting on the dashboard. Suddenly, I was cold.

Philo took a deep breath and exhaled slowly. He released the steering wheel with his right hand and reached over to clasp my hand with his. "You are everything a successful symbiont must be to do the work for which God created us. We are investigators...travelers in time...and our business is to find the truth. Many of us live a safe existence...at least I know I do. But you are a traveler in the best sense of the word and risk is your business, Petra." He turned his dark eyes on me and sought my face. "You are doing what is natural, my dear."

I bowed my head and studied my knees. For an instance, I glanced up and saw the edifice of John Umstead Hospital as we breezed past. A few patients were walking outside, despite the brisk weather. I hoped they had adequate clothing, I thought, the idea an idle one.

"Thanks, Philo. You somehow can put everything in perspective for me when I get stuck." I smiled at him, aware that my lower lip was trembling slightly, despite my efforts to quell the movement. Over three hundred years of mutual acquaintance was nothing to lightly discard.

Philo took a deep breath and his knuckles turned white as he gripped the steering wheel more tightly. "You, at times, tend to forget the unusual nature of Kipp. I think it's because you are so close to him. But his abilities are so advanced past the rest of our community, that he will absorb your distress like a sponge, whether you want him to or not. "

We left Butner proper and Philo accelerated along the two lane country road. At times, the brush alongside the paved highway slapped the bruised doors of the little car. Philo might be my oldest friend on earth, but he simply terrified me with his driving skills...or lack of. The heater worked with a vengeance, and my feet felt as if they were on fire. I glanced down to see my toes moving beneath the fabric of the worn shoes.

"I thought we were going to buy me some new shoes," I commented, recalling how this day had started with my resolution to regain some semblance of physical fitness.

"We will, but I wanted to have this talk with you first. Juno is with Kipp and is trying to help him understand the dream issues with which he's been struggling. My job, difficult as it is to deal with your hard head, was to help you, too."

I rolled my eyes up and relaxed back against the seat. A broken spring threatened to assault my left buttocks, and I tried to squirm to a more comfortable position.

"I guess, unless the Twelve tell me I can't, Kipp and I will travel again when he is whole. So I need some running shoes, Philo."

He gave a soft grunt and nodded his head.

CHAPTER 3

Between the gymnasium at Technicorps and the uneven, broken sidewalks of my neighborhood, I began a program of exercises to build muscle and rev up my naturally slow metabolism. Symbionts require much less food than would a comparably sized human due to the slow fire that burns in our bodies, thus helping us to live for centuries.

The cool weather had not broken its grip, and Kipp was still not able to walk the two miles to Technicorps. We piled into my ancient car…at least I'd managed to get some decent tires and an oil change before something critical fell off in the road one day. The drive only took a few minutes, and I dropped Kipp off at the front door while I looked for a parking place. In keeping with my new regimen, I parked as far away from the entrance as possible and walked vigorously across the lot, swinging my arms to help with the cold as much as to burn calories.

I made my way directly to the physical therapy area and nodded to Tom Hughes, the veterinarian who was supervising Kipp's recovery. Tom and I went back many years, and I knew him to be a competent symbiont who remained on top of the most current research available to minister to the medical needs of the lupines in our ranks.

"Hi, Tom," I said.

"Cold out, isn't it?" he replied, looking at the bright red

circles on my cheeks from the exposure to the brisk air. Turning, he led me to the pool where one of the larger male therapists was working to support Kipp, who was dog paddling in the warm water. They had tried a harness before, but Kipp didn't like the feeling of confinement and insisted on another method. It was about all I could do to get him to accept a leash and collar when he was posing as my loyal dog to all human eyes.

Kipp turned his head at my approach and lolled his tongue out in a moment of mock panting. But he was very strong and vigorous and pushing against the water today, harder than before. I tried not to wince with pain when empathetically feeling the damaged areas of his shoulder pull in response. Tom, on the other hand, was staying focused on Kipp so that he could evaluate progress.

"Do you need something for pain, Kipp?" he asked, propelling the thought across the distance.

"Nope," Kipp grunted in reply. "I don't like the way it makes me feel," he added, so that Tom wouldn't assume he was just being tough. "And you don't need to hover like a mother hen," Kipp added, his amber eyes finding mine.

I gave a half wave and decided to head up to the gym and work out. I saw a few humans who were employed at Technicorps and was amazed, as always, that we symbionts could disguise ourselves to this degree so as to be unnoticed by the dominant species on the planet. When they looked at me, they saw a young woman—anywhere from mid twenties to mid thirties in age—with a dash of freckles across a too large nose, hazel eyes with flecks of gold and green and a tumble of dark hair that fell past shoulder level. The humans thought the lupine presence just indicated Technicorps to be a pet friendly environment and several brought dogs from home to rest in offices or cubicles; one brave spirit had an aquarium containing a 4 foot long corn snake named Lucy. I respected most forms of life on the planet but confess that snake was not one of my favorites. Kipp, on the other hand, found her fascinating and tried to divine what was going on in that slender serpentine head. After hours of frustrating himself, he decided snakes thought about food, and that was about the end of it. Dogs, on the other hand, were more complex and enjoyed the role of pack member with humans. Kipp, before his injury, would engage some of the canines in typical dog play. But he confessed to me that the dogs were uniformly confused by him...the smell and appearance seemed right but not his life energy.

After lifting some weights and running on the treadmill, I took a quick shower. I checked the time and realized that Kipp was not finished with therapy. Philo was in meetings all day, so there was no conceivable way to intrude upon his world. I hadn't seen Fitzhugh in a while and decided, on a whim, to visit him in the basement dwelling I thought of as his lair. In any case, it would be nice to see Lily.

Since I figured I'd worked out enough, I avoided the stairs and took the elevator. When the doors opened on the basement level, I took the familiar path of right and then left; in just a few seconds, I pushed open the door to the library and hall of records where all documentation about our species was housed. Fitzhugh, who was pushing 1400 years old, had devoted most of his life to this one endeavor. And he did so with the fervor of a fanatic. His young apprentice, Peter, had little drive and was only here because he needed the work. Besides that, his overprotective mother had forbade him to assume the live of a traveling symbiont, like Kipp and me.

Fitzhugh had once been what I thought of as my nemesis. But during the time I was preparing with Kipp to make our first investigational journey together, Fitzhugh softened towards me to a great degree. I never knew why but was relieved. However, a few of my past lapses in good judgment still lingered as barriers between me and Fitzhugh. He would never forget the episode when I altered an ancient Egyptian wall mural. I, at the time, thought the main character might look nice in a sassy fedora and adjusted the painting—call it a whim and a passing impulsivity of youth.

I gave a deep sigh. Symbionts were no less likely to be totally foolish and self-absorbed than were humans, I supposed. Age had tempered my judgment…that and my bond with Kipp. When he literally saved me, 70,000 years in the past, I had no way of knowing he would become my most critical ally. Unlike contemporary symbionts, Kipp's genes were not degraded by centuries of breeding in a relatively tight pool. Symbionts had pretty remarkable talents but all of us paled in comparison to the amazing Kipp. I felt as if I was daily learning something new about his capabilities. I was probably one of the worst choices available to be a companion and tutor to the novice Kipp, but he had fixed his connection on me, and there it remained.

A rustling sound at my feet disturbed my reverie, and a moment later I yelped in pain as a young cat wrapped her lithe body around my right leg and began biting while kicking with her back legs. I tried, to no avail, to hop my way free, but the cat was determined to make her presence known. The sound of deep laughter caused me to look up.

"I see Lily is giving you a loving greeting," Fitzhugh remarked. He was exceptionally tall and remained straight in posture despite his age. Dark eyes, still sharp as those of an owl, peered at me from beneath heavy, gray brows.

"Yeah, it seems so," I commented as I stooped down and managed to pluck Lily from my leg. "You'd think she'd be grateful to me for rescuing her; instead, I have to put up with an attack kitty."

Fitzhugh laughed again and reached out for the mischievous Lily, who, despite her behavior with the rest of us, was always gentle with the old symbiont. He draped her across his shoulder, and she began to purr so loudly I could hear her from a few steps away. Kipp had been her original rescuer, but we left her with Fitzhugh during our trip to Lands Point Colony. He fell so obviously in love with the little tabby striped wad of fur that Kipp didn't have the heart to reclaim her. The cat spent her days racing up and down the corridors of the library as Fitzhugh mock scolded her for numerous infractions of his rules.

"She chewed off the corner of one of my oldest manuscripts that dates back to ancient Greece," he commented as he idly stroked her soft fur. "I think I need you and Kipp to take her back to your house."

I knew, of course, that he was baiting me. "Oh, no way, Fitzhugh. You're stuck with her."

He gave a soft sigh and turned to walk to his desk. Unlike most of the offices in Technicorps that were predictably modern, Fitzhugh's area was filled with antiques; his centuries old desk was made of venerable English oak.

I followed him and dropped into an overstuffed chair without being invited. It wasn't too long ago that he would have run me off from his space. But now, he ignored my presence in a way that was comfortable. He knew I didn't require entertainment, and he had none to offer. His hapless assistant wandered up and was promptly sent off to fetch a pot of hot tea. Yes, there was something decidedly genteel about Fitzhugh.

"How's Kipp?" he asked as he carefully opened a large binder. Dust particles flew up from the stacked documents within and were caught in the glow of the desk light. Fitzhugh turned his head and gave a polite cough.

"He's coming along. As soon as I don't think he'll get hurt by Lily trying to climb up his leg, I'll bring him down here. He always enjoyed the library." I started to add, "and time spent with you," but I thought Fitzhugh would think I was being overly ingratiating and would snap my head off. He lacked a touchy-feely component in his makeup…except for his love for the wild thing, Lily.

Fitzhugh, Philo and Juno were the only three symbionts who knew the totality of Kipp's nature. Even though my own history with Fitzhugh was rocky, Philo trusted him completely, and my experience to date was that he was worthy of the trust. Fitzhugh helped the rest of us, through finding old documents, to understand Kipp's unusual ability to plant thoughts, telepathically, in the minds of others. This ability was probably once common among the ancients of our species but had been lost over the centuries.

Peter arrived with a fragile china teapot balanced on a tray, with two cups and a sugar and creamer service. The young man politely nodded and inquired after my health before Fitzhugh sent him on another errand. As the door to the library closed behind a departing Peter, Fitzhugh and I were left in silence. He took on the chore of pouring out, since he was the host. We both took a moment to prepare the Earl Grey to our mutual liking.

"I get the feeling something is bothering you, Petra," he began, sitting back in his chair. Fitzhugh took a sip of the tea and gave a deep sigh. "I still need to work with Peter on how to make a perfect cup of tea."

I laughed softly. "I'm sure it's fine," I commented before tasting the brew, which was hot enough to mildly scald my lips. "Very good," I added.

"You have uneducated taste buds," Fitzhugh remarked with a frown. Lily hopped down from his shoulders and began sniffing at the tea pot. No doubt, there would be cat hair in the tea before long.

I stared back at him, not willing to be drawn into a discussion of all my many faults. To him, due to the massive age difference, I seemed to be a willful, ignorant child. If only I would follow his dictates, life as we both knew it would be vastly improved. The steam from the tea tickled my nose, and I inhaled the unique fragrance of bergamot.

"But as I said, you seem unsettled," he began again. "Can I help in any way?"

I was so shocked I almost shouted in reply. As long as I had known him, I'd never encountered a moment where he offered to listen and give compassionate counsel. Usually, he was telling me and everyone else what to do, how to do it, and explain, in advance, what I would be doing incorrectly.

Impulsively, I responded. "I've been experiencing mental conflict, apparently, and unfortunately it's made its way to Kipp's dreams."

Fitzhugh took another sip of tea before carefully replacing the cup on the desk. He gave a deep sigh and sat forward, resting his elbows on the wooden surface.

"Your connection with Kipp is so unique that there will be moments that seem inexplicable to the rest of us." He peered at me with dark eyes.

I nodded my head and wrapped both hands around the fragile tea cup. My hands felt cold…that had happened a lot lately.

"We have learned to compartmentalize our thoughts and feelings, and in the give and take of polite symbiont society, we don't intrude unless invited," Fitzhugh commented. "To do otherwise would invite chaos. Kipp, in his innocence, does not understand boundaries…no, let me restate that. He is learning to respect them with us but not with you. He enjoys unfettered access to all parts of your mind…even to the dark corner where Petra Goodgame would deface an invaluable piece of history by painting a fedora where one was not planned." Fitzhugh sighed. "And in any case, it was historically inaccurate."

I rolled my eyes slightly and shrugged my shoulders. "Fitzhugh, I felt it was important to not completely deprive Kipp of what was natural to him. Once upon a time, all symbionts behaved in a manner like he does."

"I understand, Petra, and am not critical of you. I think, given the unusual circumstances, that you are doing the right thing. And I have to believe it is difficult for you to allow him to get in all those places in your mind where dark images and thoughts lurk." He sat back and resumed sipping his tea. "I respect you for that. I recognize I would not be willing to do the same."

I felt an unexpected wash of color flash on my cheeks and across my large nose. Don't cry, I thought to myself.

"So, my thought would be that the issues you both are having right now would be natural for Kipp…part of his expected experience." Fitzhugh smiled at me, a rarity. "So why don't you trust him? I personally think he can handle it."

Before I could respond, the door to the library swung back with a bang, and Peter raced in, his head down as he passed us. "Forgot my wallet," he muttered as he walked to the back of the room.

Fitzhugh looked at me and sighed. "He would forget his head if it were not attached by his neck," he commented, raising the heavy eyebrows that were matted with gray and white hair.

"For you and Kipp, your existence is shaped around time shifting and exploring mysteries. And I think that will continue for many, many years until one or the other of you decides to start a family." He ignored the startled look on my face. "I'm not unaware that you were married and a mother, Petra, but you might choose to go that route again one day in the future. And certainly Kipp might like to have his own family, complete with children."

He carefully maneuvered the tea pot and warmed up his brew; I waved away any more for myself. Lily carefully maneuvered herself until she was curled in his lap, ready for a nap.

"Kipp is not done yet, and neither are you, Petra. You don't need to totally let yourself go in this fashion," he commented, waving at my sweatshirt and sweat pants.

I began to feel irritated at his remarks, but then I remembered that he was saying nothing to me that I hadn't already said to myself. Yes, he was right. My work—mine and Kipp's—was just beginning. There were countless places to go and many mysteries to investigate.

I rose from the comfortable chair and nodded. "Thank you, Fitzhugh. I enjoyed the tea." I turned to leave. "When Kipp is a little further along, I'll bring him to visit Lily."

I started to take the elevator and instead pushed the door open into the stairwell. Maybe six flights wouldn't kill me.

CHAPTER 4

I'd spent some cold winters in my lifetime, but this particular winter in North Carolina was colder than average for the climate. Kipp, in between time at physical therapy, would hang out on the woolen rug in front of the fireplace. I, having regained my momentum, began jogging. It had been my preference for years to run or bicycle when the weather was cooler versus the humid heat of summer.

I had a human friend who did occasional handyman work at my little house, and he managed to keep me stocked in firewood due to the involvement of his brother who was clearing acreage on some land up near Creedmore. It was quite a treat, and both he and his brother refused payment. They were older gentlemen and looked upon me as one would a daughter. I'm not certain if their feelings for me would have changed if they had been aware that I was not human.

One morning, I completed my run and entered the house through the kitchen door. Kipp's mind met me as I pulled off my parka and tossed it over the back of a chair. I put a kettle on the stove, thinking a cup of tea with honey would just about make the morning complete. Rummaging in the cupboard, I found a tin with some English Breakfast loose tea, a favorite of mine due to the mild taste.

It is difficult to describe the manner in which symbionts

communicate and comprehend the language of humans. Symbionts, being natural telepaths, understand one another's thoughts, regardless of language used; the actual intent of the thoughts is communicated. It is in this manner that I could, for example, understand the thoughts of a human who perhaps spoke Japanese, a language for which I lack any sort of proficiency. Kipp, for all intents and purposes, did not possess the ability to comprehend English, my primary language. But he comprehended my thoughts. Fitzhugh told me once that no lupine symbiont had mastered actual language, besides the unique one spoken by our lupine companions to one another.

Kipp and I had found that he could not enjoy television for just that very reason. The one dimensional medium contained no thoughts to which he could connect. And with his inability to understand spoken language, watching a movie was a useless experience unless I filled my head with the images, dialog and feelings, and he tapped into my brain.

Kipp seemed preoccupied, so after spooning a dollop of honey in the hot tea, I wandered into the living room. The fire was cranking out a nice, even heat and Kipp's eyes were half closed as he stared, mesmerized, into the yellow and red tongues of flame. The large front window was covered with a mild sheen of frost that caused the light from outside to be slightly distorted as it fell across the wooden floor.

"What's up?" I asked, plopping into a wing chair that I'd rescued from some antique store many years ago. The subtle armrest was worn, with the base of the chair almost showing through the shiny fabric. Really, I thought, I needed to get this and a few other things reupholstered.

"I was just thinking about Lily," he replied. He reached his head forward to carefully lick his left paw. After doing so, he contentedly tucked it beneath his chest. "I enjoyed seeing her the other day when visiting Fitzhugh." He smiled in his thoughts. "She still thinks I'm her mother, but she loves Fitzhugh and is happy racing around the library, stirring up dust and causing mayhem."

"You seem to be resting better," I said, trying to not sound too clinical or too worried.

He turned his head and the amber eyes glowed as they looked at me. I realized I could never fool Kipp on any matter or at any time.

"I'm actually feeling the best I've felt in a long time," he responded simply. "Physical therapy has technically ended, and I'm on my own now to continue to strengthen my muscles and regain my endurance." He yawned. "I'm thinking I'll join you in some jogging…or at least fast walking," he added when he saw the look of alarm on my face. "I've been cleared to do anything I feel like doing."

I nodded my head and sipped the tea. Resting my hand on my thigh, I realized that my baggy sweats were a little baggier…maybe my efforts were paying off, too.

"Ok, Kipp. Whatever you want to do is fine with me." I rested my head on the high flared back of the chair.

I'd left the television on for noise while gone and glanced idly at the screen. It looked like *Key Largo*, an oldie that I'd not seen in a long time. Kipp turned his head towards the screen but didn't ask for me to interpret, so I sat quietly and watched as Edward G. Robinson tried to outmaneuver Humphrey Bogart.

I wasn't really paying attention to Kipp until I realized something was different…something was wrong. Kipp's mind, which was usually strangely blank during a movie, was filled with thoughts…thoughts about *Key Largo* and the characters in the movie. I realized, with shock, that he comprehended the spoken language in the film and was using it to process the events on the television. My amazement grew when the scene approached where the Johnny Rocco character was humiliating his girlfriend who was desperate for a drink. It was a subtle scene, sad and tragic, but Kipp was registering the nuances with fluidity of comprehension. He even jerked his head back when Rocco slapped Humphrey Bogart.

Slowly I turned my head so that I was staring at the back

of Kipp's, both fascinated and mesmerized by the stream of his thoughts. In a moment I saw his large ears flick back towards me.

"It's not polite to stare," he commented. Kipp stood and stretched fore and aft before circling the rug and taking his place again, this time facing me.

"Well, Kipp, are you gonna explain what's going on now?" I asked. I was sitting forward in my chair, no longer comfortable with the relaxed pose of before. My time to date with Kipp had been full of surprises, and I had the queer feeling I was about to be hit with another anomaly.

Kipp was quiet for a moment before raising his massive head to make eye contact with me. The flames from the fire reflected off of his burnished auburn coat and he looked oddly animated. A piece of wood broke into ash and a flurry of fire lit particles danced up the chimney.

"I decided," he began, "to learn English. So I spent time with Fitzhugh, and he gave me the fundamentals; I learned the rest by watching television." He tilted his head slightly to one side and waited.

"Fitzhugh didn't tell me," I replied, feeling defensive and whiney.

"Well, that's because I wanted to surprise you." He glanced away. "I didn't want to announce my plans and then, perhaps, fail, and not be able to deliver."

I wasn't certain how to reply. If truth was to be told, and it was always so with symbionts, I felt a little hurt and somewhat nettled that Kipp would not share something so important. But yet I understood his motivation. He, like most of us, didn't want to announce a grand scheme only to have the attempt crumble into failure.

Kipp rose, and I saw that his ability to do so had improved greatly; the usual wince of pain was curiously absent, and I perceived his internal grunt of approval…he was getting better, and quickly now. He walked to me and placed his broad head on my knees.

"Petra, I don't keep things of importance—or much else—from you. I really wanted to surprise you and thought you'd be happy."

I felt ashamed that I was bursting his veritable balloon of joy. Maybe Philo was right and I was much too possessive of Kipp; I had to consider the fact that my feelings revealed insecurity in me.

Bending over, I placed the side of my face on top of his soft head and put my arms around his neck. The thick, soft fur tickled my nose, and I pushed a sneeze back down deep in my throat. What Kipp had accomplished was unheard of and a remarkable occurrence.

"I'm sorry, Kipp. I was being selfish thinking that I have to be involved in everything you do. You have a right to make independent decisions and go your own way, whenever you wish. You are free."

I pushed back and we stared at one another. Unbidden, I felt tears come to my eyes and tried to hold them there but couldn't. The recent issues with our intermingled, tortured dreams as well as my lingering grief and guilt had made me more emotional than I liked. True, I wasn't the most controlled symbiont in the world, but I usually didn't carry all my baggage out front, either.

I felt Kipp's alarm at the tears, and he immediately began frantically licking the salty dampness from my cheeks.

"Don't cry, Petra," he said. "I don't like it when you cry!"

"That's only because you don't like it that I can do something you can't!" I replied, laughing lightly. "Let's go for a run and let me get my energy out in a better way."

The result of Kipp's revelation was that we decided to call a meeting between Fitzhugh, Philo and Juno. The Twelve, our governing body, were meant to have the best interests of the species in mind, but I didn't trust them due to past history. When I first arrived with a novice Kipp in tow, one of the members—a male by the name of Max Stone—wanted to take control of all decisions regarding our newest, and most talented member. Max even suggested cloning Kipp. Fortunately, Max had been shuffled off to a new location, but the thought that at least more than one on the council thought his idea was sound still disturbed me. Since Philo and Juno were on the council, I realized that whenever I met with them privately on Kipp issues, I put them at risk. But we all realized that Kipp's nature was so unique that he must be protected at the cost of the rest of us.

As was usual with my, uh, off the record collaborations, we scheduled a time for early evening, after Technicorps was technically closed for business for the day. Kipp and I walked the two miles, since we were both working on endurance. Symbionts, as a species, have a very slow metabolism and often are forced to endure severe and prolonged deprivation and starvation in the pursuit of the business at hand, so optimal physical fitness is critical. Neither Kipp nor I spoke of it, but we obviously were in training, again, but neither of us knew for what end.

The air was brisk and cold as it hit my face. Kipp, with his natural climate protection, felt happy and content as he trotted along. A couple of times, I slowed to a walk, not wanting him to overdo things yet. He'd just recently completed physical therapy and had been counseled to go at his own pace of tolerance. I knew Kipp's heart; he was not timid and would always push himself. Yes, as far as I was concerned, my strength was improving as well as my self-confidence. My legs, when I looked, appeared stronger and more toned. The weights, too, were helping my upper body. No, symbionts didn't train like a NFL football player, but we had our own needs.

Technicorps was closed but I used my badge to swipe the entry pad to a lesser used employee entrance. A blast of warmer air hit me in the face as we entered and I quickly pulled off my jacket. From the run, a mild sheen of perspiration dampened my face, and I took a minute to reconcile the abrupt change in climate.

"I'm not taking the stairs," I commented, looking down at Kipp who paced at my side.

"Wimp," he replied, laughing softly in his mind.

In a minute, we pushed back the door to Fitzhugh's lair and were welcomed by Philo and Juno. I noted some chairs were pulled together for the humanoids, and Philo placed a couple of pallets on the floor for the lupines. He wouldn't say anything, but the gesture was a thoughtful one to make the resting place for Juno more comfortable. Kipp, in his kind way, went to Juno and touched noses briefly before accompanying her to her pallet. After stiffly turning around a couple of times, she managed to find a way to plop down and ease her arthritic joints.

Peter was gone for the day, but Fitzhugh prepared some tea for us three humanoids. In a moment, I spied him walking slowly, with a tray carefully balanced on his aged hands. Philo jumped up to assist and in a minute, I was able to wrap my still cold hands around the fragile china cup; I almost sighed with relief.

"Petra, when you call a meeting after hours with our little subgroup here, I start to get worried," Philo began. "It usually indicates you want to break a rule or suggest something that will get the rest of us excommunicated from symbiont society." He took a sip of his tea and carefully placed the cup on the table. "So, which is it tonight?"

I half closed my eyes at him, trying to manage an agitated squint but it probably only looked as if I was mildly nearsighted.

"There is no call for rudeness," I replied. "And I'm not the one with the issue, tonight. Why don't you make your little sarcastic inquiry of Fitzhugh and Kipp?" I took a sip of my tea. Checkmate, I thought with satisfaction. Why did it have to be that everyone was suspicious of my motives? Let someone else take the heat for a change.

Philo raised his eyebrows and turned to gaze at Fitzhugh, who strangely ducked his head. I'd never known him to be one to flee from controversy. But then, of course, this was Kipp's revelation to be made—not Fitzhugh's.

"Kipp?" Philo looked at my companion, who was completely relaxed and sure of himself, as was typical. Kipp lacked the gene of deception and didn't understand the games many others played.

"I've learned—with Fitzhugh's assistance—to comprehend the English language," Kipp commented, glancing at Juno, whose head jerked up suddenly. I still wasn't sure why all of us continued to be surprised by Kipp. He was a perpetual onion with mysterious layers to be discovered.

Philo's expression of amazement was almost comical. Who would have known that his heavy eyebrows could scoot so far northward on his impressive brow that they would almost merge into his hairline?

"Fitzhugh?" Philo was obviously still struggling with the need to have someone tell him something comforting, something he could understand.

Fitzhugh coughed politely, a throat clearing gesture. At the noise, Lily, who'd obviously been napping somewhere, raced down one of the corridors, her little feline paws pounding a loud tattoo as she scampered our way. The delight in her little mind was evident—even to those of us who found deciphering the more primitive cognitions of animals to be a challenge—when she spied Kipp. Immediately, she made her way to his pallet and did her sinuous feline walk back and forth, rubbing her tabby body against Kipp. At one point, her posterior flashed alarmingly close to Kipp's face in the distinctly cat maneuver of presenting the rosebud, and I saw Kipp's eyes widen in alarm. I couldn't help myself and burst out laughing. Finally, Lily settled down and curled up between Kipp's forelegs, her little triangular face resting on a massive lupine paw.

Fitzhugh's wizened face relaxed as he gazed at the object of his affection—Lily, the magnificent. After a soft sigh, he turned to Philo.

"Yes, I've worked with Kipp at his request. We actually started the activity as an experiment, and he has made considerable progress. It won't be long before he will have a solid working comprehension of English." He smiled. "Of course, he can't speak it."

"Well why not!" Philo rose and began to pace. "I think that one day we'll hear that Kipp is piloting Air Force One or has become an astronaut flying to Jupiter."

Juno turned her head and watched Philo as he had a mild fit. "Why are you so upset?" she asked, her thoughts gentle and evenly flowing in the room.

"Oh, I don't know," he responded. It was clear he was disappointed in his reaction. "It's just that we seem to keep having new things to explain, and I don't know what to tell the others this time. Every time we find a new skill or talent that Kipp possesses, there are a few on the Twelve who become uneasy." He looked over at Kipp. "I don't know how to protect you."

Kipp raised his head and gazed at Philo. "I understand," he replied. "Maybe this is one time that we really don't need to involve anyone else."

Fitzhugh spoke up. "But maybe this is a skill that other lupines can learn and, if so, it is valuable. We owe it to the species to determine whether Kipp's ability is due to his genetic makeup or not."

I remained silent for the present. My concern was always to do what was best for Kipp and the rest be hanged. Even though I, perhaps, owed some allegiance to my species, I felt little and the overriding factor was Kipp. After all, I brought him from his century to this modern one and his acclimation was my responsibility. So I would listen, for now.

Juno raised her gray head slightly. "Fitzhugh, is there anything in the historical records that might help us understand this phenomenon?"

"No, and I've looked extensively. This seems to be something completely undocumented in our history."

Kipp shifted his gaze to me, and although I was staring at the amber depths of my tea as it swirled around in the delicate china cup, I knew his eyes were on me. "Petra, what do you think?" It was the voice of my best friend, my bonded partner, the one who trusted me completely— whether I deserved that trust or not.

Typically, I inserted my opinion, unable to rein in my mouth. Maybe my age was catching up with me, and I was growing some wisdom. Probably not; after all, wasn't I the rash one, unpredictable and impulsive?

"Kipp, I trust you to decide how to proceed. Since it seems to be something that affects the lupine branch of the family, I think the rest of us need to keep our counsel private and let you and Juno work this out." There, I felt pretty darn proud that I could sound like an elder statesman and less like a possessive, controlling symbiont.

He turned his head slightly and gazed at me from the corners of his amber eyes. I could hear the disbelief bouncing off the corners of his mind as he processed what I'd said to him. He gave a slight sigh and looked at Juno.

"Maybe Petra is right. If you don't object Juno, I'd like to try and teach you what I've learned and see if it is a skill all lupines can adopt. Perhaps we've never tried because we were told we would fail. After all, the ability to comprehend language doesn't mean that we must have the ability to speak it."

Philo had remained suspiciously silent. He was the leader of the Twelve and the de facto commander of our little unsanctioned subgroup. Eventually, all eyes, except for Lily's which were closed in slumber, turned towards him. He stood and walked a few steps before turning back to face us.

"I think we continue to push the limits by operating outside of the governing ability of the Twelve. The reason we have such a group is to make certain that no symbiont believes he or she is so superior that rules become superfluous." He walked back to the table and reached down for the now cold cup of tea. He picked up the fragile piece of china and held it up, turning the bone china to the light. The construct was so fine that one could see light cascading through in distorted, translucent patterns.

"This is quite old," he commented idly, a soft laugh punctuating his comment. "Fitzhugh, where on earth did you pick up this service?"

Fitzhugh leaned forward in his chair. "I found it in England two hundred years ago," he replied. "I was searching out documentary evidence of a past time shift and happened upon the most lovely little shop in the east end of London."

"I think that Kipp and Juno need to spend some time together," Philo finally commented. "I trust both of you," he said, turning dark eyes on the two lupines, "to do the right thing in terms of our species and the careful balance we maintain on this planet with the resident humans." He replaced the cup on the table, the bone china making a tiny, high pitched noise, when it made contact on the wood.

"Let's agree to meet here again in a month. But other than that, let's not speak of this again. I think we will need to avoid ongoing contact regarding this matter so that the off chance a stray thought will be picked up by a peer is lessened." Philo took another deep breath. He took a step forward and placed a large hand on my shoulder and gave it a slight squeeze. "I'm going home. My wife will get annoyed if I am late for dinner—again."

Philo was one of many of our kind who chose to not travel and bond with a lupine. He had been married for years to a humanoid symbiont and was father to several children, all of whom had left home many years ago.

I reached up and placed my hand on top of his, knowing the risks he took for me and Kipp.

"Thanks, Philo."

It would be a cold walk home, but I looked forward to the time outside; proximity to nature and few other curious minds gave me time for peace and solitude. Why was it, I thought, that my life was about to get busy again?

CHAPTER 5

It was mid-March, and I enjoyed the hasty entry and lazy departure of the daffodils. A few brave azaleas were trying to enter into the fray, but the persistent chill of the early mornings continued to cause them to think otherwise and continue their slumber. The hyacinth and tulips were showing some early competition in terms of color and beauty of form.

I woke early, the bedroom still couched in darkness. An oscillating fan on the dresser across the room soothed my nights with a dulling white noise. Thankfully, I must have done some type of inner work on my issues because my sleep, of late, was more restful. And even more importantly, Kipp was no longer plagued by the demons of my psyche. It was cold in the bedroom, and I huddled beneath the down comforter. Kipp, in response, moved his heavy bulk further upon my chest, sharing his natural warmth with me. His broad head pushed down upon my breastbone, almost to the point of pain…but not quite.

My hand drifted up and I threaded my fingers through his dense, reddish coat. If he'd been a cat, he might have purred, but instead, he gave a little grunt, and I felt his body relax.

"Can we stay here?" Kipp asked, sounding more than usual like an orphaned pup adrift in an alien time.

"That would be nice," I replied, knowing we had work to do. Despite the fact we weren't currently able to travel since Kipp remained technically in recovery, we were still on the payroll at Technicorps and had to work. Until we were able to be assigned a new mystery to investigate, Kipp was compelled to continue the debriefing that seemed to never end. It seemed the historians could not pry enough information as to his experiences as a natural lupine symbiont 70,000 years in the past.

I, on the other hand, was told to report to Fitzhugh daily and work with him and Peter on finishing translations of several manuscripts. This type of tedious assignment was not quite unpleasant but almost met that threshold. I got the impression that Fitzhugh, at times, wanted to take a ruler and rap my knuckles when I was off the mark or just inattentive. Peter, though much younger than was I, would peek at me conspiratorially and suppress a giggle. I think he enjoyed having what he thought to be a partner in crime.

Philo arranged all the schedules so that Kipp could meet privately with Juno. With his position on the council, Philo really did not have to explain the decision to anyone but made a feeble comment that Kipp and Juno were working on a special assignment. Symbionts are curious but restrained in their probing of the motives of other symbionts...so, Philo's explanation was met with neutral responses all around.

In the past, I'd been able to review numerous documents that dated back to the time following the Civil War when the animosities of the North and South were slowly healing. I had a special interest in the Civil War and hoped to make another trip to that time in history. I'd been fortunate enough to meet Grant, Hancock, Hood, Stonewall Jackson, Longstreet and even the erratic, but brilliant, Sherman, but had yet to see Lee in action. I realized the thought was self-indulgent since my primary focus was the accuracy of the historic record. But I confess to a fair amount of plain old curiosity.

However, the period of time and the battles had been

subjected to such intensive investigation, that my request would probably be turned down. The time after the war, however, included gross expansion of the west and brought together people who would have formerly taken up arms against one another. Somehow, they managed to work together to grow the country. At some point, I would have a bonus trip—more properly thought of as a vacation—and I might ask to go to the frontier west. Of course, I'd have to check with Kipp since he might have other desires.

"Pay attention, Petra!" Fitzhugh walked over and stared at the manuscript that was carefully laid out on the massive table. I tried not to wince, thinking he might pop the back of my head for good measure.

"I am, Fitzhugh," I replied. "But this is written in an obscure German dialect, and I have to read the entire paragraph to get the flavor of what was intended."

Fitzhugh shouted at Peter to go make us a pot of tea before pulling up a seat next to me at the table.

"I'm sorry," he commented, and I almost turned my chair over backwards in surprise. Fitzhugh was rarely sorry in my experience.

"I think you are doing a fine job with this. To be honest, there are only a few symbionts that would be able to do this translation." He shook his gray head in sorrow. "This young generation doesn't seem to show an interest in the humanities. Everything is about science and machines and gadgets and gizmos."

It didn't require the skill of a telepath to determine the source of his grief. Fitzhugh, at his great age, was witness to the change of culture that is inevitable if one lives long enough. Would all his work be appreciated in the future? I thought the answer to be yes but had no way to tell him lest he become irritated at having been perceived as soft and my response to be inanely coddling.

I made do with a soft "thank you", and continued my work. My mother taught languages and was master of twelve. When I was but a toddler, I recalled crawling around under her feet as she was cooking dinner while she called out rhymes to help me learn language roots. I was quite impressive with French, Spanish, German, Icelandic, Russian, Greek and, of course, English. I figured when I turned 500, I might try my hand at Japanese, since that would be a challenge.

Peter reappeared with the tea and placed the tray between Fitzhugh and me. I thought the old historian might leave, but he relaxed in the chair at my side and waited politely for me to pour. I lacked many of the dainty niceties of others of my sex but could occasionally manage to pour tea into a little cup without making too much of a mess.

Carefully, I moved the manuscript aside and made preparations to pour. Fitzhugh gave a grunt of approval at my caution. The tea was Earl Grey and the steam tickled my nose as I handed him the fine bone china cup. Blue Willow had always been a favorite of mine, and I had a few odd pieces at home, things I'd picked up at antique stores and rummage sales.

Fitzhugh looked over his shoulder; Peter had withdrawn to a back room to resume cataloging. After taking a cautious sip of the tea, Fitzhugh dipped his head down and spoke to me with a sotto voice.

"I'm keeping up with Kipp and Juno. He is working on teaching her the basic of language structure, much as I did with him. Then he will show her letters and go from there." He smiled faintly. "I only mention it because Kipp said you don't ask him about it."

I nodded my head. "That's true. I don't want him to feel under pressure to perform. Since this is just an experiment, I felt there was no rush to determine an outcome."

I felt something against my jean clad leg and looked down to see Lily as she began a complex series of figure eights around the legs of my chair and my two appendages. At one point, she stood on the toe of my running shoe, somehow balancing her body on the toe with all four feet off the ground and on my New Balance. Yes, I thought with satisfaction—I'd made the transition from stretchy pants to my jeans. The waistband was still rather snug, and

I knew I'd have imprints on my flesh where the rivets dug into the skin. Lily looked up at me and blinked her eyes—a cat kiss if I'd ever seen one.

Fitzhugh took a deep breath before sitting forward to rest his elbows on the edge of the table. He wore an almost contemplative look for a moment.

"What is it?" I asked. Of course, I could have just plundered his mind but was too well trained to be so rude. When dealing with humans, it was a different matter and all the customary holds were off.

He turned and gave a slight smile. "I've grown to the age where I have to face the fact that I've outlived most of my contemporaries." Fitzhugh gave a slight gesture over his shoulder. "Peter is a fine young lad, but he is not in any way ready to take on the responsibilities of the library we maintain. There is an enormous amount of work remaining to be done." He looked away from me. "I wanted to leave something important behind."

I felt I knew him well enough to not toss platitudes in his direction. "Fitzhugh, I know Philo will make certain that any work here continues. Period."

The old librarian gave a quick smile and glanced at me again. "I believe that, too, Petra. Maybe I needed to be reminded that I'm not the only one who values this," he said, gesturing at the room.

"But there is something else," he commented.

I raised a dark eyebrow and took another sip of my tea.

"Lily needs a, uh, guardian, in the event I don't wake up one morning." He gripped his tea cup a little too tightly, and I worried the handle might snap off.

Was that what really worried him, I wondered. Taking a risk, I reached over and lightly touched his aged, arthritic hand. "You never need to worry about her, Fitzhugh. You know that Kipp loves her, and she is always welcomed in our home."

He nodded his head and turned his face away from me while he worked on regaining composure. What a sentimental one he'd turned out to be, I thought in amazement. Who would have pegged him for all of this mushy stuff? After a moment, he seemed to have gathered himself and, after a polite "pardon me", he wandered off to the rear of the library.

I felt Kipp as he approached. That in itself was not unusual for my species but was even more acute between bonded symbionts. As he sauntered up in his characteristically lithe and relaxed manner, I basked in the waves of contentment that flowed from him. Kipp had experienced a good day, I thought.

Lily, always happy to see her surrogate mother, hopped off my foot and ran over to tackle Kipp's foreleg, kicking and biting to make her greeting known to him. I laughed softly and ducked my head at the fire darting my way from Kipp's amber eyes.

"Don't forget that I can plant a thought in her head and make her turn her affections on you," he commented, nodding at me as he began to shake his leg vigorously to dislodge the persistent cat from hell.

"No, thank you. I've already had to pluck cat hair from my hot tea and I think that is just about enough of The Lily for one day."

Kipp ambled over and rested his head on the table where I had manuscripts laid out.

"What are you working on," he asked, staring at the documents.

Remembering that he could read English language to some degree, I carefully pulled over the aged parchment and showed him the document that was written in German..or at least a dialect with a lot of German roots. With the tip of my pen, I pointed out letters and indicated some words that were similar in English. The light bulb went on in his impressive brain.

"So, several languages are interconnected," he commented, sitting back on his haunches.

"Yes, to a degree. Many have roots in Latin but sentence structure varies widely. English is difficult to learn because lots of words have so many different meanings and usages that it makes it complicated. And the rules of grammar and spelling are difficult to embrace…*I* before *E* except after *C*, and things like that."

I wanted to ask him how things had gone with Juno but resisted, not wanting him to feel under pressure. There was relief for my curiosity, when he raised the subject unbidden.

"Juno is struggling with the concept of written language." Kipp leaned over and sniffed at my now cool tea. "What's sweet?" he asked.

"Honey," I replied. Always wanting to give him new experiences, I took the spoon and drizzled a dollop on my finger tip and held it out to Kipp. He didn't hesitate and licked the amber droplet; a moment later, I felt his surprise.

"That's wonderful!" he commented. "Where does it come from?"

I spent a little time explaining about honey bees and the uses of honey, going back to ancient Egypt and the medicinal applications in terms of the antibacterial properties of the amazing substance.

"Kipp, I was thinking about something before you arrived and wondered what your opinion would be if we start some gradual preparations for a, uh, vacation. It would be a time shift, but one for pleasure and not work." I pushed the manuscript away from the edge of the table lest Lily leap up and send the half filled teacup flying. Fitzhugh, with his love of the cat, would not blame her…he would target me and my lack of foresight.

Kipp turned around a couple of times and collapsed to the floor. It was gratifying to see that his repaired shoulder seemed to absorb the impact, and I felt no pain or discomfort accompanying the soft grunt he uttered. Lily was delighted and climbed aboard his flank where she began to knead fur biscuits.

"So, where would you like to go?" he asked.

"Well, where would you like to go?" I replied, not wanting to be selfish.

"Oh, no," he laughed. "You're not gonna do that to me.

This is your idea. I wouldn't know where to suggest anyway since I've never been anywhere and don't know any good choices." He furrowed his brow a little and stared at his right paw; in a moment, he began to groom it carefully, smoothing some hair that was unruly. Turning his head, he began to chew at a claw that was too long.

"I can have Tom trim those," I began before stopping in midsentence.

Kipp was not a dog, but I'd found that lupine symbionts had two things in common with dogs. One, they loved to ride in cars with the windows down, air blowing in their faces; the other was they did not enjoy having toenails clipped. I tried once with Kipp before he pulled the clippers from my hands with his massive teeth and a cautionary, "watch it", comment.

"Okay," I sighed. "Let your toenails grow out like some old grandpa who has nails five inches long. The ladies will find you most unattractive."

Kipp tilted his head up at me, amber eyes glowing, and I knew he was having fun. "I'll just find a lady who likes long nails," he replied. Turning his head, he sniffed gently at Lily. She opened one lazy eye and blinked at him.

Fitzhugh walked up and politely greeted Kipp. Pulling up a chair, he sat with us and didn't bother with discretion; instead, he began to interrogate Kipp about the day with Juno and what was happening in terms of teaching her English. I sighed inwardly and realized that all my careful intrigue was for naught, and that I might have been better off being direct.

"So, Fitzhugh," Kipp said, "what vacation trip would Petra enjoy?" He darted a quick look at me. "She won't tell me, and I'm trying to not be rude and pry."

"That hasn't stopped you before," I commented, my lower lip starting to make its unwelcomed appearance.

Kipp just laughed at my mumblings and focused on Fitzhugh.

The old symbiont sat back in his chair and looked up, thoughtfully, before replying. "Petra told me once that she wanted to take a trip to the old west...maybe the 1870's or 1880's...somewhere in there. Not for any particular purpose except to experience the growth of the times."

Kipp glanced at my face and the heightened color on my cheekbones revealed some underlying excitement that I felt. His curiosity at the blush was interesting since he lacked the pigmentation to do so himself.

"Any particular suggestion?" Kipp asked, not taking his eyes from me. I, meanwhile, tried to keep my thoughts neutral and mentally began to review the recipe for vegetable lasagna that my mother used to make.

"Yum, Petra. That sounds really good, but I would prefer if you leave off the zucchini. I just haven't developed a taste for it." Kipp gave a casual yawn.

I stared at him through half closed lids and was rewarded with his return gaze. Fitzhugh obviously thought our staring contest to be silly and broke the impasse.

"I've always thought a trip to Tombstone, Arizona during the time of the Earp brothers and Doc Holliday might be interesting." He sat back in his chair and crossed one thin leg over another.

"Why's that?" Kipp asked.

"Well, it is a fascinating story of competing interests that involve politics, distorted media and humans with hidden, conflicting motives." He glanced at Kipp. "Not that you would be going to solve a mystery, but there is no clear history that defines the players. People of the day who were interviewed gave stories that did not mesh."

"That sounds good to me," Kipp commented, eager to prod me from my sloth.

I took a deep breath and began to replace the manuscript in its binder; I'd done all I planned to do here today.

"Kipp, the old west was a notoriously violent place. I'm not sure on a daily basis how many murders there were in Tombstone, but it was a sizeable number. It wouldn't be like we are going somewhere relaxed and fun."

"Oh, Petra, you'd be bored in a minute unless something interesting was going on. Me, too. It could still be relaxed in that we aren't going there to work...just observe and interact. How could that be difficult?"

I counted silently to ten and then stood from my chair. My back and knees were stiff from sitting in one place for much too long. I could share memories with Kipp of one vacation I took with Tula that went terribly wrong, but I realized Kipp's mind was set. Leaning forward, I placed my palms on the table top and stretched.

"Fitzhugh, do you think you could put your hands on a couple of reference books for Kipp?" I stared at Kipp. "Since you've learned to read, this will be a good opportunity to do a little study before you jump into this."

Kipp looked at me, his amber eyes cool in the dim lighting of the library. "How will I turn the pages?" Kipp might be remarkable but the issue of lacking opposable thumbs seemed to rear its ugly head more than once lately.

"Oh, Kipp. That is not a problem; I'll turn them for you."

CHAPTER 6

My car swerved along a curve in the highway as I drove from my little house to Duke Forest. Kipp's thoughts were not complimentary of my having taken that last corner a bit too fast for his liking; normally, he had his big canine head stuck out the window in absolute pleasure as the wind flattened his ears and hair. But today, we had the silly one, Lily, riding shotgun so that she could go romp in the woods with us—and she detested the air blowing in her pixie face. Fitzhugh was too feeble to accompany her outside lest she run too far ahead or trip him up by darting between his long, thin legs.

I had stopped at a fast food place to procure a repast, and as I maneuvered the car, I passed Kipp a steak biscuit, which he gently plucked from my fingers with his large, ivory teeth. His mind was filled with pleasurable thoughts as he bit into the soft, warm biscuit only to find the steak filet lurking beneath the dough.

Lily began meowing in her typically demanding way. Abandoning Kipp to the back seat to enjoy his biscuit, she climbed up the back of my seat until she perched, teetering on my shoulder. Realizing I was about to wreck the car due to all the shenanigans, I pulled over to the grassy verge and braked. Lily continued her descent onto my lap.

"Okay, okay!" I said, trying to pull off some cheese from

the biscuit I was holding. She grabbed my hand with both paws and rather delicately, I thought, began to eat the gooey cheese, licking my finger tips for good measure.

"This was your idea, Kipp, and here I have to feed the little monster," I grumbled, trying not to smile at the expression on Lily's face. Her large eyes were almost crossed as she focused on my fingers and the crumbled biscuit.

"Toss me another biscuit," was the reply from the back seat.

I managed to divert Lily by crumbing some steak on the passenger seat—I'd long since worried about the condition of the car—and reached into the bag for another biscuit for Kipp. His enormous auburn head reached forward again, and I realized he was trying not to drool on my arm.

While he and Lily were kept suitably occupied, I salvaged my own egg and cheese biscuit and sighed with pleasure. The memory of life at the Lands Point Colony was not very far from recall, and I recalled the food fare— or lack of. There was dried fish made into a stew that was almost rancid at times as well as some sort of mashed up hardened corn/nut combination with the consistency of a brick. The only benefit from the latter was the thorough tooth cleaning that Kipp received—it was like a milk bone on steroids.

Pulling the lid off my steaming coffee, I reclined back a little and closed my eyes. Yes, life in this century was simpler in many ways. Lily disturbed my pleasure by climbing into my lap again, so that she could attack the other end of the biscuit I was trying to eat. With a sigh, I tore off some of the egg and put it back on the stained passenger seat. The diversion worked and the tabby terror hopped back over and left me in peace.

"I don't know how Fitzhugh keeps up with her," Kipp commented. He'd finished his repast and thrust his head over my shoulder, watching Lily with amber eyes. "She's almost too much for you, Petra."

I knew he was being deliberately and playfully

provocative, so I took the bait.

"And why would that be?" I asked, sipping the coffee again.

"Well, you are older than I am and that takes a toll, you know," he responded.

Suddenly, his attitude turned serious and he gently nuzzled the side of my face. "I was just kidding, Petra," he commented. As was true with us, I knew the thoughts and feelings that provoked him.

"Kipp, I may be a little older than you, but I'm in good shape and plan to be around for hundreds of years. So, I'm not going anywhere." Reaching up, I looped my arm beneath his muscled neck and pulled his face against mine. The abandoned pup that lurked within Kipp's psyche would never stop thinking of his mother dying and leaving him. The fact he had survived a harsh and primitive world at such a young age was nothing short of miraculous.

The moment became unexpectedly serious; to reset our energy, I put the rest of my biscuit on the seat to amuse a gluttonous Lily and turned the key in the ignition. In a short while, we were back on the road.

Duke Forest had long been a favorite of mine, and for years I'd wandered along the trails to explore the dark green depths. One year, I took an extension course at Duke so that I could identify the flora and fauna with more confidence than achieved from having perused my little dog eared field guide I found at a yard sale.

When Lily was a kitten, I carried her in a little back pack lest she become fatigued. But she was older now and full of explosive energy from too many hours in the library. There was no need to worry about her since Kipp and I could track her primitive mind—Kipp was more talented in this arena than was I—and Kipp was physically agile enough to keep her in sight.

As I watched, her little fanny vanished like a bounding jack rabbit in a heavy growth of underbrush; Kipp, likewise, charged in, a couple of yards behind her. I could feel his satisfaction at having regained almost one hundred percent of his strength and mobility as he cornered quickly, his body low to the ground. He and Lily enjoyed acting like primitive creatures, fundamental and strong, as they coursed along the forest floor.

I had no illusions as to my body and knew all the limitations God had placed upon me, a mere bipedal creature. So, I ambled along the trail, confident that Kipp would reappear when he was ready. Since I was in constant contact with him, I could enjoy their mock hunting expedition. Lily's mind felt experiential rather than one consisting of organized thoughts; nevertheless, I shared in her joy as she spied a chipmunk. In that moment, all her hunting instincts were in play. Kipp, no stranger to the hunt since he was a carnivore by design, stopped Lily since he did not approve of hunting when there was no hunger involved. He recognized the cat was hardwired to predate, but as gently as possible, he picked her up in his massive jaws and brought her to me as a momentary distraction.

"I can't seem to do anything with her," Kipp commented as he dropped the squirming cat to the ground. She wore such a look of total distaste at being covered in lupine saliva that I had to laugh. Lily lost all interest in the now hidden chipmunk and began to groom herself to be rid of the cloying dampness. I took a seat on a fallen log, and Kipp reclined at my feet in a bed of leaves.

"Well, Kipp, she's a cat and just understands the hunt. I've always thought felines to be supremely gifted at the subterfuge of stalking. They do kill, however, when not hungry, and I realize that violates your code of ethics."

Lily finished her grooming and wandered over to curl up between Kipp's massive forepaws. He bent his head down and gave her a lick or two for consolation after his manhandling her in such an ungentlemanly fashion.

"What are the reasons for killing another creature?" he asked.

I knew he'd been reading history books about the old

west—and that included Tombstone. To say there was excess of violence would almost be an understatement.

"What did you mother teach you, Kipp?" I replied.

He looked up at me and took a deep breath. "She told me that all life was unique and sacred, and that there were two reasons to kill another creature. One would be for food required for physical survival. The other would be for self defense or defense of a member of the pack." Lily rolled over on her back and somehow curled up in a figure eight where both her face and her back were pointed north.

"Yeah, I'd say that's about it," I commented.

"Do you think everything is valuable...I mean down to the ants and spiders and fleas and ticks?"

I decided to carefully consider my reply and took a moment. Overhead, a slight wind disturbed the dense canopy which was bright green with the distinctive color of early spring; the air smelled fresh and clean. The temperature was trending milder, but it was still early enough in the season that mornings had a lingering, faint chill, a reminder of the harsh winter we'd just put behind us.

"Well, Kipp, for the life of me I'm not sure what value ticks bring to the planet's ecosystem, but if you believe in a divine creator—which I do—then you trust that all things here are a part of a perfect balance. We must accept the fact that we, as a species, are no more equipped than are humans to comprehend the thought behind the big plan."

Kipp began to swirl what I was telling him through his massive brain which, through its superior speed of processing complex thoughts, put mine to shame. I knew his mother had imprinted upon him her set of values which included belief in a higher power and the general rules of right and wrong. My Kipp was ethical to the point of being tedious.

"So, are you rethinking Tombstone?" I spied something moving on the log next to my thigh and realized it was a massive wolf spider, involved in careful examination of the gigantic intruder.

"Now, Kipp, look at this really big spider," I commented,

pointing at the moving quasi tarantula. "If I did what I wanted to do, I jump up and run screaming back to the car. Or take the other, more definitive route, and stomp it with my foot. The eight legs and multiple sets of eye are just a bit too much." I finally did stand and watched as the spider continued its journey until it disappeared from view. Resuming my seat, I reached down and caressed the soft dome of Kipp's head. "If you'd wanted to protect me, you could have jumped on that spider."

He shook his head. "I was too scared of it. And, no, I'm not rethinking Tombstone. I'm just trying to understand why an intelligent species would just kill each other off with no real rhyme or reason."

A bright yellow goldfinch swooped in and perched a few feet away from us, his bright eyes examining our odd party; the black cap on top of his golden head gave him a saucy, jaunty appearance as if he'd donned a little fedora for a night out on the town. In a moment, he was joined by a few of his friends, and they resumed flight as a small flock of animated sunshine, their wings beating the air with a soft sound.

"Kipp, humans have examined their nature for centuries. In my experience, I've seen them kill for power, control, food, survival and just plain meanness." I hesitated to bring up the recent past of Lands Point Colony, but it was there, hovering, a dark nightmare that would not put itself to bed for good. "Sir Edward killed because he became deranged and his ability to reason and use his former sense of right and wrong had vanished."

Kipp nodded his head. "I understand he was sick. It makes what happened in the end even more regrettable."

I stared at him and realized the amount of personal regret I still carried over the incident.

"You must forgive yourself, Petra," Kipp commented. "Even if we could have saved him, we wouldn't have possessed the ability to heal his sickness. The colonists would have executed him for his crimes."

I nodded my head and glanced down in the direction the

spider had taken. The spider would live, for now, but a man had died; one life spared, one taken…was that the balance of nature? I was not a particularly deep thinker overall and preferred to leave the musing of such concepts to philosophers.

Kipp, sensing the timing was right, reassured me he wanted to go to Tombstone. With that thought in mind, we drove back to Technicorps where I deposited Lily with Fitzhugh. He examined her tabby body with palpable anxiety, and I tried to not be offended; he was clearly unhinged where the well being of the little cat was concerned.

The weather was still cool enough that Kipp could remain comfortably in the car. I ran into a video store and checked out the Kirk Douglas/Burt Lancaster version of *Gunfight at the OK Corral* as well as Kevin Costner's *Wyatt Earp* and *Tombstone* with Kurt Russell. Since Kipp was developing his ability to watch movies and comprehend, I thought this might be a more relaxing venue.

We arrived home, and I pulled the blinds shut in the living room. Encouraging Kipp to take care of his personal needs, I did the same. The microwave prepared my movie popcorn, and I stretched out on the sofa while the player cued up *Gunfight*. I confess I became a little silly as I began to loudly sing along with the theme song which was one of the more ridiculous ones I'd ever heard. Kipp at one point rolled his eyes at me.

"I hope I won't be humming that for days, weeks and months," he dryly commented, as he held back on any bracing editorial comments on my voice as well as the inane lyrics of the song.

I told him the little I knew about the Earp brothers; after all, I'd been alive during their time on earth but made no trips to their locality. I did recall reading about their exploits in the cheap magazines that one could purchase that profiled people who were allegedly legends and heroes. Kipp's fascination resided, however, with Doc

Holliday. The idea that this well educated man could blend southern gentility with utter ruthlessness made him a fascinating character.

"So, was he a bad man?" Kipp asked as Val Kilmer polished off Michael Bien. Simultaneously, I was polishing off a third bag of popcorn.

"Remember that these movies are only portrayals of historical characters and events. There is no one living who was there and can tell us what really happened. And as is true with history, it gets distorted with time and agendas. For example, people who didn't like the Earps would relay negative information and impressions about them. But Wyatt's wife, Josie, was his biggest supporter and wanted history to recognize the values that she identified in him. So she wanted the story told as she remembered it."

I looked down at Kipp, who was mesmerized by the figures moving about on the television screen. "What you are watching is someone's idea of what happened. Or what that person wants us to think happened. "

Kipp broke his stare to glance at me. I was busy stuffing popcorn in my face, and he gave me an accusatory glance.

"This isn't bad for me," I began defensively.

"I didn't care about that," he replied. "I wanted some, and you are hogging the bag."

After warning him to be careful of the unpopped kernels, I put the bowl down next to him. The small dark room was filled with the sound of crunching.

We spent the remainder of the day watching the Kevin Costner film. I'd moved down to the floor at some point and cuddled under a light blanket. Kipp curled up next to me, and as the final credits rolled, I allowed myself to fall asleep. Having Kipp in close contact was like being next to a virtual heater.

My dreams were interesting, and Kipp lazily allowed his mind to follow mine as I walked down the streets of old Tombstone. A tall man, lean, with hair the color of ripe wheat and eyes as blue as a midsummer sky, approached me. His full mouth, beneath a leonine mustache, twitched in a slight smile as he acknowledged my presence.

"Good day, ma'am," he murmured, tipping the brim of his broad western hat in a courteous gesture.

I was dressed to the hilt in a period costume down to the slight bustle anchored over my butt. An interesting invention, I thought, wondering who on earth had figured women needed any more packing in that area than was necessary. In my hand was a silly little parasol, and I carried it to shade my supposedly delicate skin from the harsh sun.

In my dreams, I nodded my head in response to what seemed to be Wyatt Earp and passed him. Suddenly, a loud noise rang out. I turned in alarm to see Wyatt fall to the ground. Looking up, I saw a small cloud of smoke that revealed the location of the shooter, who seemed to have fired from the edge of a storefront. People began to shout in alarm and were running in our direction. A man ran past me, accidently jostling my arm as he did so. He turned, briefly, to look at me, and his slender face wore a look of horror. I realized the thin man was Holliday. I awoke with a start.

Kipp stirred at my side. "What's wrong, Petra?"

I shook my head, not certain what awakened me. Finally, I commented, "We must be cautious, as always, Kipp, to not change history."

He was quiet and pushed closer to me, resting his head on my chest. The house was silent, save for the ticking of a nearby clock. It must be early morning and nearing sunrise, because I could hear the sounds of birds as they began to roust themselves for the upcoming day. I stared up at the ceiling. Overhead, an antique light fixture winked back at me, some of the crystals catching fragments of ambient light in what seemed to be an otherwise dark room.

"Is that possible?" he finally asked. "Don't we always change it in some way?"

I sighed deeply. It was too early for philosophical discussions, and I felt a little hung over from too much television and excessive amounts of popcorn. No doubt the salt had left me sluggish. I'd probably drink so much water today that I would slosh while walking.

"In that others get to know us when we time shift, then, yes, we always change something." I took a deep breath and threaded my fingers through Kipp's dense pelt. He was so familiar to me now that I realized I could find him merely by touch if he were in a crowd of thousands of lupine symbionts.

"When we were at Lands Point Colony, we were instrumental in the death of Sir Edward," Kipp said, persistent with his line of questioning.

"That's true," I commented. "But apparently we didn't change the overall progression of history. The colony, and all its inhabitants, vanished." I turned a rueful smile towards the ceiling. "I guess you could say we failed. We never did find out what happened to all those people."

"I still worry about Perdy and Alice," Kipp said. His thoughts turned sad.

"I know, Kipp. Me, too."

CHAPTER 7

———— ◆ ————

"Let's go visit baby George," Kipp announced after we finished breakfast. A long workday loomed ahead at Technicorps. I would be in the pit with Fitzhugh as I struggled to decipher manuscripts, while Kipp met with the group who continued to gather information about symbiont life 70,000 years in the past.

"I'm not sure I want to do that," I began, an unpleasant whine accompanying the thought. Abruptly, I stood and took my cereal bowl to the sink. With dismay, I noticed I'd allowed my woefully negligent housekeeping to rear its ugly head, and the sink was full of dishes. I made a space to get to the sink stopper and plugged the drain. After squirting some detergent into the sink, I began to run hot water.

Kipp looked up from where he rested on the wooden floor. "I was going to comment that the place looks like a pig sty but hated to sound critical." With that remark, he rolled on his side and began to stretch, his large body consuming almost a quarter a length of the room.

I turned from the sink and gave him an impressive stink eye which he ignored. Leaving the dishes to soak for a few minutes, I went to the dryer and removed a load of clothes that had been hiding there for a couple of days. Dumping the mass on the kitchen table, I tried to shake out what wrinkles I could and mashed things into fairly neat stacks.

Kipp opened one eye. "I think I prefer my life to yours. I don't have to change clothes or wash clothes or even wash dishes. I can just run outside, chase down a rabbit, have dinner and come inside to take a nap."

"Don't gloat, Kipp," I commented. "And since we live in a highly populated area, I'd suggest you not start hunting the local wildlife up and down the street. It might get the attention of the authorities and neither one of us need that."

As I washed the dishes, I reconsidered my initial and knee jerk response to Kipp's thought that we needed to visit George. Going to the cemetery was not something I did often but usually felt better when I did make the journey. Actually, I was feeling more energized with this little spurt of homemaker productivity. Kipp might have been more surprised than was I, when I turned to him and told him we'd take a loop by the cemetery on our way to Technicorps.

Less than an hour later, we left the house. The longer than usual walk was good for both of us—I was still trying to deal with three bags of popcorn from the previous day, and Kipp was strengthening his body. After leaving the immediate vicinity of habitation, we turned on a road that took us out into the countryside. The cemetery was situated on a lovely sloping hillside; the piedmont of North Carolina was filled with rolling hills spaced between level expanses of green grassy areas.

Even though we'd not been here since before we left for our assignment at Lands Point Colony, Kipp remembered exactly where baby George rested. At Kipp's insistence, I had brought a few early roses from my garden. They were a deep red in color, usually the color of life. In a moment, we found the granite marker where George was buried. A recent storm had deposited some leafy debris on his little plot, and I bent to brush the area clean. Then, I placed the roses at the base of his headstone.

Kipp did not need to inquire as to my thoughts and feelings, but I knew he was curious as to the relative lack of emotion I experienced. The pain of losing my baby never left me, but I'd learned, in typical symbiont fashion, how to compartmentalize the feelings. It was a necessity for my kind due to our long lived nature. How could any sentient being go on for hundreds of years if grief was a predominating issue? Such a thing would not be compatible with existence.

The ground was slightly damp with dew; fortunately, I was wearing a longer anorak and tucked it beneath my rear end and took my seat. As I gazed out into the countryside from the hilltop vista, a gentle breeze pushed my dark hair back from my face. Kipp sat next to me, and I put my arm across his massive back. Idly, I began to scratch his skin, my finger tips finding their way through the thick pelt of fur. This was my life as I'd chosen it. I was a bonded, traveling symbiont. At this time, I had no desire to marry again or to assume the mundane existence of my peers who showed up at Technicorps with a large cup of coffee in a decorative traveling mug. I wasn't a thrill junkie by any means but also had no desire to avoid the nature given to me by God. Yes, we symbionts had a purpose on earth.

Kipp followed my thoughts in his relaxed manner. With Tula, my bond had been more restrained since we both followed the contemporary rules for our kind that respected the mental boundaries of courtesy and respect. Kipp's thoughts intertwined with mine to the degree that I was forced to focus so that I could keep straight what belonged to me and what was Kipp's.

"There's an amazing diversity of life, isn't there?" Kipp asked. He poked his head forward and touched the edge of one of the roses with his delicate nose.

"Watch for the thorns," I cautioned.

"Why does it have the sweet smell?"

"I guess to attract bees for pollination, but I'm not sure," I responded, picking up one of the stems and examining the flower. I pulled it in close to my nose and inhaled the distinctive scent of the rose.

Kipp allowed his curious mind to relax and tried not to

think for a few moments. For one with such an impressive and busy brain, it was no easy feat.

Before long, we stood and continued our walk towards Technicorps. By the time we completed the large loop, my cheeks were flushed with a healthy glow, and Kipp was panting. Yes, our endurance was building. After saying goodbye, Kipp headed off to the lab, and I made my way to the basement.

Fitzhugh was waiting for me, a scowl on his face. The source of his agitation was a mystery since I just arrived and hadn't yet had the opportunity to screw up anything.

"You are late," he began before turning away and walking towards the massive work table. A manuscript waited for my arrival. I suppressed a smirk as I noticed a pot of tea that Fitzhugh had thoughtfully provided.

"Hopefully, the tea is not cold," he muttered.

Lily arrived to greet me and began to wind her sinuous body between my legs. I reached down to pet her and was welcomed with a bite. Forget that, I thought to myself. Why Kipp and Fitzhugh were in love with this impulsive, out of control monster was a puzzle to me.

I'd been working a few hours and my back had developed a decided cramp. Standing, I took a moment to stretch and walk around. The library was painted in a deep green color that seemed reminiscent of Victorian times when houses were often decorated with intense colors. Peter was off on his lunch break as well as having been given the task of running errands for Fitzhugh. It was quiet, and I began to walk slowly up and down the aisles, glancing at the stacks as I did so. A notation on the end of a binder caught my interest, and I pulled it carefully from the shelf. Like a kid who was afraid I was about to get caught nabbing an illicit cookie from a jar, I peeked around to see if Fitzhugh was watching. He must have been in his office, and I pulled the binder and took it to my desk. From the dates on the binder's spine, the information inside was gleaned from the year 1863 and was in reference to the American Civil War.

Two hours later, so lost was I in the story that unraveled before my eyes, that I failed to hear the light step of Fitzhugh.

"What are you up to?" His deep voice almost vibrated with disapproval.

I twisted my head around and peered up at him, determined to not let him bully me. All symbionts had a right to this library, and he did not own the contents. Fitzhugh, of course, read my primitive and defensive agitation, and his heavy brows drew together as he frowned.

"Who was John Gold?" I asked.

Fitzhugh's gnarled hands drew to his hips as he stood, looking down at me, in consideration. He could play nice and chat or be obstreperous; either way, the ball was in his court. With a deep sigh that seemed to come from the bottom of his solar plexus, he pulled out a chair at the table and took a seat.

"John Gold was a talented symbiont who became obsessed with the history of the Civil War. He, if he is still living, would be about six hundred years old."

Ah, I thought. A mystery! I could feel the interest in me build like a hunter tracking prey. But I knew Fitzhugh, and he detested being pressed. So, I waited. Patiently.

Fitzhugh cleared his throat. "Gold was not a contemporary student of that war and actually was kept occupied with multiple assignments over the years that the war was ongoing. As I recall, the leaders at the time felt his curiosity over the war could lead him to draw conclusions not based upon fact...but more on feeling. So he was not permitted to travel to that time and locale."

"But he went anyway," I commented. Having been accused over the years of being somewhat of a rebel, it was nice to find that there were some of my species who really were rebels, in the truest sense of the word.

Fitzhugh glanced up at me. "It's nothing to celebrate." He leaned forward and folded his hands on the desktop. The surface was polished until it gleamed and not a trace of dust or particle of cat hair was in evidence…a true miracle by my measure of thought. "I'm not certain, Petra, that you get it, even after all these years. The slightest miscalculation and history can be changed."

I felt the hot flush of blood beneath the skin on my face and was momentarily surprised by the surge of anger I felt. Before I could reign in my tongue, I replied, "And it would be nice, if once, just once, you would give me some credit for being a competent, thoughtful person. All I seem to hear are your numerous criticisms of me and all I do." I could have added that he was not my mama but recognized the childish tone associated with that particular utterance.

The hapless Peter took that moment to arrive, his hands occupied with a couple of large, paper bags from the supermarket. Fitzhugh was no doubt restocking the mini kitchen with a few goods. Peter, though not as talented a telepath as I or Fitzhugh, immediately picked up on the anger, which suffused the library like a sour odor. Without speaking, he kept walking past us and headed straight to the back. Fitzhugh and I both turned, watching the young man's rapid retreat. Then, unexpectedly, my eyes met Fitzhugh's.

"He's not as thick headed as I thought," Fitzhugh commented, his mouth twitching with suppressed humor.

"No, seems like he is able to quickly assess a situation and make a bold and decisive decision." I nodded my head. Carefully, I closed the binder and decided to put the story of John Gold and my curiosity to bed. I wasn't headed anywhere near the American Civil War and had work to do on the tedious translation of the manuscript I'd been given.

My eyes were bleary eyed when I was able to complete my work several hours later. I'd traded up the hot tea for a pot of strong coffee, courtesy of Peter. Thankfully, he didn't try to engage me in conversation about what had occurred between me and Fitzhugh. I knew Kipp was near, and I detected the familiar thoughts of Philo, too.

"Hi, Petra," Kipp said, approaching and sticking his massive head up to my chest. His jaw opened in a lupine smile, and he pressed his chin against my sternum in his typically chest crushing greeting.

I briefly rested my cheek on the top of his warm, soft head. "Hi," I replied, peering up to see Philo standing at the edge of the desk.

"So, are you thoroughly sick of reading and translating?" Philo asked, laughing softly as he took a seat. He knew better than most that I was not a detail oriented person and preferred action and movement to sedentary contemplation.

"I thought of vomiting but knew Fitzhugh would yell at me and make Peter clean it up, so I managed to be good." I rested my elbows on the table and stretched forward in the chair a little.

I inquired politely as to Kipp's day and was relieved to hear that his hours on end of debriefing by various specialists were drawing to a close. He continued with his covert work with Juno but admitted the effort to teach her English was slow.

"The brain is an interesting organ, Kipp," I commented. "You weren't given the burden of having been told you were incapable of learning the language. Juno, for all her existence, has been told that lupine symbionts can't learn or interpret language. So, not only is she trying to understand what you tell her, but also she is having to unlearn having been told that she can't do what you are insisting she can do."

Kipp tilted his auburn head slightly in consideration of my words. "I hadn't thought of that, Petra. You have a valid point."

Philo politely cleared his throat. "I've arranged a time for you both to meet with the Twelve and outline your request for a, uh, vacation trip." His dark eyebrows scooted up on his high forehead. "Am I to assume you still want to go to the old west...Tombstone, to be specific?"

I rolled my eyes. "Kipp seems determined, despite the

negative comments I've made. It would be too simple to go
to the beach and lie out on the sand for a few days." As I
spoke the words, I knew Philo deciphered the real meaning
of my words. I could no more sit and be idle and quiet than
I could flap my arms and fly like a little sparrow.

Philo smiled at Kipp and shrugged his shoulders. "I don't
know how you stand her, Kipp. She's always been difficult
and cantankerous, but you're stuck with her, my lad."

The two of them proceeded to have a conversation about
me and engaged in a mock debate over my liabilities as
well as my apparently limited number of personal
attributes. I nodded my head and rolled my eyes again. My
fan club, I thought.

I wasn't sure why, since I prized myself on being able to
contain myself, but I suddenly was overwhelmed with
emotion as my love for Kipp boiled over in an unexpected
surge of intense feelings. He jerked his head towards me
and abandoned his humorous dialog with Philo. Anxiously,
he poked his large muzzle close to my face and I felt his
wet, cold nose as it examined the curve of my jaw, leaving
a little moist snail trail of dampness on my skin.

"Petra, we were just kidding," he began, before I
interrupted.

"I just love you," I said, my voice husky with spoken
emotion.

Philo reached over and grabbed my shoulder with a large,
gentle hand. It was a wonderful moment with a fullness of
feeling that came from the heart. Symbionts had the most
amazing ability to be totally honest with one another and
lacked artifice, despite the shell of falseness we wore with
our human friends. Tilting my head back, I glanced at Philo
and realized that a tear had escaped my eye to trickle
slowly down my face. Kipp nestled closer, if that was
possible, and tucked his head beneath my chin.

CHAPTER 8

A week passed before our meeting with the Twelve. As the day approached, I became increasingly nervous, the fact of which did not escape the notice of Kipp. Short of a debriefing following our return from Lands Point Colony, I'd managed to avoid the perusal of our governing body. True, Philo assured me that the overall temper of the group had changed with the exit of Max Stone. But I knew there would be some aggressive hotshot angling for power. It seemed, even in the world of symbionts, that there would be a few who operated from hidden motives. It smacked of something uncomfortably close to what humans often did to one another and I cared not for it. But there would be no further time shifts condoned by the Twelve without the occasional meeting. Perhaps, I was too conventional to make the leap and go rogue.

It was Saturday, and I spent the morning trying to pull my house into some type of order. Kipp's lack of assistance finally irritated me, and I made the decision he could share in the work load.

"I want you to go through the house, find anything that looks dirty, and bring it to the laundry room and toss it in the floor." I was quietly pleased that I had found a job he could manage.

Kipp, excited to be put to use, made several trips back

and forth, his toenails clicking sharply on the wooden floors.

"Don't forget the bathroom towels," I commented, aiming my thoughts at the back of his head. A minor jerk of his ears acknowledged my last order.

In a short time, I had enough to fill the washer and started a load. Arming myself with a water-vinegar mixture, I began wiping down the kitchen counters. Kipp returned and plopped down on the floor behind me.

"What's this word?" he asked.

I turned to see he had brought a book I borrowed from Fitzhugh on the old west and managed to place it carefully on the floor. Somehow he used his nose, tongue and paws to open it to the place I'd marked with a torn envelope. Shoving aside a grimace in the hopes he'd not defaced the book in any way, I requested he spell the word.

"R-e-p-u-b-l-i-c-a-n," he slowly ticked off the letters.

I gave him the correct pronunciation and went on to explain political parties and politics in general.

"So why do humans need them?"

I considered my reply as I washed a glass and placed it on the draining board.

"Humans have a tribal nature. So they tend to form groups that have similar beliefs for their alliances. Political parties pull together larger coalitions of like minded people…or at least that is what they are supposed to do." My thoughts took a negative turn. "But they also pull together people who desire power and control and not necessarily in the best interest of the larger group of individuals."

Kipp grunted and read further. I was quietly impressed at his skills and mastery in such a short period of time. If we had the ability to test the IQ of lupine symbionts, I had no doubt that Kipp would be classified as a genius. I held no fantasies as to my own greatness, and knew I was average at best.

"You're impressed, aren't you?" Kipp asked, pulling his head up to gaze at the back of my head.

"Don't get cocky," I replied, playfully splashing water his way and forgetting for the moment my concern over the pristine nature of Fitzhugh's book.

Within an hour, we were restless for the outdoors since the weather was spectacular. I donned my running shoes and layered lightly so I could modify my garments to the temperature as well as my level of exertion, and we took off.

I began my slow jog after a brisk 15 minute walking warm up. Kipp was holding back, but I recognized he was bristling with energy and could hardly contain himself until we could get to the open meadow a mile away where he could stretch out and run. We drew a couple of glances, mostly due to Kipp's unusual size...a dog with his bulk was always eye catching. Despite his hatred of the leash and collar, I kept the leather lead draped casually across my arm since there were leash laws, and I had no desire to be cited due to a complaint.

The late morning sun was reaching higher in the sky, and despite the mild temperature, I felt my skin begin to warm as the blood surged to my large muscles in my legs. There was a heavy, but not cloyingly so, floral scent from the abundance of flowering plants. Overhead, the leaves on the tall trees intermittently blocked the sunlight, and the dappled pattern created a checkerboard effect on the rough sidewalk ahead.

Finally, we made it to the large meadow, and I released an eager Kipp, who was almost dancing on the end of the leash. He sprinted away, as would a thoroughbred horse from the starting gate. He was my Seabiscuit and the bell had just been rung. Kipp began running in large circles, looping close to me each time he made another elliptical lap. His large ears were flat against his skull, and he looked more wolf-like than usual as his muscles rippled beneath the auburn colored fur. Yes, my powerful Kipp was back!

I decided to take a breather while Kipp showed off, and I sank down into the tall grass. There was a mild dampness since the sun had not been intense enough to burn off any lingering dew, and I brushed my palms against my worn sweat pants. Kipp eventually approached me and plopped down in the grass, his tongue lolling comically from his big jaws. He stretched out on his side, and I reclined against him, my head finding the soft pillow of his flank.

I confess, I think I drifted off into a light sleep, so comfortable was my bed of fragrant grass and Kipp's warm body. The soft sound of voices murmuring caused me to awaken as some fellow travelers made their way to our meadow. Kipp's head rose in interest, and the voices began to fade and retreat in the distance.

"I think you scared them," I commented.

"I'm just a big pussycat, and you know it," he answered with a soft laugh. His thoughts turned serious. "Why are you so worried about meeting with the Twelve?"

I shrugged my shoulders but there was no way to evade his query; it was easier to lie to myself than it was to Kipp.

"Well, you know I have history with them, Kipp. They typically disapprove of me and my methods. And only because of Philo and Juno do I still have some, uh, cachet with the group."

Kipp raised his head and looked at me. "I think you enjoy the role of rebel and outcast," he commented. The comment hit close to the mark, and I almost winced. Was I that shallow and superficial? If so, it was an unpleasant aspect of my character. I felt Kipp's damp nose nuzzle my face as he managed to maneuver his body in a horseshoe shaped curve.

"I didn't mean to hurt your feelings, Petra. I don't think that you deliberately try to cause trouble. But it's easier for you to limit your relationships with others. Some of us need a lot of friends and a big group of supporters; you are more comfortable with a little group."

I half closed my eyes and gazed upward. The sky was a deep blue, almost cloudless, and overhead a single turkey buzzard circled, his head occasionally craning around to stare down at us. I wondered if he could smell us.

"Yes, he can," Kipp replied. "We are not moving, and he is checking to see if he needs to stop by for lunch."

Shaking my head, I laughed softly. Kipp had a decidedly more off beat sense of humor than had Tula.

The remainder of the weekend passed by too quickly for my liking, and I recognized this was only due to my anxious anticipation of the meeting on Monday with the Twelve. Never one for ceremony, I pulled out my jeans; my only concession was a button front cotton blouse versus a t-shirt or sweatshirt. I owned almost no jewelry, and Kipp made note of that fact while I dressed. He lay on the bed in the tumble of sheets and comforter, licking his paws, his amber eyes flicking up to watch me, as always, with intense curiosity.

"What are those things human women wear on their ears?" he asked.

"Do you mean earrings?"

He gave a mental shoulder shrug. "I guess so." After a second, he added, "I think they are pretty."

"Do you want me to get my ears pierced?" I enquired. In a moment, I had to explain what that meant and laughed at the horrified expression on Kipp's face.

"Why would humans punch a hole in their flesh for self adornment?" He tilted his massive head a little.

"They do much more than just that, Kipp." I raised an eyebrow at him. "But I'll save that for another day."

He rose and hopped off the bed. Once down, he stretched fore and aft, his paws slipping a little on the wood floors. Then he yawned so wide that I could see all of his back teeth. It was no wonder to me that when Kipp had been called on to muster up an aggressive display, others were impressed by his potential. From their way of thinking: big dog, big teeth, big ouch. Even when we met in primitive times, he managed to scare off a duo of wolves that likewise came to the conclusion they did not want to tangle with whatever the heck he was.

"You are so pretty, Petra," he commented. Of course, I recognized he loved me in his childlike way, and that I would always be beautiful to him.

I reached down and ran my hand through the soft fur on the dome of his head. His coloration was unusual for our lupine brothers…Kipp always would be distinctive, if not for his appearance, then for his remarkable mind and amazing depth of character.

It was raining so we took to my battered car, and I crossed my fingers as the key turned in the ignition. To my surprise, it sprung to life immediately with a perky roar of the engine, and we left for Technicorps. Kipp demanded I crack the window, and he put his large nose to the aperture, snuffling at the fresh, damp air that pushed in through the opening.

I let him off at the door and, after parking, ran across the parking lot, dodging large puddles as I scampered to the cover of the front entrance. Kipp was watching a person approach with an umbrella. He looked up at me, inquiringly.

"Yes, I have an umbrella. It's at the house, of course, in the front closet." I stared him down.

We were at the waiting area for the large conference room in less than a minute. The large wall clock indicated it was two minutes before nine o'clock. At least I'd not been late this time.

"Relax, Petra," Kipp's reassuring thoughts drifted to my brain. "It'll be okay."

I glanced down; Kipp, in so many ways, was my teacher while I reverted to the role of eager pupil. It was supposed to be the other way around, according to the Twelve, but they—even Philo and Juno to some degree—still did not recognize Kipp's innate abilities that vastly eclipsed the rest of us. He was my superior in all ways save experience. I lacked the ego to struggle with this reality.

The door to the conference room opened, and we were greeted by the tall form of Philo, smiling as usual. He, knowing my history with the group and my natural aversion to authority figures, typically attempted to begin meetings that involved me with a cheerful introduction and a breezy manner. We'd been doing this sort of thing for many years, and I did not need to point out the fact that often the meetings would dissolve into an unpleasant pile of bad feelings and resentment. If I'd not been such a talented traveler, the group would have probably sent me to the library to be closeted like a hermit with the aging Fitzhugh...out of sight, out of mind.

I took a deep breath and grounded myself by running my hand gently down Kipp's spine. He wagged his tail in response, and we preceded Philo into the large room. Looking around, I realized I'd never liked this room, with its sterile, modern appearance. Maybe I was better off with Fitzhugh in the dark, Victorian lair he had constructed in the basement. The one saving grace, however, was the large series of windows that overlooked the lovely garden where I'd spent much time meditating over the years. I spied my favorite tulip poplar lurking outside, beckoning me like an old friend to come play. Kipp followed the whimsical meanderings of my mind with humor.

Philo ushered me to a chair, and Kipp took his place next to me on the raised bench provided for the lupines. He, courteously, nodded his head to Juno who sat across from us. He and I both knew many of the symbionts present, since the composition of the Twelve rarely changed. However, the big new factor was that a female had taken over the position formerly held by Max Stone, my nemesis in all ways that mattered. To say I hated him would be pretty much accurate. Human morality teaches that it is wrong to hate, but I had always taken the position that to pretty up a strong emotion with the word 'dislike' was being false and ridiculous. If it was hate, just call it that.

Philo was still in the leadership role, but the Twelve was grooming the younger female to eventually take over the position at whatever time Philo chose to revert to his passion, which was research. Like so many in the human world, my peers were thinking that younger equated to better. I worried that they were tossing maturity and experience out the window as they strove to infuse new blood into the mix. I knew next to nothing about this new player, who was conspicuously absent.

A door to the rear of the room opened, and I turned my head to watch as a tall, breathtakingly beautiful humanoid symbiont walked in. She had the grace and bearing of a dancer or maybe an athlete. Her hair was a vivid copper hue and hung down her back like the mane on some wild, untamed animal. Brown eyes stared out of a face that was a perfect oval of creamy, flawless skin. With care, I shuttered my thoughts after giving Kipp a quiet caution to do the same. We would keep our hand carefully concealed for the moment.

The female took her place at the opposite end of the table from Philo and, smiling, nodded to those present. She saved the direct gaze for Kipp and then for me, almost as an afterthought. It was no surprise that she had been told that Kipp was the remarkable one, worthy of respect and perhaps research. I was nothing new…another contemporary with an adequate skill set but nothing amazing. The glance she gave me was not quite dismissive, but it came close. Kipp experienced a minor twinge of irritation before I reminded him to bank his feelings.

As I did so, I felt the twitch of her mind as she followed the exchange between Kipp and me, an indicator that she did not follow the usual symbiont protocol of politeness. This was unexpectedly intrusive and an unwelcomed wrinkle. She'd not been formally introduced but had already met her match with Kipp. He slammed his mental doors and relaxed at my side, passive and calm.

Philo cleared his throat and spoke. "Petra and Kipp, I'd like you to meet Andrea Collins, the newest member of our group." He looked around the table as he mustered up a smile.

Knowing him as I did, I recognized his anxiety without having to probe his mind; it was evident in his body language as he first put his palms on the table and then removed them to cross his arms at his chest. He did not care for our newest team player but was compelled to play the part of a gentleman and welcome her as we all acted civilized with one another.

I nodded my head and made a comment of welcome. Kipp half closed his eyes and remained quiet. It was marginally rude, and I suppressed the amusement I felt. Kipp's boorish behaviors would be tolerated but not any coming from me.

The female's dark eyes traveled from me to Kipp, and it did not take a talented symbiont to feel her gently probe his mind. I glanced at Philo and saw him drop his gaze to the polished table top. He did not approve of her methods, that much was clear to me.

"If you want to know something, you need to ask it out loud and not try and pry it from me," Kipp commented as he swiveled his massive head to stare at Andrea. "I don't like you trying to go places you've not been given permission to visit and will only let you know what I choose to give up freely." He was completely and utterly in control of himself, and the thoughts were delivered without malice or defensiveness.

Andrea sat up straighter in her chair, if that were possible, and stared at Kipp for a moment before laughing. She had a deep, throaty laugh that no doubt was attractive to those of the opposite sex. Fortunately, Kipp was a lupine and just wasn't interested.

"Why, Kipp, I meant no harm. I was just trying to get acquainted." She placed her hands on the table, and I could see perfectly manicured, oval nails that were painted a pale coral color. Without thinking, I glanced down at my own set of nails and recognized their ragged, unkempt nature. I could not find any similarity between myself and Andrea save the obvious one that we were of the same sex and species.

Kipp glanced at me and lolled his tongue out in the gesture I recognized as his manner of laughing. Darn it, he was having fun while I was sweating bullets.

"I'm perfectly happy to get acquainted, but you don't need to go prying into my head to do that." Kipp cocked his head at her. "I thought symbionts are compelled to observe restraints with one another."

I looked across the table at Juno and her eyes met mine. Despite the fact her dark orbs were clouded with cataracts, she still could deliver more expression with a glance than could many others. There was something in her bearing that warned me to let Kipp handle himself. She knew, as did Philo, of my protective nature when it came to Kipp. I took a deep breath and relaxed my clenched fists.

"The only symbiont I allow unfettered access to me is Petra; that will not change," Kipp commented.

He felt strong and confident from where I sat. And I suppose in the overall scheme of things, he could be just that. As far as our species was concerned, he could not be forced to do things against his will. About the most terrible thing that could afflict us was to be separated from our bonded partner. And if they ever tried to do that, I would leave the community and strike out on my own with Kipp, if he so desired. I literally owed my life to him and would be whatever he needed me to be.

Andrea Collins had regained her composure, and I felt her completely withdraw into herself. She turned her smile on the others. As I watched her, I wondered what chain of events had brought her to this place. She obviously was greatly skilled, perhaps on a level to approach the masterful Kipp. Was there a thought that she could forge a symbiotic bond with him and change the future course of our species? The question was in my mind but along with it came the soft voice of Kipp. He had chosen me, despite my flaws and would not be swayed. Even if he could bond with Andrea and go forward and make a new history for our kind, he would refuse out of loyalty to me.

The remainder of the meeting was uneventful as pleasantries were exchanged. At the conclusion, I felt depleted and somewhat dejected. Yes, Kipp and I had been given permission to make our vacation travel to the old west, but the entire venture had lost some of its zest as far as I was concerned. I wanted to go to my little house, the one that was filled with reminders of the past. The collections of old bottles and knickknacks, the picture of my mother and of baby George…yes, I needed to go home and walk around my place on earth.

CHAPTER 9

Sitting back, I stretched my tired, cramped back against the stiff resistance of the chair. For the first time, I fully appreciated why a soft, inviting chair would not be conducive to attentiveness towards one's work. I rubbed my eyes so vigorously with my hands that I would have been unimpressed to see my eyeballs pop out and roll across the table. Before me stretched another one of Fitzhugh's manuscripts; if I were to finish my translation before Christmas, I would consider that to be my present to me. This sort of tedious work was really not something from which I gained pleasure despite the fact I had the aptitude. For a moment I wondered if the fact I was doing such a stellar job—and gaining the approval of the Twelve—might lead the governing body to consider me to take Fitzhugh's place one day. Such a thought was abhorrent to me, as accustomed as I'd become to a life of more activity than the sedentary pace kept in the library.

I told Kipp that I would let him set the date for our trip as long as he gave me sufficient warning to have Suzanne prepare a wardrobe for me as well as the other accoutrements required. Usually, I gave her just enough time to complete preparations for a trip, but no more than was necessary. She worked best, I'd found, when under intense pressure.

It was getting late in the day, and I had the sense that the floors above my head were systematically emptying as symbionts and humans left for their respective homes. In the back of my head, I could visualize a home surrounded by darkness, a welcoming light attracting bugs as it glowed above the front door. For many, there would be someone at home to bestow a kiss on a fatigued cheek. I'd had that, too, when I was married. But that was a long time ago…a soft sigh escaped my lips.

Peter had left earlier in the day, and Fitzhugh spent his afternoon closeted in his office. I was a little surprised to open my eyes and see his tall form at my elbow; really, he had the most remarkable talent for silent creeping.

"Philo and Juno wanted a brief meeting with Kipp and us," he commented. "I'll make tea." He turned to disappear without giving any explanation.

I shrugged my shoulders at his thin, retreating back and closed my eyes again. It was but a few minutes later that I felt the familiar ticking of my mind that heralded the approach of Kipp. The door to the library was opened by a lupine muzzle which was followed by a large shock of auburn fur.

"Hi," he commented, pacing to my side. "You are tired."

"Fitzhugh is killing me with this stuff," I replied, gesturing at the manuscript.

"Maybe we need to set a date for our vacation?" Kipp asked, tilting his head to gaze at me.

I reached down and smoothed the fur on top of his head. The upright ears seemed even larger and more attuned to me than usual. "Your call, Kipp."

The door opened again, and in strode Philo and Juno. I could not help but notice that Juno looked tired, too. She was really approaching the place that her arthritic joints were causing her to be mentally distracted more often than she wished. Philo moved ahead and thoughtfully arranged a large cushion on the floor. Kipp walked over and nuzzled Juno gently as she circled and finally plopped down, hard, lacking the coordination to make a graceful descent. A soft grunt accompanied her landing.

"You don't need to worry about me," she commented, meeting my gaze. "I'm old and my hips ache, but I still want to be here and be involved."

Had I been that obvious? I knew she was not intrusively reading my mind so all I felt and thought must have been written on my face. I nodded my head in response.

Philo cleared his throat and waited while Fitzhugh set down a tray with a pot of tea and three cups for the humanoids. Whatever the blend, I hoped it contained a jolt of caffeine because I felt as if I was about to fall over on the table and sleep for a week.

"I called us together," Philo began. "Fitzhugh, you weren't with us at the meeting we had with Andrea Collins, but I gave you a briefing. As in the past, I think we use our little, uh, unofficial group to discuss things that impact Kipp." Philo looked at each of us, pausing to make eye contact. "I think we have a joint investment in looking out for Kipp's best interest." He took a deep breath. "I think, overall, that the Twelve wants what is best, too, but unfortunately the direction can become distorted through personal agendas."

I kept my eyes down, my thoughts shuttered. Juno surprised me by focusing on me like a beam of intense light. Finally, she said, "Petra, what are you keeping from us?"

How she detected what I thought I'd so carefully hidden, I did not know. Glancing up, I made eye contact with Kipp, whose eyes were half closed. No one could penetrate his walls when he chose to keep private.

This tiny conclave that consisted of Philo, Juno, Fitzhugh, Kipp and myself had evolved into a safe place of discovery and amazement as Kipp revealed skills and talents that were once natural to symbionts but had been lost in antiquity. He could, for example, insert thoughts and manipulate dreams. It was a good thing that I trusted him completely since he could manipulate me at any time, and I'd never be aware of his having done so.

Kipp finally yawned and gave me a slight nod.

"Uh, the other day, Kipp was doing something that was a little unusual," I began before quickly realizing that I was speaking in riddles. I looked up to see Philo frown in annoyance. "When we were meeting with the Twelve, Kipp was communicating with me but managed, somehow, to block it from the rest of you."

Fitzhugh had taken a seat across from me at the table. He leaned forward, placing his thin elbows on the table. "Are you saying that Kipp was having an active dialog with you that the others in the room did not hear?"

I looked down at Kipp who managed to appear slightly bored. He, as always, was modest about his talents.

"Kipp, tell them."

"I didn't care for Ms. Collins. So I decided to block her from listening to what I was saying to Petra." Kipp glanced at Juno who had opened her dark eyes wide. Kipp managed a slight wag of his tail and leaned forward to nuzzle her face gently.

Philo shook his head from side to side. I noticed, with some tenderness, that his hair line was finally receding a little, and that the gray lurking at his temples was making inroads into new territory further back on his scalp. He was not old, by any measure, but he was a maturing symbiont past middle age. He looked up at Fitzhugh and raised his eyebrows.

The old man in his role of keeper of the history of our species knew just about everything that had befallen us over the years…good and bad. He took a sip of his tea and gave a soft sigh of pleasure. Peter must have happened upon a very nice blend of tea.

"As far back as our history is recorded, we, as a species, have practiced and perfected a non intrusive manner of communicating with one another," Fitzhugh commented. "I only read your thoughts if I have been given permission, so to speak. To brazenly charge in and take the thoughts of another would lead to chaos and probably a sound fist fight more often than would be helpful." He looked at Kipp and his face softened. "But right now, if Kipp is communicating to Petra, I would not be able to block awareness of the fact." He tilted his head and asked, "So are you, Kipp?"

"No, not now." Kipp was relaxed and self-assured.

Juno raised her gray head. "Tell us how you do it, Kipp."

"Well, to be honest, I was irritated at Andrea. She was pushing at me, wanting me to reveal more of myself than I wished. So I blocked her and began talking with Petra." He looked at the floor. "Some of it wasn't nice, so I'd rather not repeat it."

I spoke up. "Since I don't have the ability to block, I just listened to him and tried to keep my mind blank. But it wasn't easy because he was saying some funny things about Andrea."

Philo took a deep breath. "We need to be careful, my friends. I knew Max Stone was an issue because he looked at Kipp like one would a commodity…something to develop, mine, sell, etc. But Andrea covets Kipp for a symbiotic bond because she recognizes she is a supremely talented traveler…and she wants the best one of our species to be her partner." He looked away for a moment. "Her flaw is her narcissism and arrogance."

"Her other flaw is her big caboose," Kipp commented.

Philo's mouth twitched, and he tried not to laugh as he assumed a stern expression. "Kipp, it's serious."

"And why? She can't make me do anything I don't want to do. Period. So for me it's not serious at all."

I sipped my tea and recalled a time when I fought like a tiger to defend Kipp when he was a novice and innocent in our ways. The baby had grown up and needed no one to defend him any longer. There were tears behind my hazel eyes, which probably looked suspiciously bright in the semi darkness of the library. We, as a species, were flawed, but I hoped that we were always trying to grow in positive ways. Maybe the Max Stones and the Andreas were the reality checks needed from time to time.

Fitzhugh decided to change the subject for a minute. "Kipp, since we are focusing on some of your hidden talents, how is it going with Juno?"

The elder lupine smiled in her mind and glanced at Kipp.

"She has the ability to learn letters and recognize written words," Kipp replied. "So I don't think the talent is localized to me. I think that, historically, someone assumed lupines lacked the ability since our vocal cords don't let us speak the language we read."

"That's amazing!" Fitzhugh exclaimed. "I think this is one thing we need to share with the others since it opens up an entirely new chapter for our lupine partners."

"I agree," Philo commented.

I decided it was time to wake up and become a part of the dialog. "And how will you handle it if they wonder what other amazing talents of Kipp's have been kept from them?"

Philo shrugged his shoulders. "I think we can honestly tell them that Kipp accidentally discovered this talent, and that we allowed him to work experimentally with Juno. That is the truth, and we can tell anyone who inquires that Kipp has not worked with Juno on any other skills acquisition."

I shrugged my shoulders. "I'm fine with that suggestion as long as it doesn't put Kipp at risk. On the surface, it sounds pretty safe."

Fitzhugh raised his eyebrows in a polite inquiry if I desired more tea. I shook him away. It was getting late, and I was tired; the caffeine from the tea would be an unwelcomed companion in the wee hours of the morning. As I darted a quick glance at his lined face, I realized that my friends in the world were currently clustered in this room. It had been a long journey with Fitzhugh, who once seemed as if he despised me. But there had been considerable softening, and I recognized we trusted one another. Philo and Juno were constant, unshakable, and I knew would fight to protect my back at all costs. How had I allowed my world to become so small, I wondered?

Kipp's head went up, and I recognized his amber eyes were gazing up at me. The others in the room were politely avoiding my sentimental reflection but Kipp had worked his thoughts intrusively into mine. I experienced something approximating a mental hug from my partner. I felt my mouth twitch in appreciation and gave a subtle nod of thanks.

The walk home was pleasant. It was rather late, but this area was considered relatively safe for a woman to take a stroll after dark. In any case, I was accompanied by what appeared to be an enormous dog and didn't concern myself that any bad guy would think me to be an easy target. Glancing up at the canopy of stars, I gazed at the full moon suspended overhead. Having made so many trips back in time, I reflected upon the people I'd visited and their various interpretations of the composition of the universe. With the knowledge I possessed, it was beyond my mind's ability to process the fact that space stretched to infinity. When did it all start? I realized that neither the symbiont brain nor the human brain could comprehend such things. Kipp pushed his massive, warm body against my leg and twisted his head to stare up at me. His mouth dropped open in a pant, and his plumed tail waved like a flag in the slight breeze.

"Don't worry, Petra. I'm not smart enough to figure it out either."

I laughed in response and felt somewhat gratified that Kipp was unable to wrap his superior brain around the concept.

"But the moon is beautiful, isn't it," he commented.

We walked along, enveloped in a cocoon of darkness. A mild wind ruffled Kipp's fur and pushed my hair over my shoulders. The trees overhead—children of the ancient forest that populated this part of the country once upon a time—swayed back and forth, the leaves speaking in a soft rustle. I stumbled on a rough patch of sidewalk, and Kipp moved his body protectively against my leg. There were times I envied my partner his superior instincts of hearing and sight…and this was one of those times.

"Why do dogs howl at the moon?" I asked unexpectedly.

Kipp furrowed his brow. "They don't, really. If you notice, they howl when there is not a moon, too. But there is no particular reason that dogs or wolves howl at any celestial body. They are just talking to each other."

"And you understand them?"

"To a point, just as I understand Lily…on an instinctual level."

In a whimsical moment, Kipp left my side and scampered up a grass-covered hill. Laughing softly to himself, he tucked his haunches and sat rigidly upright, head pointed to the heavens. Stretching his neck, he let out a mournful, night piercing howl. Turning my head, I saw a couple of porch lights snap on as people regressed to thinking they lived in the midst of the wilderness.

The remainder of the walk home was quiet and introspective. While Kipp took a discrete trip to the back yard, I opened a can of soup and began warming it on the stovetop. By the time Kipp returned, I had his dinner in a bowl, and he managed to devour his food in less than sixty seconds. I'd turned on the television in the living room and lost sight of Kipp as he left the kitchen. At his request, I'd found a John Wayne western since Kipp remained focused on all things old west. I brought my soup on a little tray and munched on crackers while it cooled to a tolerable level.

"Why does he walk like that?" Kipp asked, cocking his head slightly as he watched the Duke amble across a saloon floor.

"It was just part of what made him distinctive," I replied. "For a big man, he walks with small, short steps, and it changes his gait in a way that gets your attention."

"Is he popular?" Kipp asked.

"Well, he was—and still is. He's been dead for a number of years, but he was a huge, iconic star. He rarely played a bad man, and even if his character had a questionable past, he played a man of honesty and conviction."

Kipp licked his paws and settled down, without moving, for the next couple of hours. I was in and out and managed to wash a load of clothes as well as clean the bathroom.

When the movie ended, Kipp stood and stretched fore and aft.

"Watch, Petra." With that, Kipp began a short-stepped swagger back and forth across the floor in a parody of Wayne's style.

Laughing, I commented, "Well, Kipp, I think you have a career in movies." The fact I lived with a crazy lupine was indisputable.

CHAPTER 10

At an awkward meeting with the Twelve, Kipp and I were formally given approval by the group for our vacation. Andrea Collins spoke only once, and if her rigid posture and closed mind were any indication, she still held a measure of anger towards Kipp and his rejection of her overtures. It was regrettable we'd inadvertently made an enemy of her, but it was the reality and something with which we must cope.

Kipp proceeded, with an almost fanatical dedication, to watch every western movie he could catch as well as read books related to the history of the day. He, in time, became a huge fan of John Wayne and referred to me as 'pilgrim' for a week solid until I asked him to have mercy and stop.

Since I was compelled to work, I continued to assist Fitzhugh in deciphering and transcribing manuscripts and found, with pleasure, that my relationship with the old symbiont continued to evolve. I was slightly surprised to find I no longer dreaded his company and acknowledged his growing appreciation of my skills and dedication. I may not like the tedious nature of the work, but I was talented and could do a good job. This I say with no false modesty.

"Tell me more about what happened to John Gold," I requested during a brief break while we enjoyed a pot of tea.

Fitzhugh massaged the bridge of his prominent nose. I had a sense he was rubbing away his irritation at my query. It was unclear to me why he was so avoidant about the subject.

"Gold was being trained by me to take over my role." Fitzhugh's dark eyes darted to make a brief, fleeing eye contact with mine.

I was confused, and the feeling must have shown on my expressive face.

"I had some plans of retiring and leaving all this," he said with a soft laugh as he waved his hand to indicate the massive library.

I sensed he did not want to elaborate and bit my lip to contain the curiosity that boiled up in my brain. Instead, I nodded my head.

"Gold is—was—my nephew, my sister's youngest son. He was my favorite, and I think he had a great deal of affection for me." Fitzhugh dipped his head. "It was a terrible betrayal when he vanished with his symbiont, Ula. Actually, he was a talented traveler but the governing body of the day did not think he had the right temperament and judgment. John was always impulsive—brilliant, but impulsive. They planned to take Ula from him to insure he would not time shift since he threatened to go without permission. He disappeared before they could accomplish that."

I knew he was sad and disappointed over the choice his nephew had made. It seemed that Fitzhugh trusted him, and Gold had violated that trust.

I couldn't contain my curiosity and asked, "Why were you retiring, Fitzhugh? You love this and have dedicated your life to chronicling our history."

"My sister was ill and had limited time left. I planned on taking her somewhere she would enjoy and letting her live out her life with whatever pleasure she could gain." His face fell, and he looked older than previously.

What a big, old sentimental softie, I thought. He was typically full of bluster but beneath the crusty shell was a marshmallow core of kindness. I saw it in how he treated Lily, too. In response to my having conjured her in my mind, the little monster arrived and began weaving around my legs. I recognized this was her prelude to an attack and tried to shift in my chair. Instead, she hopped up on the table and began a tippy toe prance across the precious manuscript. Fitzhugh ran his hand lightly along her spine and smiled as she arched to impossible heights.

"What amazing creatures are cats," he commented, his voice soft. "She curls up on my pillow at night and taps her paw gently on my face." He glanced at me. "I always am made to wonder if she thinks herself human or does she believe I am a cat." He cleared his throat in embarrassment; obviously, this sort of dialog had gone on too long for his comfort level.

"How can I be of assistance in helping you and Kipp prepare for your old west trip?"

I told him that any maps or descriptions of the topography would be helpful. Since neither Kipp nor I had been there before, we would have to focus in on an entry point in time using study of the landscape. This, of course, was not unusual for symbionts, but it did make for a more unpredictable journey. Due to miscalculations in the past, I'd experienced more than one close call in terms of definitely being in the wrong place at the wrong time.

With Fitzhugh's promises ringing in my ears, I left him and made a stop at the workshop where Suzanne created the costumes and accoutrements required by all of us— whether an assigned work trip or a vacation journey. She met me in her typically breezy manner as she ushered me into her chaotic workroom. Brushing aside a book of fabric samples, which fell heavily to the floor, she gestured to the unveiled chair and took a seat opposite me.

"Kipp and I are taking a trip to a western town in the 1880's, specifically Tombstone, Arizona."

Suzanne's eyebrows rose in interest, but she only nodded as she took a large gulp of her caffeine charged coffee. Her bright red lipstick left a stain on the rim of the white, ceramic mug. She recognized I was a seasoned campaigner and waited for me to give her the necessary details.

"I will be travelling as a well off widow and plan on landing in a town nearby Tombstone. It will be one where the stagecoach routinely runs. So I will need an outfit befitting a wealthy young widow." I paused and rolled my eyes upward. "Since the times were treacherous, I expect to be a victim of robbery, and you need to think of some manner in which we can conceal large sums of gold coins and other currency that would be obtainable in the day." I stared at her. "I don't want to run short. My plans are to open an account at the bank and establish the fact I can take care of myself."

She shrugged her shoulders. "I know it's not my business, but why would you go to such efforts to appear wealthy? I mean, won't that draw attention to yourself?"

I sighed. "Yes, I realize I usually take the lesser, more unobtrusive role. But in this case, I don't want there to be any reason why I can't keep Kipp at my side. So, no matter where I am, I need to be able to purchase his presence." I smiled. "I have also had the thought that my wealth will buy solitude, and since this is a vacation, I want to be able to observe and relax."

She smiled. "I see. Well, we can sew some hidden pockets into your garment for currency. And I'm thinking that a nice collar can be fashioned for Kipp that works like a money belt." Suzanne put her hands on her hips. "No one will mess with him." After another moment she added, "But we will make certain we furnish you with a reticule that contains money so that if—or when—you are robbed, you can easily give up some money to the bad guys."

I nodded my head in agreement. She promised to begin work on the research required to furnish me with an appropriate outfit for traveling as well as money. Anything else needed, I would procure once I arrived.

My mind pinged, and I realized Kipp was searching for me. Mentally, I asked him to meet me in the garden out back. In less than five minutes, I was seated on the lichen covered bench beneath the shade of the yellow poplar that had graced this garden for at least eighty years. In my manner of personifying inanimate objects, I felt the tree to be a wise guardian of the activities of the symbionts hive. My romantic thoughts were interrupted by Kipp.

"Hi, Petra. So, Suzanne has started? We are really going, aren't we?" Kipp's comments flowed in rapid succession. He rested his large head heavily on my knee.

I laughed softly. Kipp's enthusiasm was infectious, and I felt my interest rise.

"Yes, and you and I have serious work to do and it starts tonight."

"Tombstone, Kipp, was a rough town, initially founded around the discovery of silver ore in the vicinity." I sat back in my favorite wing chair, a cup of hot tea in my hand. Kipp settled down on the oval wool rug that rested on the worn floors.

"Is silver important, Petra?"

I smiled at him.

"Silver is an element of the earth. It is considered valuable and is used for many things, both industrial and otherwise." I gestured at the small Luckenbooth brooch— the one given to me by my husband as a token of love— which I often wore about my neck. "This necklace is made of silver," I added.

"So, it is a soft metal," he concluded with his usual keen mind.

I nodded and sipped my tea. It was quiet on my street, and I relaxed in my chair. Soon, I would be off again. My neighbors, humans all, thought me to be a professor who travelled to universities on a lecture circuit. I'd carefully kept my publicized range of interests vague and obscure over the years. Soon, I'd be forced to move since my much too obvious lack of aging would draw suspicion to myself. At Technicorps, we solved that issue by transferring humans and symbionts on a rotating schedule that was calculated by a computer. At some point, my name would come up on the grid, and I'd probably be relocated halfway around the world. For a moment, I felt anxiety, wondering how I would make it without Philo, Juno and, now, Fitzhugh. Over my several hundred years of life, my course had intersected with that of Philo and Juno many times; of late, I'd become more attached than was wise for one of my kind. My thoughts and worries on the subject would have to wait for another day.

"There was a lot of money in the town due to mining and the stamp mills," I commented. "But also, there were ranchers who had cattle and horses. And there was a serious business in cattle rustling, where men stole cattle and took them to Mexico for sale. Also, there were houses of gambling and prostitution."

Kipp assumed his favorite sphinx-like pose and relaxed his large ears back. I knew he was ready for what I planned for him tonight.

"Tell me what you've learned about Tombstone and the various players," I requested. Privately, I hoped my own research on the subject was thorough enough to correct any misinformation he might have. It seemed time to allow him to take the lead for a change.

"There were four Earp brothers who lived in Tombstone: James, Virgil, Wyatt and Morgan. Most of today's historians think they were minor characters overall in the western theater, but there was a surge of interest in them—especially Wyatt—that began when a biography was written about him early in the next century." Kipp tilted his head. "It's impossible to know what is fact and what is fiction, and many issues were in dispute."

I nodded my head. "It is always thus with history, since all observers have a slightly differing perception. When in doubt, stick to the facts."

"The Earps went to Tombstone to attempt to make a fortune in the mining business. Their main work skills were law enforcement and owning saloons and gambling parlors." Kipp glanced up at me; his amber eyes caught a spark of ambient light. "It seems that they most likely made a living doing some of all three things."

"What about them personally?" I asked.

"They were tight knit and clannish. And the general thought was that they trusted each other completely, even if the intensity of their bonds damaged marriages and other relationships. The exception might have been Doc Holliday. Wyatt seemed to trust him implicitly."

"What did you find out about Doc?" I took another sip of my tea, which had cooled. Happy I'd brought the teapot with me, I poured a warm up and enjoyed the fragrant steam that tickled my nose.

"He is the one I'd most like to meet, I think. He was well educated and seemed to have come from a cultured family. The Civil War and the resulting period of reconstruction appear to have devastated his home life and played havoc with his health." Kipp stood and stretched for a moment before circling to lie down again. Even though his shoulder was healed, he easily became stiff if dormant too long.

"Petra, I haven't had time to research his health issues, yet."

I decided to spare him the work. "Holliday had tuberculosis, which is an infectious lung disease. Nowadays, it is curable but back then there was no effective treatment. It finally led to his premature death."

Kipp took a deep breath. "The most consistent descriptions of him were that he had few friends, was completely fearless and was doggedly loyal to the people with whom he had attachments. There is still dispute over whether he was one of the most prolific killers of his time or if he, as did many, inflated the numbers so as to draw fame to himself."

"I know a few other facts, if you would like me to share," I commented. "Doc was classically educated and could behave as a genteel Southern gentleman one moment and as a vicious killer the next. He was high tempered and unpredictable. To make things worse, he drank more whisky than most and was known to ingest two to three quarts daily. He could speak Latin, French and ancient Greek, which I would think made him stand out more than a little from his peers, many of whom were illiterate."

Kipp nodded his head. "He made his living as a gambler and, on occasion, as a dentist. He first met Wyatt in Dodge City and something transpired that made him decide to be loyal to the end." Staring off into space, Kipp added, "I guess Doc would be the best kind of warrior to have on your side. Since he knew he was dying, he had nothing to lose."

I decided to add the other bits and pieces that were residing in my brain. "When he left Georgia, he went to dental college in Baltimore. After that, he headed west and began making a name for himself as an adequate dentist, an insatiable gambler and a killer. He never married but traveled often with May Kate Horony, otherwise known as Big Nose Kate Elder. She was probably a prostitute."

Kipp really didn't understand the human need for the sex trade industry, since he was unable to equate the giving of money or goods in exchange for an act of intimacy. At least, that's how Kipp viewed sex. Male lupines didn't become sexually active until they were fully mature and Kipp wasn't quite at that place in his life yet. I'd had one birds and bees discussion with him…something that was painfully awkward for us both. Maybe I'd be spared another one and could coerce Juno to explain lupine sexuality to my Kipp.

I decided to breeze past the moment and added, "When Doc left home, he basically disappeared and had no contact with his family except for, maybe, a cousin. No one knows the type of relationship they had, but she apparently joined a convent and became a nun. And lore has it that Holliday converted to Catholicism shortly before his death."

I stood and stretched; the day had been long, and I was fatigued. Kipp knew my signals for bedtime and followed me as I turned off lights, rinsed out my tea cup, and placed it in the sink. Opening the back door, I stood aside and watched as Kipp drifted down the steps into the yard. He disappeared behind some bushes, and I took time to breath in deeply the night air. It wouldn't be too much longer before the air I breathed would be dry and dusty; the natural humidity of the east coast would be an afterthought. Kipp rejoined me and we returned inside.

In less than five minutes, I climbed into bed and tried to get comfortable while Kipp did the same. He struck his preferred pose of resting his long muzzle across my chest, sighing while I gently scratched the top of his head. That seemed to be the one spot on his body he really couldn't reach without an unusually acrobatic maneuver.

"We have a lot of preparation, Kipp," I said, my tone cautionary. For all the excitement of a time journey, they were always fraught with danger, despite all reasonable cautions to make the event as seamless as possible. The overhead fan pushed a comfortable breeze on my face and the mild humming noise from the motor made for a pleasant white noise in the small, dark room.

"We'll get there," he promised, bidding me a good night as his eyelids drifted shut.

CHAPTER 11

Kipp continued to nail down his facts, and we spent each evening reciting information gleaned from almost every likely source. When we weren't doing that, we were working at Technicorps or engaging in exercise to maximize our fitness. My experience told me that the most important thing I could do was to be physically strong. Possessing factual information was critical, too. But the defining quality of my species was to be adaptable and innovate quickly in compromised situations. In other words, we had to think on our feet and create a narrative to fit the evolving situation. With modesty, I say that my ability to do that rather well was why I was allowed to travel and many were not.

It was Saturday, and we'd spent most of the morning in abject laziness as an insistent spring storm that caused the windowpanes to vibrate in response to rolling, deep thunder passed our locale. I should have quizzed Kipp but didn't want to expend that much energy, and he was busy watching "Rio Bravo" on AMC. Clearly, Kipp was not out of his John Wayne phase yet.

By noon, the weather front had pushed out and so had the wagon train leaving Rio Bravo, so I nudged Kipp with my toe and suggested he stretch for a run. He jumped up, tail wagging, eyes bright. I completed my stretches, too, and we were out the door in less than ten minutes. The sun overhead was filtering through the thick humidity and a mild layer of steam floated up from the wet pavement. It wasn't summer yet, but the damp warmth made it feel a little like July in North Carolina.

"Explain politics and how that influenced the fight going on between the Earps and Johnny Behan," Kipp requested.

I was grateful to be a telepath since I could answer his questions without having to speak while running. In no way was I fit enough to do that.

"Well, politics and the people who use it for power and control have not changed for centuries…and that goes across nations and cultures." I made a slight course correction and crossed the street when I saw a man up ahead who was walking two enormous bull mastiffs on the sidewalk I was using. The dogs began to strain at the leashes upon spying Kipp.

Kipp glanced up at me. "They'd like to kick my butt and probably could do it. There's two of them and one of me."

"Two," I said, smiling. "I'd go down with you, Kipp. We'll fight to the end together, if need be."

We soon left the unhappy dogs behind and headed away from the clutter of houses. A few cars passed us and even a couple of cyclists, but for the most part, we were on our own.

I went on to explain that Arizona was first a territory and that the two major political parties—the Republicans and Democrats—were vying for local control so as to influence the decisions that would lead to statehood. From my reading, the Earps were Republicans and garnered the support of John Clum, the editor of the Tombstone Epitaph newspaper. Behan, then the county sheriff, was supported by Harry Wood and the Tombstone Nugget. Unfortunately, it was illustrative of how, if there is not an unbiased press reporting the news in a fair manner, the distorted information presented as undisputed facts can influence the public.

"There was a lawless element that appeared to have the

backing of the county sheriff, Behan. They were known as the cowboys and were a loosely knit collection of several smaller groups. In response to the crime they brought to Tombstone, a law and order group called the vigilantes were formed and tried to support the city marshal, who, for a time, was Virgil Earp. All the Earp brothers took their turns in law enforcement in Tombstone." I let my thoughts drift off as my visual appreciation of the passing scenery delighted my soul. Kipp, however, was still focused.

"I read about the cowboys. There was Old Man Clanton and his sons as well as the McLaury brothers." He rattled off the names of Bill Broscius, John Ringo, Frank Stilwell, Pete Spence and a few others. "I was struck over the number of conflicting reports regarding the history of those men. Some thought them to be fun loving scoundrels who dabbled in illegal activities while others regarded them as the hub of organized, violent crime."

I laughed. "Well, Kipp, you've just figured out why we do what we do...symbionts, I mean. For every event in time, there will be more than one opinion as to what happened. Part of our job is to clarify these narratives and record them."

Kipp grunted softly. "I like being on the side of truth."

The remainder of the weekend was spent with me trying to catch up countless chores. I hadn't given Philo an exit date for my time shift, but it would be relatively soon. Maybe it was a holdover from what my mother taught me, but I disliked departing on a trip with things left in disarray at home. Philo always took care of the business side of my existence while I was gone.

Kipp and I began a nightly routine of studying the various maps of Arizona. I'd made the decision that we should time shift to Tucson and travel by stage to Tombstone. My thinking was that I'd need a little time to prepare a wardrobe and to make certain both Kipp and I were mentally settled, since this would be our first trip together after a fairly long period of inactivity. We looked at overhead views of Tucson and included old photos in our study. I'd looked up the latitude and longitude; Kipp and I would lie in bed at night, focusing on the coordinates and mentally synching with one another.

After another week passed, I visited Suzanne for an update. Her hair was standing on end as usual, and I thought I detected a long buried pencil stuck somewhere in the midst of the dark strands. Some time back I'd engaged in a quiet office pool that speculated how many days it would take Suzanne to discover the pencil hidden in her tresses. I always tried to give her breathing room since she really was a true, creative presence. But to enhance her motivation, I gave her a deadline of two weeks hence that I'd need her to have completed my garments and Kipp's collar. Her blue eyes rounded in dismay, and as I left her workshop, I felt as if the orbs were drilling holes in my back.

"Kipp, what is your conclusion on the roles of men and women in the 1880's West?"

He was lying next to me; it was early—too early to go to work—but we'd both been awakened by dogs barking nearby. I'd always loved this time of day when everything felt new and fresh.

Kipp rolled over on his back and twisted his head to look at me. "I don't know what to think. It seems men had a variety of occupations—some legal and some not. And sometimes men did several things, like the Earps, to make money. I'm sure in other parts of the country, women had occupations open to them, but it seems in these new growth towns that many of them were forced to work in saloons and gambling halls. And I think many of them sold sex for money."

His distaste of the subject was evident. In the world from which he'd emerged, such a thing was unheard of.

"Life was hard, no doubt. And it still is, in many parts of

the world. There are cultures where women are not valued; I think it is improved from what it once was, but there are still many issues for the human species."

Kipp stretched his neck and arched his head back slightly. Outside, I heard a crow cawing and Kipp's ears picked up with interest.

"I like to compare the ways men and women's thoughts differ," he commented. "Both can be very organized and analytical as well as chaotic at times. But there is a difference, something I can't put into words."

I laughed. "Well, you wouldn't be the first to try and fail. Poets and authors have tried for centuries to capture the differences to no avail."

With that last profound comment, I finally made myself leave the comfort of my bed and wandered to the bathroom to splash water in my face. Raising my head, I saw the reflection of Kipp in the mirror. He was conflicted, disturbed, but not sharing openly. I trusted he would do so when he felt he needed my counsel.

After a simple breakfast, we left for Technicorps. I spent most of the morning with Fitzhugh; midday, I visited Suzanne at her request. She was ready for a preliminary fitting of my travel garments.

It is an oddity of symbiont travelling that we can take with us anything in close contact to our bodies during the time shift. Bulky objects, such as a suitcase, wouldn't make the trip. With that thought in mind, Suzanne planned on making three outfits in addition to my traveling attire; these she would roll into a bundle and contain it in something like a backpack for the journey. I would have anything additional made for me once I arrived.

I collected Kipp, thinking he would enjoy this part of the preparation, since he was the impetus behind the Tombstone journey.

"Hi," I called out to Suzanne. Her voice floated back to me from somewhere behind a partition. Her head finally appeared over the half wall, and she beckoned for me to come to the fitting room. Kipp trailed along behind.

"Let's review what the wardrobe of the day would include," she began. She held up a white, very fine woolen camisole. "Women would put on a camisole with a pair of attached drawers or knickers. On top of this would be a foundation garment, much like a modified corset, but not as extreme." She took a seat on a high stool. "The look in the early 1880s, was a high bust, fairly narrow waist and a bustle in the back. Thankfully, the wide skirts were gone, and there was a more conservative footprint." She smiled. "Feel relieved you don't have to wear a hooped foundation for a skirt that makes you look like the Liberty bell."

She held up something that looked like a basket with two long ribbons. "This is a bustle."

Kipp's head jerked up with interest. "What do you do with that?"

Suzanne walked over and anchored the basket over my fanny and tied the ribbons around my waist. Kipp began to laugh so hard he actually fell out on his side in the midst of the fabric swatches and tumbleweeds of discarded thread and fluff. His churning feet finally tangled in the mess on the floor.

Slowly I turned and put my hands on my hips. "Watch it, Kipp, or we'll create a bustle for you, too."

Suzanne ignored us both. "So, you put on the camisole, knickers, the foundation garment, the petticoat, the bustle and then the dress." She stared at Kipp. "Too bad you don't have hands or you could help her, Kipp."

I ignored them both. "What about hair styles?"

"Well, you are out west and not in the middle of high fashion society. So, I think you can get away with pretty much anything. And you'll have a hat, anyway. But a popular style was to part it in the middle and pull the sides back severely; then the back could be wound in a chignon or allowed to cascade in curls. The hat would have a ribbon to tie under the chin."

Kipp was quietly relieved that he was a lupine and spared all the falderal. I often envied my lupine brothers and sisters, and never more so than now. To a fashion minimalist such as me, these dress styles seemed silly, and I would never possess the patience or dexterity required to coax my unruly hair into cascading curls, as Suzanne called them.

I stepped into the dressing room and divulged myself of jeans and a t-shirt. Beginning with the camisole, I drew it over my head and pulled the little ribbon cord to ruche up the neckline. Placing my legs in the drawers, I pulled them to my waist and used buttons to attach them to the camisole. Looking in the mirror, I had to laugh since I looked like I was wearing a modified union suit. Feeling silly and knowing Kipp was wondering, I pulled back the curtain and ran, with my knees high up, throughout the dressing area. Suzanne was not appreciative of my high jinks at the expense of her carefully created concoctions. However, Kipp fell on his side again, hysterical with laughter.

Slightly breathless, I returned to the cubicle and managed to get the corset on; this one laced up the front so I didn't need assistance. I pulled it tight enough so that my bosom rose to impossible heights. No modern foundation brassier could manage such elevations. With the bustle resting on my backside, I pulled the dress, which was a nice, middle tone green color, over my head. With perhaps a slight modification to the day—since Suzanne knew I'd be dressing myself—she put hook and eye fasteners up the front with some decorative buttons and a concealing flap of fabric. It was, at least, simple to take on and off.

I walked out and did a little pirouette. Suzanne walked over and began to tug at the fabric, then stepping back with a critical eye. She picked up a pad and made a few notes of things she wanted to adjust.

"You'll have four garments total, including the one you travel in. Once you arrive in Tucson, I'd recommend you go to a store that has readymade clothes or a dress maker and get a couple of skirts and blouses. That will be the simplest thing for you to get on and off."

I inquired about shoes and she brought out a pair of

leather ankle boots that had buttons up the side. After instruction with a button hook, I felt relatively ready to go solo.

"You'll have one neutral hat, and I'd suggest you buy a hat or two, too. After all, you are traveling as a well off woman."

I hadn't thought of it previously, but I'd need a plausible reason why I arrived with such few belongings. But being the adaptive symbiont that I was, I quickly concocted a story in my mind that my trunk had been lost. Therefore, I had only the few things in another smaller piece of luggage that travelled with me.

That night, Kipp and I finished dinner and watched the local news. I think we both were pretty much filled to capacity with all things old west. But I knew Kipp had been pondering the most intriguing question of the period in history that lay before us.

"Yes?" I inquired, knowing Kipp hovered on the cusp of a query.

He settled on his worn woolen rug in the living room, after circling carefully a time or two. "So what really happened at the OK Corral?" he asked, turning his massive head to stare at me. "Everything I read is conflicting, but all of the movie accounts seem to portray the Earps as heroes."

"Well, of course, none of us know. But if we are fortunate in our timing, we may be able to see history as it takes place. There was a pretty big industry in the following century to portray the Earps, especially Wyatt, as the quintessential lawman who always did the right thing for justice. But during the day, there was a true divide between the factions and truth was literally in the eye of the beholder."

I was tired, more so than usual, and headed off to bed. Kipp trailed after, his paws padding softly on the wooden plank flooring. The sound of the soft ticking of his nails on the hard surface followed me, echoing in the narrow hallway. After brushing my teeth, I turned on the fan and climbed into bed. Kipp hopped up to be at my side, his muzzle across my chest. His mind was busy, active, still full of questions.

"Kipp, go to sleep," I commanded, too weary to continue to have his thoughts occupy my fatigued brain.

I must have fallen asleep in a couple of minutes, but a restful sleep was to elude me. On occasion, I had disturbing dreams. Kipp had, in the past, displayed another amazing talent when he actually entered my nightmare and changed the outcome in my mind. Our subsequent discussion led to my assurances that I was strong enough to handle bad dreams and that, indeed, dreams, both good and bad, were important and that I preferred him to keep his lupine nose out of my subconscious meanderings. But on this night, I might have reconsidered.

I, in my dream, was attired in the pretty green dress that Suzanne made for me. It must have been my mind's creation of Tombstone, and I was walking down a wooden sidewalk, a jaunty little scrap of a hat perched on a mass of improbable curls. A cluster of men were off to my right; I recognized them as cowboys, from their stereotypical attire. One of them detached from the group and walked forward to intercept me. Looking around, I noticed that Kipp was missing from my side, and I felt a mild dart of anxiety. Without my symbiont, I felt as if I were incomplete and would lack the mental dialog needed to deal with a potentially difficult encounter. But the man was smiling, his teeth flashing beneath a dark, sweeping mustache, and I continued forward.

"Hello, ma'am," the man said, stepping in my path to block me. "I think you are new in town, and I'd be pleased to show you around." He smiled again, his face dark from the intense Arizona sun. "I'm Bill Broscius," he added, tipping the edge of his wide brimmed sombrero, a style of hat the group seemed to favor.

I nodded in response and smiled, but internally I could feel my anxiety build. Where was Kipp? Finally, I managed a response. "Thank you, Mr. Broscius, but I can manage."

With that dismissal, I made to walk around him but was startled when he grabbed my arm, his large hand encircling my upper arm.

"You don't understand, miss," he said, his voice low. "This is a dangerous town full of bad folks."

I was not particularly tall or strong, but I managed to twist my arm free and stepped back from him. The blood of agitation was causing his color to deepen, and I saw his mouth twitch in frustration and suppressed anger. I knew his thoughts, of course, and my rebuff had embarrassed him in front of his friends. Curly Bill fancied himself as somewhat of a ladies' man. From behind us, a voice sounded, soft but commanding.

"Step back from her, Bill."

Both Curly Bill and I turned to see Doc Holliday standing ten feet away, his hands casually at his sides. He was minus a coat and wore a white shirt with a high collar, the tails of the shirt neatly tucked into dark trousers. The nickel-plated Colt 45 revolver he carried was holstered at his waist, his right hand resting dangerously close to the handle.

Doc was minus a hat, and a slight wind tousled his blonde hair, which was a little long for the day, and a few strands fell across a broad forehead. Beneath a neatly trimmed mustache, his lips compressed, and his blue eyes narrowed. He was thin to the point of gauntness, but in no way did he appear feeble or impaired. The lethality of the man was evident. I took a deep breath and in my dream could smell the faint scent of some cologne he was wearing.

Curly Bill was mentally reviewing his options. He had no desire for a gunfight with Doc but also didn't want to lose face in front of his friends. Bill respected Doc and did not have the hatred for him that, perhaps, an Ike Clanton did.

I felt the familiarity of Kipp and looked across the dusty street to see him sitting in front of the Occidental Saloon. His eyes met mine, and he nodded. I knew he was telling me that he was there, in my dream state, but wouldn't intrude and manipulate the natural progression.

Bill was speaking. "Doc, there's no reason for you to get riled up. I was trying to be sociable to the lady and escort her safely to her destination." His words were polite but his thoughts were twisting like a vortex of wind in the desert. A smile curved upon his lips. "You know, Doc, there is a lot of riffraff in town, and we wouldn't want the little lady to be offended by some of these rough boys."

Doc, on the other hand, was not agitated; indeed, he was calm, deliberative and calculating. I followed his keen mind and recognized he was without fear. The stray thought occurred to me that I'd read accounts of Doc having a hot and impulsive nature, but that part of him was not evident today. Maybe he was sober, and that made the difference.

Bill squared his body and his right hand dropped casually to within an inch of the butt of his pistol. He was confident, no doubt, but there were few that were completely certain of their skills against Holliday.

From across the street, the other cowboys began to stir and started walking to our location. I felt the need to do something, anything. Since I was closest to Bill, I reached over and lightly placed my hand on his forearm.

"Mr. Broscius, I would appreciate your escorting me safely to the Grand," I commented, my voice low. Glancing at Holliday, I saw his face relax as he gave an almost imperceptible nod; he saw through my behavior and recognized I was defusing a powder keg.

Curly Bill looked down at me and smiled, the white teeth flashing again. The only reason my interruption was working was because he really had no motivation for a gunfight with Doc. He was quietly relieved even if he wouldn't admit it due to his need to keep the façade intact.

Noticing that the other cowboys continued their walk toward us, I made my next move. Holding out my arm, I glanced at Doc.

"Mr. Holliday, I would appreciate your taking my other arm." Improvising quickly in the manner of symbionts, I added, "I took a bad step earlier today and my ankle was

twisted. It will help me to have the assistance of you both."
Kipp's voice of laughter rang in my head from his vantage
point across the street. He, more than most, knew my
aversion to helplessness and was amused by the part I
played of vulnerable female.

I'd placed Doc in an awkward position since he was
forced, if he bore any residual characteristics of a
gentleman, to take my elbow and assist me as if I were as
helpless as a kitten. I stepped off the wooden sidewalk and
into the dust of the street. My two escorts, without
speaking, helped me along. The sun overhead was brilliant,
and I stumbled as I looked up and was temporarily blinded.
Doc tightened his grip on my arm in response, and I looked
down to see his thin, but strong, fingers encompass my
upper arm.

A soft but insistent sound began to buzz in my head. In
the manner of one who resists the siren call of the alarm, I
attempted to ignore the increasingly loud tone until Kipp, in
frustration, licked my face.

"Wake up, Petra, and turn off that racket."

Turning my head, I raised my hand and pushed tangled,
dark hair from my face. The alarm clock annoyed me, too,
and I finally located the button to switch it off. Despite the
rude awakening, I felt myself to be in some sort of deep
stupor. Wakening in the midst of a dream state was much
the same for symbionts as it was for humans.

Another day had dawned, and I had work to do.

CHAPTER 12

———— ◆ ————

Kipp and I really didn't process the dream as we walked towards Technicorps. It seemed to me to be a fairly straight forward story of me wanting to avoid provoking any sort of confrontation that could spiral into violence. In retrospect, I think it had to do with the knowledge that I must not change history, either deliberately or inadvertently. Before we separated for the day, Kipp nuzzled my hand gently.

"I love you," he commented, gazing at my face.

"I love you, too, stinkweed," I replied, laughing to relax the moment. Kipp worried more than he needed to about me.

A message awaited me at the library. Peter was the bearer of interesting news when he told me that Andrea Collins had asked me to come to her office when I showed up for work. I was mildly curious but not interested in the least. However, she was one of the Twelve with the authority to call me to her office if the whim struck. Apparently, it had.

I made a brief trip to the ladies room and checked my appearance. Pulling back my lips, I inspected my teeth for food particles. Usually, I didn't bother with makeup, and I looked a little pale this morning, although the pattern of freckles across my nose was vivid. No doubt, my disarray and self-neglect would be a nice contrast to Andrea's perfection. Using my hand, I finger combed my hair and tamped down the frizzies. That was about all I could do on short notice.

In less than five minutes, I was at Andrea's office as her receptionist buzzed to let her know I was waiting. Kipp's mind searched for me anxiously as he inquired as to what was happening and did he need to come. I warned him away with the admonition to block his thoughts for the moment. Until I had a better feel for Andrea, I didn't want Kipp involved.

The office door opened, and the perfectly oval face peered down at me. She was close to six feet tall and was wearing three inch heels. Either she enjoyed being statuesque or she liked the powerful effect she possessed by staring down at most of us.

"Petra, thank you so much for coming," she commented. Her tone was low and musical.

I nodded my head and preceded her into the office, keeping my thoughts tightly shuttered. Even though her mind was politely closed, I knew she was exceptionally skilled, maybe on a level only rivaled by Kipp, and didn't want her to pry anything from me.

Once seated, she offered me coffee, which I accepted. Even if I didn't care for her personally, I was not so hard headed as to turn down a cup of hot brew. There was no predicting what sort of horrific blend of beverage I'd be forced to drink in Tombstone.

Andrea chatted on pleasantly, querying me about my work with Fitzhugh as well as the preparations for our trip, Kipp's and mine. I tried to keep my answers brief and factual.

"What name will you use?" she asked. Creating a name and persona was one of the more enjoyable parts of preparation for a time shift.

"Petra Totheroh," I replied, smiling.

At her raised eyebrows, I explained. "I was watching a couple of Charlie Chaplin movies and saw that his cinematographer was named Rollie Totheroh. I liked the way the name sounded."

After this polite exchange, Andrea began telling me about herself, obviously with the mindset that I needed to know.

"I was very happy to be transferred here," she began. A perfectly manicured hand drifted down to the table as she captured the cup of coffee. I noticed she had changed the nail color from coral to a pale pink. As before, I resisted the urge to stare at the ragged nubs that adorned the terminus of my fingers.

"I'd been moved around parts of Europe for years, and my number came up to relocate to the United States. I actually had been here before, but it was a couple of hundred years ago and things were much different." She laughed and smiled. I waited patiently.

"Have you wondered why I don't have a symbiont?" She stared at me. Of course, it was useless to lie to her.

"Yes," I commented, taking a sip of the hot, bracing coffee. This preamble bore the hallmark of a longer discussion, and I relaxed back in my chair. Perhaps it was productive for me to know this woman who could be a helper or a nemesis.

Her perfectly composed features changed for a second as her eyes dropped. "I had a symbiont…Cassie…but she became ill and died many years ago." She looked up. "You understand, that after such a wonderful friendship and bonding, one is hesitant to try and recreate that synergy."

I felt no need to pretend. "Yes, I felt lost after Tula was killed." Feeling a flash of sympathy, I added, "But I would encourage you to try again since you may experience something just as wonderful, even though it is different."

Her mask was back in place. A strand of copper hair fell over a slender shoulder, and she turned her head slightly.

"Funny you would say that since my interest is obviously directed at Kipp. We don't need to play games and be coy, do we?" She gazed directly but avoided being intrusive with her thoughts. Obviously, she trusted me to be honest.

"No, coy doesn't work for me," I answered. "Kipp is not a commodity to sell or trade." I stared at Andrea. "He is intelligent and self directed and charts his own course, Ms. Collins."

There must have been a candle somewhere because I caught a whiff of sandlewood and maybe patchouli. Andrea rose gracefully and made her way wordlessly to a side table. I saw a flash and realized she lit the candle. Her behavior was meant to drive home the message that she was skilled enough to monitor my thoughts without my knowing it. I didn't care for the exercise and stood.

"I am leaving now," I commented, feeling a flush of anger on my cheeks.

She opened her eyes wide and walked towards me, hands relaxed at her sides. "I was trying to be a good hostess and make you comfortable," she commented.

I took a deep breath and inhaled the candle scents as well as the acrid odor of the spent match.

"No, you weren't," I replied. "You were threatening me and don't think I don't know it. I may not have your skill level—or even Kipp's—but I'm not stupid and know when someone's playing with me." I turned to leave but her soft voice caught me.

"I can be of help to you, Petra, or I can be a hindrance. It's entirely your choice."

I took another breath and replied, my back to her. "I'm done with you."

I was back in the library in less than a minute. It was no surprise that Philo was there, as was Kipp.

"Let's go for a drive," Philo suggested. "I'll be out front in five minutes."

I was still steaming but allowed Kipp to herd me like an errant cow to the elevator. "Come on, Petra."

In four minutes, Philo turned his car from the front entrance of Technicorps and began to rapidly accelerate. Privately, I wondered how many speeding tickets he'd racked up over the years. I laughed softly. Probably, back in horse and buggy times, Philo drove in just this same manner, wheels in the air as he careened around a corner on a macadamized road. When we had achieved enough distance that even the supremely gifted Andrea could not follow our thoughts, Philo began to slow and eventually pulled the car over to a shady verge. The windows to the little car were down, and we were treated to a nice cross breeze.

I didn't wait for either of them to ask. "Andrea summoned me to her office and treated me to a little unwanted, uninvited intrusion into my private thoughts. I didn't care for it and told her so." I rushed on with my commentary. "She may think she'd the hottest new thing since sliced bread, but I don't like her, and she shouldn't be able to just show up and take over my brain."

Kipp propped his chin on the edge of my headrest. "That's not all that bothers you, is it?"

I raised my hand up and scratched him gently beneath his jaw. His mouth dropped open and a little puddle of drool made its way to my shirt. Philo was silent, his dark eyes on me.

"She did it without my knowing just to let me know she could." From my standpoint as a contemporary symbiont, she had violated me. To say I was offended was a gross understatement.

Philo raised his eyebrows. The windows to the car were down and I watched, amused, as a slight breeze tousled his already unkempt hair. The same wind pushed Kipp's fur as would an errant breeze on a field of ripe wheat.

"I am forced to report this to the ruling council," Philo said, his voice soft. I started to interrupt but he waived me off. "No, Petra. Our species decided long ago that we have certain rules of conduct with one another. You and Kipp are exceptions with one another due to, uh, unusual circumstances. But the rest of us are held to a standard. Andrea, by violating that, shows she is not appropriate to be a member of the Twelve. Our international body will want to review her membership."

"And I'll have to make a statement which she will deny," I replied. For one who hated politics and intrigue, it seemed I ended up in the middle of too many highly charged issues.

I longed for the sanctuary of home.

"She may think she's good, but, Petra, you know we really can't lie to one another. It just never works out." Philo sighed. "Don't misunderstand; I don't cherish this, either. She'll accuse me of wanting her position, or some such nonsense. Symbionts such as Andrea don't go easily because of a fault in their egos."

Kipp pushed further forward, his massive head fully between us in the car. "Let's go get ice cream." He turned slightly to Philo. "And despite whatever is going on with Andrea, Petra and I are going on vacation and don't plan on delaying it."

Philo laughed as he turned the key in the ignition.

"This is good," Kipp commented as he polished off his second bowl of vanilla ice cream. "What did you get, Petra?"

"Strawberry." I was whittling down the scoops and was perilously close to the waffle cone. I knew he wanted to taste mine but was being polite. "Here," I offered, scooping some of the ice cream on my finger.

Kipp thrust his head forward and delicately licked the pink treat off my forefinger. He immediately made a face that was the lupine equivalent of a frown.

"Yuk!"

Philo effortlessly had changed the subject to other matters and was reviewing anything I'd need him to take care of while Kipp and I were gone. It was a short time later that we returned to Technicorps; Philo had an afternoon meeting and felt settled enough to be in proximity to the unpredictable and dangerous Andrea. Kipp and I decided to take a small detour through the garden before going inside. Even though we'd pushed into summer, the weather was blissfully mild; some large clouds were forming to the west, and I thought I smelled rain on the horizon.

"Why didn't you and Philo marry?" Kipp asked. He lay

on the freshly mown grass and permitted himself a lengthy stretch.

"What left field did that come from?" I replied. "And you know Philo is married, Kipp. Why would you think of such a thing?" After a pause, I added, "And, yuk, Kipp. He is a friend, and I don't think of him in that way."

Kipp rose and shook vigorously; cut blades of grass flew into the air before he took to his sphinx pose and cut brilliant amber eyes to my face. "You have a great deal of affection for one another," he replied.

"Yeah, but kind of like a brother and sister." I paused before adding, "Kipp, stop worrying about me. I'm happy with life. You really don't need to manage me."

Two weeks later, Suzanne called me in for my final fitting. The green gown for traveling was completed as well as the other outfits. As promised, she fashioned a hidden pocket beneath the basket frame of the bustle and secreted appropriate period currency there.

"I hope no one tries to take your bustle," she commented, smirking. "If a man gets that close, you'll need to slap him or Kipp will need to bite him." Kipp, lying nearby, emitted a mock growl and displayed all of his ivory teeth—with the exception of a rear molar or two.

I thought the bustle bank idea was pretty clever and remarked upon the fact. Suzanne's cheeks reddened from the compliment.

"Come here, Kipp," she requested as she got down on her knees. He rose and came to sit in front of her. He was so massive that he was slightly taller than was she. She held out a decorated leather collar.

"I know you don't like anything around your neck, but this is a money belt, for all intents and purposes." Turning it over, she pointed to the flap that, when pulled back, revealed gold coins. "You and Petra don't need to be worried that you won't be without resources."

Kipp stared at her and then at me. "I wasn't worried."

"Yeah, Kipp," I replied. "But I can't run down a jack rabbit for dinner; and I can't go naked down the streets of Tombstone."

He laughed. "But the latter might be fun for everyone else."

Ignoring him, I addressed Suzanne. "We are having a send off party tomorrow at my house, if you can come." She accepted, as she had in the past.

The next evening, I finished straightening up the living room in anticipation of guests. Symbiont tradition held that close friends would gather the night before a time shift to wish the departing pair good fortune. It typically devolved into a roast of sorts, in my case, with embarrassing stories being told of my past misadventures.

Kipp padded after me. "I'm not sure why you are cleaning up since the place will be a wreck when they leave."

I picked up a pillow from the sofa and fluffed it before replacing it in an artistic fashion on the armrest. "You are correct; it's just what we do and a part of history."

A noise went off in the kitchen signaling the coffee had brewed. Simultaneously, the doorbell rang and I went over to admit Juno, who was laughing at something Philo had said. Kipp darted forward with delight and touched noses with his old friend. Then, like an ancient courtier, he accompanied her to his favorite woolen rug and hovered anxiously as she got her body comfortably positioned.

"Tom couldn't come," Philo commented. "His son is playing baseball and had a game tonight."

Fitzhugh followed Suzanne inside, and, much to Kipp's delight, Fitzhugh released an anxious Lily from a fabric cat carrier. She almost literally tore out of the contraption and ran around the room until Kipp cornered her and licked her triangular face in a soothing manner. Lily, in response, began to curve between his legs, her back arched to impossible heights.

I beckoned everyone to be seated. In one of the many

peculiarities of symbiont culture, it was our responsibility, Kipp's and mine, to provide food and entertainment and then clean up after everyone left. I'd made a large pot of vegetarian chili for the humanoids and boiled chicken and rice for Kipp and Juno.

Philo arched his eyebrows. "Something smells good, Petra. Is it your vegetable lasagna?"

I shook my head in the negative.

"How about that amazing vegetable soup you make?"

He went on listing multiple things until I became slightly cross with him.

"It's chili, and I worked all day on it."

I retreated to the kitchen to prepare drinks for all and was surprised when Philo trailed after me.

"I've made a preliminary report to the governing council on that business with Andrea. They, actually, weren't surprised and it seems that there have been past concerns over her ethics. I think they have moved her around hoping she'd fit in somewhere because she is so talented. But this may have been a last straw, and I think they'll find her a research spot somewhere and avoid leadership roles." He took a deep breath. "I didn't want you to worry about it while you are gone."

I nodded my head and filled another glass with ice cubes. "Thanks, Philo. It's good to know that I won't have to deal with that when I get back."

Our small group spent the next four hours in laughter and storytelling. For Kipp, this was amusing since he didn't share in our collective history and was still learning about what it meant to be part of a larger community. And he was even more startled when the typically composed Juno decided to reveal a tale that would seem to be antithetical to her nature.

"Yes, I know it's difficult to believe, but I was once young and agile as are you, Kipp." She nodded her gray head. "I was partnered with Joshua Green—you remember him, of course, Philo."

Philo nodded his head and smiled. "You two were a pair, Juno."

Kipp was resting on his haunches with Lily reclining on her back between his massive forepaws. "In what way?"

Fitzhugh spoke up, his voice sounding mock disapproval. "They were always in trouble, doing something that was forbidden."

"Juno!" Kipp exclaimed, his eyes aglow. "I have a renewed respect and admiration—a lupine after my own heart."

She laughed in reply. "Josh and I got into some serious mishaps, but he was clever enough to always dig a safe retreat…somehow."

The rest of us maintained a respectful silence for a moment before Juno broke it, obviously not wishing to cast a pall on the festive occasion.

"I'm slightly envious of this trip you two are taking. I've never been to the old west and to experience such an iconic—and highly controversial—moment is a wonderful opportunity."

Kipp looked up at Fitzhugh. "Why has no one been to Tombstone before?"

The old symbiont sighed and his eyes rested for a moment on Lily. Against his bidding, a tender expression took the place of the normally harsh one.

"There are so many periods and moments in history to visit and so few of us to make the journeys," he replied. Smiling, he glanced at us all in turn. "There are six symbionts in this room and only two of us can travel. And that is a relatively optimistic statistic for our species."

The evening began to wind down and, as was typical, the others left after wishing us good fortune and compelling us to be careful. Fitzhugh corralled Lily with my help, and she was returned to her little carrier for the ride home. Philo paused to give me a hug, and Juno touched noses with Kipp.

After the door closed, I looked around the room in dismay. The symbiont standard of tradition had been met; Kipp and I were left a total disaster to clean. It had never occurred to me before, but perhaps this had started as a method of decreasing anxiety and to help draw the focus onto other things. The most successful time shift would occur with a relaxed pair of symbionts who had their minds cleared of other issues.

Kipp followed me back and forth as I carried dirty dishes to the kitchen. As I began to wash, he sprawled out on the floor and engaged me.

"Do you have worries about Andrea?" he asked, eyeing me with one amber orb.

I placed a clean, dripping glass on the draining basket. "No, Kipp, I really don't. I trust Philo when he says it will be addressed. None of it is my problem, when you think about it."

He gave a grunt in response. In less than half an hour, the dishes were clean and put away. I wandered into the utility room and checked the dryer. A towel and a pair of my jeans languished, lonely and abandoned in their metal cocoon. I folded them and left them on top of the dryer. A walk through the living room completed the tour…all pretty much seemed back in some semblance of order.

With Kipp on my heels, I walked to the bathroom and, after stripping off my clothes, took a long, hot bath. The water was soothing, and I used the time to meditate with deep, rhythmic breathing in order to relax and empty my mind. Finally, I turned off the water and stepped out of the tub. Kipp rested on a little rug nearby and looked up at me.

"It is inexplicable, isn't it, how our species would branch off as it has with us looking so unalike?"

I finished drying off and wrapped a towel around my damp hair. "I think you picked the correct word—inexplicable. I guess this is one of those things that our species can debate but in the end, this is simply who we are. I was raised to believe we are the product of an inspired Creator. So if He has a purpose for my life and yours, who are we to say?"

Kipp grunted softly. He remained silent, and I could feel his mind beginning to shift into a time shift mode of concentration. I was certainly willing to allow him to expend the energy to take the lead and observed as he pulled up imagery in his brain of images from the pictures of Tombstone as well as map depictions from photos and satellites. He was my superior in all ways, and it was nice to relax, for a change.

After blow-drying my hair, I began to dress for the trip. It only took me fifteen minutes to get the layers of garments in place, including the fanny pack-bustle bank. Standing before the mirror, I parted my dark hair down the middle and pulled the sides back where I coiled the mass into a neat chignon. Maybe I'd attempt the cascading curls at some point—but not today.

Suzanne created a very clever over the shoulder pack that contained my other garments. When turned inside out, it looked like a period carpet bag so as to help me blend in with the styles of the day. Calling Kipp to my side, I buckled the money belt that masqueraded as a collar around his thick neck. He rolled his head a little, not liking the feel of the unfamiliar equipment. He craned his neck and glanced at me.

"I guess if you have to wear that corset and bustle, I won't complain about this."

I tried to pull my skirts out of the way and lay down on the bed. The bustle created an unnatural curve to my lower back that was both unwelcomed and uncomfortable. Kipp hopped up and took his place at my side. Pulling the shoulder roll of clothes tightly to my side, I motioned Kipp to get closer. I crushed my new hat across my chest, and Kipp anchored it with his muzzle; I rested my arm across his back. We began deep, synchronized breathing as we began to relax. Kipp's mind effortlessly wove into the patterns of mine until his thoughts were indistinguishable from mine. The symbiotic bond had begun.

It happened in the miraculous manner that I hoped I'd never take for granted. Feeling as if my body gracefully jackknifed, I fell back into a funnel, a vortex with no beginning and an uncertain end. Kipp's mind reached out to reassure me and guide us to our destination.

CHAPTER 13

The thundering in my ears resembled the sound of rushing wind but in actuality I recognized the familiar beat of my heart as it rang out a rapid tattoo. Kipp's pointed muzzle pressed against my sternum until I felt certain my breastbone would shatter in response. All around us was dark, and it took my eyes a few seconds to adjust to the new surroundings. Kipp, with his inherent lupine gifts, was able to put the pieces together with more alacrity than was I.

We appeared to be in a barn, lying on the floor in a pile of dirt and straw. Inhaling deeply, my nostrils were frankly assaulted with the scent of horse dung, saddle soap, unwashed human bodies and other smells of uncertain origins. Kipp's large ears flickered with interest as he sorted out the various odors and connected them to the likely sources.

There was something sharp digging into my back—other than the bustle—and I reached beneath to pull loose a medium sized rock. Kipp, after inquiring if I was okay, stood and engaged in a vigorous shake. I saw dust particles fly, along with hair and straw, in the dimly lit barn. I sat up, and after allowing my head to clear, I stood, my legs slightly wobbly from the time shift. Kipp mentally frowned, since I'd not been unsteady when we traveled to

Lands Point Colony. He stepped forward and braced his large body against my legs.

"I'm fine, Kipp," I commented and paused to stretch. Obviously I'd gotten some sort of leg cramps during the journey but would walk out the aches with time. Removing the shoulder roll of clothing, I carefully unpacked the few garments, turned the sling inside out so that it took on the appearance of a regular carpetbag, and replaced the clothes. After dusting off the straw and dirt from my dress as best I could, I looked for an exit. The barn appeared to be closed up for the night, but the outline of a door beckoned to my right.

With Kipp at my side, we walked outside and found ourselves in a narrow alleyway; packing crates, barrels and discarded pieces of timber littered the path, but in a moment, we found ourselves on a main thoroughfare. I could only hope we were in Tucson, and that the year was 1881. A lone man approached, and I met startled eyes when he spied what appeared to be a dog the size of Kipp at my side.

"Excuse me, sir," I began. "I arrived here earlier today and have not had the opportunity to obtain accommodations. Can you direct me to a well thought of hotel that can meet the needs of a lady?"

He removed his hat as would be customary, and I got a better look at a lined face, weathered from the sun. Blue eyes peered out from slits in his face.

"Why, of course, ma'am. I'd be glad to walk you over to the Marquis Hotel, if you will permit my accompanying you." He added, "Tucson after hours can be a little rough for a lady traveling alone."

I was relieved that Kipp and I had at least hit the geographic mark. And even more, I was happy that this man seemed to have no questions for me—or at the very least, manners silenced his tongue—thus sparing my still addled brain from having to construct a plausible story. The man looked down at Kipp.

"Your dog might be a problem, ma'am."

I smiled up at him. "Hopefully not; he's very well behaved."

"I'm Steve Hill," he said.

I held out my hand, hoping it appeared to be a delicate gesture. "I'm so happy to meet you, Mr. Hill. I'm Mrs. Petra Totheroh." I added the title so that he'd have no misconceptions about my status.

"I run the dry goods store here, Mrs. Totheroh. And I hope you won't find me rude when I ask what you are doing here alone." A crease of anxiety took its place with the other myriad crisscrossed seams.

Kipp and I could read his thoughts with ease, and I was relieved to find only honest consternation and concern on his part. How fortunate was I to find a decent man who had old-fashioned values solidly instilled into his being.

He ushered me off the elevated wooden sidewalk and began to lead me across the dusty street. Raising my head, I saw some points of action along the boulevard despite the lateness of the hour. There was what appeared to be a saloon, if the yellow lights, loud, raucous voices and the tinny sound of a piano were any indication. I made out the tune of 'O Dem Golden Slippers' and recognized it as being a popular song in the early 1880's.

"Kipp—my constant companion—and I were traveling out west in search of a change of scenery. Unfortunately, my trunk has been misdirected, and I have only this one bag. I was too fatigued when we arrived to search out lodging." I hoped he'd not ask me how I arrived since I didn't know if a train ran through Tucson or if it was only service by coach. I'd been a little sloppy with my research; when I asked Kipp, I realized he'd not paid attention to an important detail.

"Well, we have several dressmakers, a milliner, and the general store carries some dresses that are already made up. So, unless you are strapped for funds, I think you can replace things fairly quickly."

I smiled up at him and was rewarded with the same in return. His thoughts towards me ran to paternal in nature, and I followed his memories as he recalled his daughter who would be about my age (he thought!) if she had lived past the smallpox epidemic that hit Tucson many years in the past.

We arrived at the Marquis Hotel, and he stood back, holding the door, to let me enter the lobby. Kipp stayed at my side, and this behavior drew the stare of the clerk. We walked to the desk, and I saw the man puff out his chest in indignation that I would bring a dirty animal into his lobby. I knew, from his thoughts, that he didn't care one way or the other but that this might be a way to extort money from me. Well, he had the right person, and that was one of the reasons I came amply supplied with cash.

The desk clerk was about my height, which made him slightly less than average for the times. His dark hair was severely slicked back with some sort of pomade, the fragrance of which I could detect in the many scented environment that seemed to define Tucson.

"May I help you?" he asked, putting an emphasis on the 'you'. It was obvious I'd have to exert a little effort to get Kipp a place in this establishment.

I took my time and looked around, hoping to project an attitude of critical superiority. After all, I was posing as a wealthy woman who no doubt had stayed in fine hotels. This place smacked of new growth and young money; the carpet was new but not woven of the best wool. Brightly gilded fixtures gleamed as the oil lanterns flickered with the softness of uncertain light. Kipp was clearly fascinated, and I smiled as I followed his train of thoughts as he compared reality to the constructs he'd seen on television.

Pulling my shoulders higher and back, I replied, "I am Mrs. Totheroh, and I would like a room—preferably something large, such as a suite."

The clerk shifted his weak, watery gaze to Kipp and looked up, silent.

"Now Elliott, you be civil to the lady and do as she asks. The dog stays with her, and I bet she'll be willing to pay a little extra for the privilege." Mr. Hill spoke up, a chivalrous knight in my defense.

Elliott shrugged his shoulders and shifted his eyes to Steve

Hill. "Now, Steve, you know I can't do that. The owner will fire me." He leaned forward and whispered. "He don't allow animals in the place after that gambler rode a donkey up to his room and let it spend the night on his bed."

Hill's mind was filled with the humorous memory, and it was all I could do to not laugh as I read his thoughts.

"Mr. Elliott," I began, "I am prepared to pay twice what the rooms are worth and will pay for a month in advance. In addition, I also will reward you and the other workers here for all the accommodations you make on my behalf." I looked down at Kipp who stared back at me and wagged his tail. He'd learned the role of submissive, happy dog. "My Kipp, as you can see, is quiet and well behaved. You will have no trouble from him or from me."

Elliott's thoughts were racing. He didn't want to draw the ire of the owner but at the same time realized he might be viewed on favorably for the double rate a month in advance. The best—and most expensive—suite was available. He decided to take the gamble.

"Alright, Mrs. Totheroh; I'll take a chance on your dog being as well mannered as you say—you being a lady and all." His thoughts, however, ran otherwise and he definitely wondered if I was a Madam. Kipp found the very thought offensive and bristled until I ran my hand down his fluffed fur to settle him.

"It's not personal, Kipp," I admonished my partner.

"Okay," he responded. "I just didn't care for his insulting thoughts about you."

Elliott handed me the register which I signed, Mrs. Jonathan Totheroh and guest. Then he came from behind the counter to personally escort me to my rooms. My friend so far in this vacant land—Steven Hill—took his leave, tipping his hat as he exited. Elliott took my carpetbag and preceded me up the wide staircase. I stumbled once, not accustomed to the long and voluminous skirt, but manage to catch my balance before taking a header down the stairs. Kipp nuzzled me anxiously.

The suite consisted of a small sitting room and a larger

bedroom that overlooked the main street of Tucson. A nice extra was that a hip bath was hidden in a small alcove artfully concealed with a screen. Some hot water, and I could bathe! Elliott made a minor fuss of lighting the lanterns and assured me that a maid would bring fresh water in the morning and attend to the chamber pot. Kipp was fascinated at the latter reference, so I supplied a definition in my mind. It was difficult to not laugh at his horrified reaction.

As Elliott left, I placed a coin in his hand; his small, pale eyes glanced at it quickly, and I felt the avarice race through his body. He thought he could make lots of money off of me if he played his cards right and was sufficiently obsequious. His curiosity about me and my situation was apparent to even a novice symbiont, which I most certainly was not.

"Mr. Elliott, if it would not be too much of a bother, I would appreciate if you could have a dressmaker here in the morning. I have become separated from my trunk and will require some things."

His eyes opened wider as the unsolved mystery of my presence deepened. But he bent slightly at the waist and departed.

Kipp and I stared at one another, exhausted but pleased. So far, we had made the journey unharmed. And what was even better was that the timing could not have been more perfect.

"Kipp, the date on the hotel register is July 25, 1881. The actual gunfight at the OK Corral takes place on October 26, 1881."

"So what do you think we should do?" Kipp was still uncertain with this sort of thing, despite his superior mind and talents. I was the flawed but experienced professional.

"I think we need to keep a very low profile here. Just our presence and the fact I obviously have some money draws attention." I took a deep breath and realized the corset was unpleasantly tight across my chest. With that in mind, I unbuttoned the dress and let it slip off my shoulders. There was an indention in the wall over which a curtain covered the area. This served as a closet and a series of pegs were arranged for hanging clothes. Taking my dress, I managed to hook it on a peg, hoping to air it out and let the wrinkles fall away. Next, I rid myself of the nightmarish corset and bustle. That left me in the comfort of the camisole and drawers.

"I'd like to keep to this room, with some limited time out, but no real excursions. We'll use that time to ground ourselves and become accustomed to the flow of energy here. I'll also be working on a small wardrobe and planning our coach trip to Tombstone."

Kipp nodded and sank to the floor. "If the history I've read is fairly accurate, in March of 1881, a group of masked men held up the stagecoach that was en route from Tombstone to Tucson. It was carrying a chest of gold and one Bud Philpot was killed during the robbery. It was thought by most that it was a gang of cowboys, but there was a concerted effort to frame the Earps, and even Big Nose Kate implicated Doc Holliday to Behan." Kipp looked up at me. "She later denied the entire event, but that was the beginning of the end of their relationship. Doc hated Behan and felt betrayed, even though Kate was probably drunk and angry when she made the accusation."

I'd sat on the bed and dipped down in the soft, cotton ticked mattress. It was fairly comfortable for the date and time in which we found ourselves.

"Kipp, things are boiling in Tombstone, and we will have to keep our wits about ourselves. We can observe and interact but must watch one another to make certain we don't influence history, which must naturally evolve."

After checking if Kipp needed to go out, which he didn't, I lay back, so tired from the time shift that I didn't bother to pull down the covers. Kipp quickly hopped up and took his place at my side. We both fell asleep in less than five minutes in a dreamless sleep that was born from exhaustion.

A polite tap on the door awakened me; I glanced up at the unfamiliar ceiling, which was white paneled with dark beams crossing the pale expanse for support. Kipp's head shot up, leaving a warm imprint on my chest.

"Just a minute," I called. With foresight, Suzanne had included a dressing gown for moments such as this, and I donned it in less than thirty seconds and went to the door. A young woman—more properly a girl—stood in the aperture, a timid smile on her face.

"Good morning, ma'am," she said with a little curtsey bob. Elliott had told her to treat me with courtesy and respect and promised that I would reward her with money just as I had him. Someone like this tiny mite would struggle all her life for the basics; I felt a dart of compassion.

Kipp looked at her, wagging his tail, aware that his size would be a threat. He, too, felt gentleness in response to this child. His thoughts merged with mine as he recalled my having told him how difficult this world could be for women.

"And you are?" I asked, smiling.

"Oh," she stammered, her face coloring at the obvious lapse of manners. "I'm Emily, ma'am. Mr. Elliott told me to take special care of you." Her hair was pulled back from her face, but dark wisps, having escaped the confining ribbon, feathered around her oval face. Her eyes were large and dark, like those of a passive doe.

I did not care for fancy titles and would have liked her to call me Petra. But I knew that would be inappropriate so I heard my voice tell her that my name was Mrs. Totteroh. I gestured at Kipp.

"Emily, this is my dog, Kipp. He's very friendly, and I don't want you to be worried about him."

She was anxious but took a step forward. Her thoughts recovered an old memory of a dog having chased her and bit her on the calf of her right leg. Unconsciously, her right hand drifted down to the area, and she rubbed it through the cotton muslin of her dark skirt.

Kipp, knowing his job, walked forward with that silly, open dog smiling face and managed to put his big head beneath her tiny hand. She smiled as her fingers registered the softness of his fur.

"He seems okay, ma'am."

I had a list of requests for the child and would see to it that she was compensated generously. Since I'd followed Elliott's thoughts on the matter the previous night, I realized he would shake her down for a cut of her tips. I had a plan for that, too.

"Emily, I'd like you each morning to bring me a modest meal; Kipp likes any sort of meat and eggs, too. I might ask you to do the same, later in the day."

Her dark eyes opened wide. "Are you staying in, Mrs. Totheroh?"

I nodded my head and took on a somber expression. As always, I felt some regret at the contrived deception, but it was time to create the story.

"Yes, dear. I hate to trouble you so, but I've just recently lost my husband and made this trip out west as a way to try and divert my sad thoughts." I looked over at Kipp. "I don't know what I would have done without my loyal Kipp to keep me company."

Emily's face took on a sad expression. "I'm so sorry to hear that, ma'am. I'll be happy to try and make you comfortable here."

She showed me a back staircase used by the servants by which I could escort Kipp outside for his needs. Emily assured me that she would take care of a dressmaker and a milliner as well as make certain we would have meals delivered as long as we wished. Of course, she had no way of knowing that our food needs were minimal due to our unique metabolism, but already it was a relief to me to be able to hide out with relative ease while we learned more about the times and players. Kipp was more eager than was I to mingle, and I assured him that we would eventually be engaged.

Later that afternoon, a round, short elderly woman with a riot of gray hair that was bundled on top of a large head appeared in my doorway. Her head had a slight, but noticeable, palsied tremor.

"I'm Mrs. Hall," she announced herself in a brisk, no

nonsense fashion. She appeared to be significantly past middle age but exuded waves of competence. Indeed, she assured me she'd been making dresses for ladies for more than thirty years.

She'd brought a little leather bound book and carefully documented my measurements and some comments about fabrics and colors. I found her to be more than a little bossy—but in a helpful way—when she instructed me as to what colors would be the most flattering for my complexion. I didn't care, of course, and was happy to let her bring forth her creative nature in all its glory.

"I am planning to remain here for but a brief time before I travel to Tombstone," I commented, in response to her comments as to when she would have my mini wardrobe complete. My next comments were probably odd, but I made them anyway. "Mrs. Hall, I really have little interest in the dresses and am of practical need of clothes since my trunk was lost. It will please me to leave all in your capable hands." I paused for effect. "Of course, I would like you to make haste with this project and will compensate you extra for your time and effort." I threw out a sum and knew I hit the target when the woman's eyes opened wider.

Her face reddened slightly. Her thoughts betrayed her dislike at being told what to do but the other side, for her, was that I was willing to pay her more than she would make in six months of work...or more. She nodded her head.

"I have a skillful girl apprentice to assist. There is nothing else that I can't postpone for a couple of weeks while I work on your wardrobe, Mrs. Totheroh."

The next visit was from the milliner, and I shared the plans for my dresses and left it to her nimble mind to prepare at least three hats that I could use. Thankfully, that would be a little less involved than was the seamstress, and all she required was suggestions of colors that I might wear. My only instruction to her was to create something stylish, knowing that would be expected.

CHAPTER 14

August, 1881, was making its last appearance in the desert country. I'd spent very little time, over my life, in the southwest. It was, characteristically, very hot during the daytime in August, but the night temperatures would drop to cooler numbers. I understood why people sought this area of the country for more comfortable living if one was afflicted with respiratory conditions. The low humidity and fewer colonies of molds and spores provided a more healthful environment for the human lung.

Emily, a dear, sweet girl, continued to almost exclusively labor to meet the needs of me and Kipp. She even volunteered to walk him, and this I reluctantly allowed at the urging of Kipp. He wanted opportunities to examine the culture, and what better place than at the side of a native of the day? In order to thwart the avaricious Elliott, I would give Emily a predictable gratuity, knowing he would obtain at least half of the amount. Then, I slipped her an additional one, which she carefully concealed in her worn, leather buttoned up shoes.

"You do not owe him for your life," I told her. The idea of liberated women was new to her, but I enjoyed watching a fire begin to ignite behind the darkness of her eyes. "Women have to be smart," I told her. "Let him think he is controlling you but you must know, in here," I said, gesturing towards her heart, "that you are free of him."

She had arranged that one of the porters, a strong, strapping young giant, would bring me enough hot water for a hip bath. Up until now, I'd only taken what might be referred to as bird baths and felt more than a little grungy. As the young man departed, Emily assisted me into the bath and began to pour water over my hair, which was in need of a serious scrubbing. The fragrance of lavender overtook me, and it was nice to find that there was actually a rather fine milled soap available in Tucson.

Kipp lay nearby, watching us. His eyes were half closed, but, as usual, he was intently focused on me and Emily.

"Petra, I like this child," he commented, as he casually licked a paw. Finally, he turned on his side and sighed deeply.

"Kipp, don't even start to think about it." I knew my tone was harsh but there was a good reason to caution my bonded symbiont. "We cannot interfere in her life any more than minimally…such as now. We take the risk if we do so, that she will evolve differently than is predestined."

"I know," he responded. His head lifted. "It seems wrong at times to not be able to make a difference in the life of someone."

I knew he was thinking about Perdy and Alice and others from the Lands Point Colony. Emily poured another container of water over my hair, and I saw the soapy suds fall into the bath below. Her thoughts were sweet and simple; even though I presented myself as wealthy, she had no whiff of avarice in her tiny body. She was content that she could meet my needs and keep me happy. I knew she would have served me just as well had I paid her less, so to some degree, she was internally motivated to do a good job—just because.

"Kipp, you made a difference to the colonists. Unfortunately, we'll never know what changes occurred due to our presence, but for reasons unknown, after we left, the colony was doomed. We failed, I think, to determine why it fell off the face of the earth." I looked over at him.

"But there is no doubt in my mind that Alice felt very close to you. In that moment in time, you had a purpose, and it involved comfort."

He had turned on his side and watched me with one eye open. The long, plumed tail thumped the floor a couple of times in acknowledgement.

"Where did you get your dog?" Emily asked, her voice interrupting my telepathic dialog with Kipp.

Startled, I constructed a story. "He was a gift from my late husband." I paused, adding, "It is the reason he is so special to me."

Emily nodded her head. "My parents are both dead," she commented. "My mama gave me a necklace, and it is all I have from them. So I understand."

A bolt of guilt shot through me. I was creating a moment; Emily's was real. This was the downside for those of us who traveled, if we had any semblance of a conscience. Our roles were carefully fabricated but yet we interacted within the tapestry of human experience. Kipp was giving me a mental nudge.

"Emily, dear, go over to my dressing table and bring me the small, velvet container." I stepped out of the tub onto a folded towel and began to dry myself. My dressing gown was within reach, and I pulled it around my body.

The girl returned with the box I'd requested. Taking it from her, I opened it and found a small brooch that I'd found at an antique store to bring along as a part of my wardrobe. It was shaped like a star with a small blue topaz in the center and what were probably white topaz stones radiating out from the core. Smiling at Emily, I reached forward and carefully pinned it on the fabric of her blouse, centering it at her throat.

"Oh, Mrs. Totheroh," she commented, her cheeks taking on a rich flush of color. "This is so pretty; I don't have anything nice like this."

"Well, now you do." I patted her on the shoulder.

Kipp began, mentally, to try and figure out the circle of fate and at what point in time had I given the girl the brooch, only to find it at a later date in an antique store in Durham, North Carolina. His spinning thoughts, of the sort that have no beginning and no end, almost made me dizzy until I commanded him to stop thinking.

Later that afternoon, I was paid a visit by Mrs. Hall who brought a dress that was close to completion. Professional that she was, a proper fitting was in order. I was pleased and thought Suzanne would be fascinated by the period fabric as well as the hand stitches that she tried so hard to emulate. I determined, when Kipp and I returned to our time, to make certain I took along at least one of these creations.

Kipp kept insisting on going out more often with Emily. I was trying, deliberately, to stay out of the limelight and knew my presence would attract attention. But Kipp was, to the locals, simply a big dog, and he would be ignored.

He went down the back stairs with Emily late one afternoon as she took him to attend to his needs. I relaxed in the cotton stuffed chair in my room; a vigorous breeze stirred the curtains, which billowed inside. With the wind came the sounds of people and horses on the street. The smells were, as always, abundantly present in a time when people did not bathe on a daily basis. It seemed odd that here in the desert the wind would feel damp with moisture. I knew enough to realize that a storm was approaching.

Kipp's mind remained curious and observant.

"Where are you?" I inquired.

"We are walking on the sidewalk across from the saloon that is down the street from the hotel." That helped me to pinpoint him since there were several in Tucson.

Suddenly, I felt his alarm; at the same moment, I heard a gunshot ring out followed by the shouts of people on the street.

"Kipp!" I shouted in my mind. Not waiting for his response, I jumped up and raced from my room and down the rear servant staircase. Finding myself in a side alley, I turned and ran towards the street. Up ahead, I could see a small crowd milling, some people pushing and shoving. By this time, Kipp answered my alarm and I knew he was unharmed, but I ran forward, nevertheless.

At the end of the alley, I turned and began to elbow my way rather aggressively through the crowd. I had to get to Kipp and Emily. I read Kipp's mind as curiosity changed to concern, alarm and then horror. As graphic as if I'd been watching a movie in the comfort of my home, I saw the scene unwind. A gunfight had ensued outside the saloon and a man had been shot in the throat. Kipp and Emily watched as the life bled out of the twitching body.

When I reached the pair, Kipp was standing protectively, as was his nature, in front of Emily, who stared, open-mouthed, at the spectacle. Unfortunately, she'd seen this sort of thing many times in her young life. Kipp, too, had seen death but not on such a wholesale basis as his petite companion.

Kipp's eyes met mine.

"Are you sure you want to continue this vacation?" I asked, crossing my arms at my chest.

He nodded his head slightly.

"I knew it would be rough," he answered. "Mama didn't raise no slacker," he commented, trying to repeat something he'd heard on one of his many movie moments.

I ignored him and walked forward to Emily. Removing the shawl from about my shoulders, I placed it across her thin back and began to usher her to the hotel. A large man, dirty and unkempt stepped in front of me and blocked my path. The odor from his body almost made me retch. He grinned down at me from his superior height, and I was rewarded with the sight of a mouthful of decaying teeth. I might not eat for a week, I thought to myself.

"What's your hurry, pretty girl?" he commented to me. He stuck his leering face close to mine and exhaled whiskey coated breath. His thoughts ran to the obscene but at least he didn't give voice to everything floating about in that huge melon that was carefully balanced atop broad shoulders.

"Let the lady pass," a voice rang out and I turned,

gratefully, to see Steve Hill standing just behind me.

"Let him handle it, Kipp," I commented. I didn't want Kipp to acquire any sort of reputation at this point and time. And even more, I didn't want an angry native to shoot him.

It was almost impossible for Kipp to follow my command, but he managed to stay behind my skirts. He recognized if he was killed in trying to protect me, I would be stranded here and could never return home. His gallant nature was inherent but he had to learn to think and not react. When he did the latter during our recent Lands Point Colony adventure, he'd just about been killed as result. I took a deep breath and relaxed when I felt him do the same.

I wasn't sure what cachet Hill had with the big, stinky ogre, but the unnamed man stepped aside and allowed me, Hill at my elbow, to walk unmolested down the sidewalk. Kipp and Emily followed close behind.

Hill's thoughts were fascinating. He was confident and sure of himself but had no desire to provoke conflict. Kipp, curious soul that he was, pushed a little deeper into the memory bank and hit pay dirt.

"He was a gunfighter," he commented. "But it was a long time ago, and he came here to be done with that part of his life." Kipp took one last look out on the street; a cart drawn by a tired, dusty mule arrived to tote away the dead body. "Hill knows he has a temper and works, with effort, to contain himself." Kipp smiled inwardly. "You really remind him of his daughter, and he feels protective of you."

Hill was of the right age, I thought. Without resorting to Kipp's intrusive methods, I recalled that a lot of men who fought in the Civil War—on both sides—left military service at the conclusion of that conflict. Many, with no other marketable skills, made their living with their guns. The country was aggressively growing, and there were more conflicts than could be counted over territory and who owned what.

Later that evening, as I tried to fall asleep, Kipp prodded me to answer questions that had lingered following the death of the man that evening.

"Petra, I've been present more than once when human beings have died. The first time was covered in horror, and I couldn't get past that thought. It was the same way with the second. But this was a little different."

I turned to look at him. His large, rufous head was resting on my chest, and the almond shaped amber eyes resembled chips of precious jewels glowing in the room. The ambient lighting of modern society was missing; a full moon overhead cast an eerie, silver pall on Tucson. Kipp's eyes must have picked up some of the moon's flowing light.

"What was different?" I asked. My hair was splayed on the pillow, and the faint fragrance of the lavender soap helped to relax my mind as well as my body.

"The man who died tonight…as he was dying, he thought he saw some type of…" Kipp paused, unable to put words to the image. "I guess it was like a doorway," he finally concluded. Kipp was unsettled, an unusual state for my best friend who was typically so grounded as to be predictable. "It was just different," he added, shifting his weight slightly on the cotton mattress.

We'd covered some discussions about spirituality before; Kipp, with his keen mind, would never be content with simple answers. I sighed. Sleep must wait a little longer, I thought.

"Kipp, I know you were raised with a moral mother who instilled right and wrong in your being. It's not my place to tell you what to believe. I believe we have a purpose here on earth. When we die, many believe we have a soul—our essence—that remains in existence in some other dimension.

"A wonderful aspect of humanity is the amazing diversity of beliefs about just this issue. And, to some degree, symbionts have divergent beliefs. So, I can only tell you my thoughts, and you must figure out what is right for you."

I ran my hand along the crest of his head and watched as his eyes closed. "Time to rest your mind, Kipp."

If for no other reason than my unwilling presence at the

demise of more than a few humans over my many years on earth, I recognized something defined and inexplicable followed death. I thought it best for Kipp to continue to watch and experience the moments telepathically. Maybe in some future time, he would find ease with the matter.

He snuggled closer; outside, the temperature was falling as night progressed. Kipp's heavy warmth was welcomed, and I mentally made a journey back to the time when we met. It was cold, much colder than this night, and I felt without hope that I would survive. Losing Tula left me adrift and abandoned in the prehistoric past with a terrifying global event in play that would transform warmth and light into frigid darkness and usher forth death on a massive scale.

Kipp smiled inwardly as he recalled our awkward first moments—he, an orphaned pup of the times; me, a weary traveler from another age—before we realized that our days of being alone and adrift were at an end.

The sounds of the piano in the saloon down the street were soft but I could hear the pianist pick out "The Bonnie Bank O' Loch Lomond". He managed a reasonably decent job despite the fact the instrument was badly in need of tuning.

I knew the words to the song and softly began singing to Kipp as he drifted off to sleep. Another full day had passed; we were that much closer to Tombstone.

CHAPTER 15

Running my hands down the seams of my new dress, I tried to smooth the fabric over the stays of the corset. Mrs. Hall made delivery on two garments and two more were in production. The yellow of the ribbons from my hat were a perfect match to the dress. The fabric was a nice weight that would see me into fall. I hoped Kipp didn't intend on staying much past November.

Pausing at the doorway to the Kinnear and Company Stage Line, I peered through the rippled glass and noted happily that the sole occupant of the office seemed to be one clerk who was hunched over a cluttered desk. Kipp looked up at me and assumed his dog role.

Pushing the door open, I swept in with the hopes I conveyed money and influence. I was playing the part of a woman who was accustomed to getting needs met with as little commotion as possible. The clerk stood and his eyes took in my nicely made dress. His thoughts were clicking as he tried to decide if I was a decent woman of means or a well dressed whore. He was leaning toward the latter since there seemed to be a multitude of employment venues for prostitutes.

"I'm Mrs. Totheroh," I began, tilting my head up as I gazed at him. Kipp walked next to me, wagging his tail despite the fact he felt I had been grossly insulted by the darker thoughts swirling in the mind of the clerk.

The man was thin to the point of emaciation, and I deduced he probably had some type of severe health concern. He experienced an 'aha' moment as he recognized my name, one which had been dropped frequently due to town gossip.

"How may I help you, madam?" he asked, bowing slightly in a quaint, genteel fashion. I suspected that was his next option at a polite response since he was not wearing a hat to tip.

I looked around the small office and gestured at the chair opposite the clerk's desk.

"May I sit?" I asked, arching my dark eyebrows.

He became flustered and darted around the desk to hold my chair for me. His mind revealed the discomfort many felt towards Kipp. A smaller dog would have caused less attention. Kipp looked up at the man and wagged his tail again, dropping his jaw with a silly dog grin.

"I'm Saul Fortenberry," he said, resuming his place behind the desk.

"I need to engage a coach to take me to Tombstone," I commented, not wasting time with small talk. "Ordinarily, I would be content in a public vehicle, but I need room for my dog. As you can see, he is quite large."

Saul's pale eyes shifted towards Kipp. His mind turned to profit and avarice, and he was figuring how much he could charge me without protest on my part. He assumed I would have no idea what a reasonable cost would be. However, since I was following his thoughts, I knew exactly the definition of reasonable.

Kipp smirked internally. "I don't think Saul gets many requests like yours," he commented. "He thinks he can retire after today." Kipp's thoughts turned serious. "You realize, don't you, that word will leak out ahead of this trip, and we are sure to be waylaid."

"Which is why I have plenty of money to pay whatever demands are made…and don't forget the bustle bank riding on my fanny." I darted a glance at Kipp. "You wanted this trip; don't tell me you are losing your nerve."

"No way," he replied. "I just didn't want you to get scared."

Saul's words regained my attention. "The charge will be two hundred dollars," he commented.

I narrowed my eyes. "I will pay one hundred and twenty five dollars."

He shook his head and laughed, the sound resembling that of a braying mule—unpleasant and annoying to the utmost.

"Madam, you don't know what is involved."

I stood. "If you are not interested in my business, then I will go elsewhere."

He panicked and stuck out trembling hands as if to ease me back down in the seat.

"Now don't go off in a huff. I will reduce our price to one hundred sixty dollars; the extra will help cover the costs of the shotgun rider." He sat back and stared at me.

"Will that be necessary?" I asked, opening my eyes wide.

"Mrs. Totheroh, the journey is a difficult one and dangerous, too. Routinely the coaches are held up by bandits. But if you want to go to Tombstone, a coach is the only way to get there."

His unpleasant thoughts were difficult to avoid, even if I'd been motivated to try. It appeared that Saul made extra money by occasionally directing highwaymen towards particularly lucrative coach trips. The ill-fated Sandy Bob stage was once such an expedition due to the Wells Fargo box of gold that was aboard, bound for Tombstone.

Kipp suppressed a growl of disapproval as we followed the man's cascade of thoughts; eventually, he reached the conclusion that we were really not worth the bother and risk of a high jacking. I might have some money, but there would be no large cash box on board, and the robbers typically wanted a sizeable pay off to compensate for the danger incurred. Realizing I'd been holding my breath over the suspense, I slowly released the air from my lungs.

I finalized arrangements with the clerk, and Kipp and I

were free to wander about Tucson. Since we'd be saying goodbye to this town soon, I decided to walk down to the small store kept by Steve Hill. A small bell tingled as I opened the door; Hill, from behind his counter, looked up and smiled, exposing even teeth that gleamed from his dark face.

"Mrs. Totheroh," he greeted me as he walked from around the counter. Gesturing to a couple of chairs circling a small table, he indicated I should sit.

"And how has your time been in Tucson?" he asked.

As we chatted, I took notice of his tender thoughts towards me, continuing in the paternalistic manner he'd shown earlier. Despite the heat outside, the shaded interior of his dry goods store was pleasant in temperature; I looked around at the neatly stacked cans and boxes that filled the shelves. Mr. Hill obviously had an eye for detail and pride in his business.

"I will be leaving for Tombstone in a week," I replied, noticing a frown gathering on his dark face.

"It's a dangerous journey," he commented, looking down at the table top.

Kipp had sprawled out on his side and monitored Hill from this passive state.

"Yes, Mr. Hill. I'm aware of that, but it is my destination, and a trip I must make." I paused and rested my elbows on the table. The hat I was wearing must have made me look vulnerable with the yellow ribbon tied beneath my chin because Hill choked back an emotional response. But his thoughts immediately went to Saul Fortenberry. He suspected Saul's involvement in past hold ups, and Hill planned on paying Saul a little visit. It would be an unpleasant encounter, no doubt.

"In any case," I resumed, "I wanted to thank you for your kindness towards me and Kipp." Kipp, in response to his name, played his dog role by thumping his tail on the floor. "Your help certainly eased my path."

I'd succeeded in embarrassing him, and he gruffly responded with a brief answer. Kipp and I took our leave and returned to the hotel. The street was hot and dusty, and the interior of the hotel gave a slight reprieve although it was not much of an improvement. I knew, with the coming of night, the tables would be reversed, and the temperature would become unpleasantly cold.

Elliott nodded in his ingratiating manner as I passed him; Kipp almost lost his composure as the desk clerk's thoughts descended into the territory of lascivious and plain old nasty. The thoughts escalated as his eyes began to burn a hole in the area where my bustle moved gently as I climbed the staircase.

"Kipp, stop focusing on him, please, just for a minute." I was mildly irritated with my best friend and partner. Once in the security of our suite, I removed my hat and sighed over the freedom of not having the ribbon clutching my lower jaw.

"Kipp, you are the most talented symbiont I've ever seen," I began, dropping into the cotton stuffed chair.

"But?" he asked.

"But, you must focus on learning to be less reactive to humans' thoughts about me. Your overreactions can put us in danger because you lose objectivity." I stood and unbuttoned the top of my dress and pulled it from my shoulders. It dropped to the floor, and I hung it on one of the pegs so it could air out. There was a little dirt on the hem, and I would ask Emily to attend to it, with a large gratuity to go along with the request. I almost cried when I managed to unhook the last eye of the corset; my rib cage would never be the same. Kipp was in a thoughtful mood and now, as always, took my comments with a sober mind.

"Maybe this vacation is helpful to me in more than one way," he commented.

I resumed my place in the chair, and he came to sit in front of me. His large ears were upright and the auburn fur almost bristled with the energy he felt. I remained silent, waiting.

"When we went to Lands Point Colony, I overreacted when I thought you were in danger and, as result, was nearly killed. My behaviors and lack of clear judgment put you at risk, too." He flexed his haunches and dropped to the floor. "Now we are here and not working; I can take the time to focus on how to use my telepathy to monitor humans and separate my responses from actions." He tilted his head slightly. "You call it compartmentalizing."

I smiled. Kipp's life experiences were actually quite limited to date. His primitive reactivity was natural and to be expected.

"Kipp, all things must be learned. There is nothing wrong with what you do. It just doesn't mesh well with being a traveling symbiont where we are dropped into all sorts of cagey situations."

He nodded his head. "I want to master the skills," he replied.

I let my head drop back. A mild breeze found its way through the open window and cooled my damp skin. Along with the air came the smell of heated horses, unwashed bodies and a peculiar mixture of food odors—some good, some not.

"Don't let yourself become so detached that you are robotic, Kipp. That's the real trick for us—being detached from human emotion but fully engaged with one another." I looked at my companion. "It's a learned skill, and you will get there."

A soft tap on the door interrupted our dialog. Emily was checking to see if we needed anything. I asked her to see to my dress and noted her pleased thoughts; she enjoyed working and responding to requests. Even at her young age, she had resigned herself to a life of service but instead of being sullen or embittered, she turned it into an opportunity to take pleasure in a job well done. What a splendidly nice young lady, I thought.

Kipp stood and went over to push his large noggin beneath Emily's small hand. She was comfortable with him, now, and gently caressed his ears.

"Mrs. Totheroh," she began, uncertain of herself. Her gentle, dark eyes timidly sought the planes of my face.

"Yes, dear?"

"I wanted you to know that I'm not wearing the pretty brooch you gave me because Mr. Elliott might wonder where I got it." She stuttered slightly. "I didn't want him to think I stole it or something."

That would be Elliott's take on it, no doubt.

"Dear, it was a gift, and you may do with it as you please." I reached out and patted her arm. While she told me that she wore the jewelry to church, Kipp's thoughts pushed into mine.

"Petra, I thought of a way we could help her that might not interfere with history."

I immediately felt on guard but asked him to go on.

"Mr. Hill seems to be a decent man. He obviously has kind, protective thoughts towards women, and we know he lost a daughter in the past. Maybe he would let Emily work in his store?" Kipp finished with a rush. "Elliott will always mistreat her here."

"Gee, Kipp, I need to think about that."

He turned to look at me while Emily walked over to retrieve the dress that needed spot cleaning.

"She'd still be here in Tucson; she would work for someone, just like she does now." His thoughts had taken on a slightly whiney tone; Kipp's ears flattened back slightly. "I know we, inadvertently, changed progression of time when we were at Lands Point Colony." He looked out of the corner of his eyes at me. "How is this different?"

I took a deep breath. The whole concept of noninterference was a difficult one to manage. I'd found it seductively simple over the years to justify, out of a sense of doing good, managing a human's life. Maybe I'd matured past it…or maybe I had become inured to suffering.

"No, you're not hardened," Kipp responded to my thoughts.

With the adeptness of my species, I managed to have a verbal conversation with Emily while having a mental one with Kipp. The girl finally exited, taking my soiled gown with her.

"I have a proposal," he commented, with the knowledge I was inherently too curious to not snap at the bait.

I nodded my head and narrowed my eyes.

"Let's walk to Hill's store, taking Emily with us. Once we are there, we can extol her virtues and monitor how he responds. From there, we will let nature take its course."

I stretched out my legs, grateful the leather boots were off my feet for a few hours. Emily had thoughtfully brought a pitcher of lemonade, the sides of which were beaded with condensation, and I took a sip from the cut crystal glass. As I held the glass to the light, I noted a tiny chip marring the otherwise perfect rim. It was as many things appeared: imperfect but seductive.

"Okay, Kipp," I finally responded. "But you have to promise to not implant any covert thoughts in his head. Either he thinks of the idea on his own, or he doesn't."

Kipp managed to concoct an injured expression at the very thought that I would imagine he would pull the highly questionable and usually forbidden stunt of implanting thoughts in a human.

The next morning, I overslept and only awoke to a soft tapping at my door. Kipp was up and on the floor in an instant, his plumed tail waving a welcome to Emily, who hovered on the threshold. She carried a tray with breakfast for me and a bowl of chopped chicken for Kipp.

I felt awkward at having been caught unawares and fumbled to pull on my dressing gown. Kipp, having no such issues with humility, buried his head in the chicken bowl.

"Emily, Kipp and I are going to walk down to Hill's store in a bit and thought you could go with us." She looked confused, so I quickly improvised. "I am going to make a few purchases and might need your help." Lame, but it seemed to work since she nodded her head.

An hour later our happy little trio set out; I felt uncomfortably conspicuous in my fine clothes while Emily wore plain homespun woven togs. But it was part of the tableau we'd chosen, and I could not vary.

It was warm, but as the month had worn on, I noticed that the blast furnace quality to the climate was marginally subsiding. There was the threat of rain on a couple of occasions, but there had been no measurable rainfall since my arrival. The street was covered with fine dust and the particles seemed to find their way everywhere, including into my shoes and under my chemise. As Kipp trotted ahead, I could see sand shake from his dense coat.

We turned into Hill's store and once again I was greeted warmly. The ex-gunfighter was pleasantly courteous to Emily, who was typically shy in an uncertain encounter.

Now that I was here, I wasn't sure what I should shop for and decided to browse about in the pre-manufactured clothing section. There were some rather nice, simple skirts, and I picked a couple that I thought would fit Emily. Without my having planned it, the trip became a shopping trip for the girl. Steven Hill, not wanting to appear overly involved in the selection of women's clothing, hung back until I asked his opinion.

"Mr. Hill, I was thinking that Emily needs a couple of attractive skirts to wear," I commented, turning my head to the side and pursing my lips in consideration. I looked up at the older man, who had a slightly worried look on his weathered face. "Of course, I doubt Mr. Elliott at the hotel would approve. He seems to completely dominate my dear Emily." My eyes opened wide in what I hoped was a beguiling expression.

The girl, meantime, blushed high on her slender face and looked down at the skirt that she was examining at my instruction.

"I would like to think she has more opportunity than has been afforded her by that clerk, who seems to have a limited view of her capabilities." I was struggling now, and Kipp tried to intrude and make some suggestions.

"Butt out, Kipp," I responded. "I'm doing my best without asking him to hire her." But as Kipp and I jousted back and forth, I realized that Hill had turned his focus on the girl and felt a surge of compassion for her circumstances and station in life.

Hill smiled at me and then at Emily. "I think, Mrs. Totheroh, that Emily deserves some nice clothes. And it is kind of you to consider her."

Kipp felt satisfied and almost gloated. "You see, Petra. I think you sowed a seed, and maybe Hill will decide to intervene with her after we're gone."

I wasn't so sure but had done all I could to put her in the spotlight and hope. In any case, Kipp and I were scheduled to leave in a couple of days, so our time here was drawing to a close. In retrospect, I'd secluded myself for the most part and conserved my energy for the upcoming Tombstone encounter. With the exception of Emily and Hill, to a lesser degree, I'd not made any acquaintances in Tucson of any significance. The next stop, for Kipp and me, was Tombstone, Arizona.

CHAPTER 16

The stage coach lurched along the hard packed rough dirt road that led from Tucson to Tombstone. There had been a change of horse teams in Contention, and we were following the same path as had the ill-fated Sandy Bob stage some months earlier. Our drive was a laconic, lanky man whose lined face was almost completely obscured by a dense brush of facial hair. His large brimmed hat was jammed down so far on his head that all one could see was a pair of pale blue eyes. Pete, as he was called, was efficient and knowledgeable, and that was what mattered. His shotgun rider was perched on the box next to him and seemed to be a much younger man. My read of his thoughts was that he enjoyed the danger and adventure involved in this sort of work and was too early in his life to yet feel his mortality.

During our break in Contention, I took the men aside and instructed them that I wanted no heroics from them in the event highwaymen waylaid us on the road ahead. From my perspective and Kipp's, we wanted no one harmed in what for us was a vacation trip. Pete's blue eyes widened when I told him that I was planning on an extra payment for him and Dave, the shotgun man, in the event we arrived safely in Tombstone.

"I'm not carrying a lot of money, but if we are stopped, I

can pay some cash just to let us pass," I commented.

Pete glanced at Dave before turning his eyes back on me. His mouth was working with effort as he attempted to suppress a big spit of tobacco juice until his negotiations with me were at an end.

"Ma'am, no offense meant, but if we are stopped, I'll appreciate it if you let me handle things. Maybe we'll be okay, since we're not carrying a Wells Fargo box or anything like that." No longer able to delay the inevitable, Pete paused and spat from the side of his mouth. The spittle popped up a little cloud of dust when it hit the ground.

I nodded my head and reached my hand down to pat Kipp's large head.

"I like him," Kipp commented to me in our telepathic manner. "He is brave and confident, but there is something, uh, real and humble about him. He should be afraid but just takes the risk as a part of his life and job." Kipp, feeling impulsive, walked forward and gave Pete a gentle head butt.

The man laughed and reached down to ruffle Kipp's large ears. "Nice dog," Pete commented.

Kipp twisted his head around and looked at me. "Maybe I should try to pat his head and tickle his ears?"

I ducked my head, suppressing a laugh.

In a short time, we were back on the road. After we passed Drew's ranch, we began up the steady incline that had been the location of many criminal escapades in the past. The grade of the road forced the team of horses to slow; if Pete had driven them harder, the result would have been exhausted animals on the downside of the slope.

All that was visible from the window to my right side was the scene of unending desert; the sun was tilting towards the west and shadows were beginning to lengthen off in the distance. The blue sky was drawn through with steaks of lavender and deep violet, much like a piece of fine silk fabric. By now, Kipp and I had become accustomed to the gentle rocking of the stage; it was oddly hypnotic and I yanked my head up when my chin abruptly dropped to my chest. I glanced at Kipp who reclined across from me, his large body occupying the entire bench seat.

"I'm glad we came," he commented. "It is interesting, and I'm enjoying the change in scenery."

I nodded my head; Kipp suddenly jerked his neck and his ears pricked upright. He was so superior to me in skills, he picked up on the thoughts of our drivers before I did. From their dialog, it was apparent we were being followed by men on horseback. Because of the slowness of the team, it would only be a matter of minutes before the unnamed pursuers would catch us. Kipp turned his head slightly.

"They are bandits…highwaymen," Kipp commented.

I wasn't able yet to clearly pluck the thoughts from the air, as was Kipp.

"They have targeted this stage…but not because of us. They think we have a gold box on board."

I laughed softly. "Well, it seems that Steve Hill's warning to the clerk at the stage company worked. They aren't after us, thinking I have a lot of money."

Pete's voice drifted back to me.

"Mrs. Totheroh, we are being forced to stop. You just stay inside and stay quiet; let me handle this."

I was perfectly content to do just that and sat back on the bench, which was padded but not sufficiently to stave off hind end fatigued. I looked at Kipp, and his eyes narrowed.

"My butt is sore, too," he commented. "I'm grateful to not be saddled, literally, with a bustle."

The rocking motion gently subsided, and had we been in an automobile, I would have been listening for a tiny squeal of brakes to accompany the stop. Instead, all I heard was the jangling of harness bits and the stomp of an equine foot.

"Driver, you know what we want, so you can go ahead and toss it down." There was a pause before the low, gravelly voice added, "And tell your boy to put aside his shotgun."

Dave's thoughts were agitated and combative since he wanted to bring a fight to the robbers. But he succumbed to Pete's instructions, and I heard the clatter of the coach gun as it hit the wooden planks of the box. The sound of Pete's spitting was loud in the quiet desert air, and I saw the missile as it passed by my window. The sweet smell of tobacco actually wafted past my sensitive nose.

The bandits were careful to not use names, but I realized that they recognized Pete from past times they had encountered him as a driver. He had, occasionally, put up a fight when carrying Wells Fargo gold boxes, since he was being well compensated to make a delivery unsullied. I, of course, had told him the opposite: don't fight and let's survive the trip to Tombstone.

A shadow fell across my window as a horse drew close. I saw a large equine eye and caught a whiff of hot, sweaty horse. Pushing my spine against the thinly padded seat, I hoped for invisibility. I glanced at Kipp; his eyes were rounded with the thrill of the moment, and his large mouth dropped open in a pant. Well, he'd wanted excitement, and we were slap dab in the middle of it.

I could see the rider as he dismounted; he cautiously approached Pete and Dave, watching them for any action. With a whistle he signaled another rider who apparently approached from the rear of the coach and began to examine the boot. All that it contained was my small trunk and carpetbag. The robbers, with one another, were using names in their minds, although they carefully avoided verbalizing them. Kipp's head darted up as he heard one of the men thinking 'Frank'.

"Could that be Frank Stillwell?" Kipp asked me.

I shrugged my shoulders.

"So what are you carrying?" the man's voice echoed out. The desert, with the lack of trees and shrubs, was a perfect void with no inanimate objects to disrupt sound waves.

"I've got a passenger today," Pete responded. "Just a lady," he added, "and I'd be grateful if you'd leave her alone." I knew that Pete had a handgun concealed beneath the jacket he wore and could see his hand moving towards the gun. Despite what I'd told him, he was not going to let the highwaymen disturb me, if he could prevent it.

It was then that I felt the touch of a symbiotic mind weaving its way through the wooden walls of the coach. My eyes opened wide, and I stared at Kipp, whose head jerked up in surprise. It was obvious one of the robbers holding us at bay was a symbiont.

Over my four hundred plus years, I'd experienced many moments with my fellow species and recognized the existence of good and evil did not just reside with Homo sapiens. I'd recently experienced the intrusion of Andrea Collins into my mind by use of a method that was thoroughly discouraged by our group. It was subtle, to be sure, but still an unwelcomed event. But nothing in my past prepared me for what was about to happen.

A forceful telepathic mind began an investigation of me that pushed past the normal and acceptable boundaries and began to shred its way into the hidden rooms that I concealed from all, save Kipp. I desperately tried to close off my mind, but it was immediately clear that the other symbiont was more powerful than was I, and I quickly lost ground to his assault. And yes, it was an assault, just as if a human attacked another of his species. I gasped and clutched with my fists at the empty air; my eyes seemed to lose their normal vision, and I heard myself whimper softly.

Suddenly, Kipp was there, teeth bared in outraged fury. Over the relatively short time I'd been associated with him, there had been moments where he displayed gifts of our species that had been lost over centuries due to the consequences of a limited gene pool. But Kipp, fresh from the ancient world, was the genuine article, functioning as God had intended us to be.

Kipp hopped over to my side of the small coach interior and began licking my face in a frantic attempt to gain my attention away from the unknown attacker. In my mind, I could hear Kipp growl again, fearsome and powerful. I don't know how he did it, but he pushed outward with his mind and slammed a door that effectively closed off the unwanted intrusion of the stranger. Kipp and I both recognized a burst of surprise followed by a wry mental chuckle. The other recognized Kipp's impressive talents and respected them.

I leaned forward and rested my sweat covered forehead on Kipp's shoulder. He pushed his head to the window and narrowed his eyes as he looked off to the southwest where a lone man sat upon a horse, silhouetted by the late afternoon sun. The man—no, make that a male, humanoid symbiont—turned his head slightly and watched Kipp. A hand drew up and touched the brim of a hat in a sardonic salute. Something akin to envy crossed the yards between us and both Kipp and I realized that he had no symbiotic partner...at least not any more. I started to tell Kipp that he should not impulsively protect me before he turned to stare at me and uttered a quiet "shut up" command.

"I'm blocking him for now so don't distract me," Kipp finally commented. He resumed his attitude at the window. The lone figure finally gave voice to his humanoid companions.

"Boys, let's go. There's nothing to be had here."

The man who was in closest proximity to me was visibly irritated since he was looking forward to stealing any jewelry or money I might have. But there was a fear of the lone man and the name given to him in the minds of the others was 'Johnny'.

I looked at Kipp and he glanced back, once. Could it be Johnny Ringo, I wondered? If so, he was notorious as a coldblooded killer of such an unpredictable temperament as to strike fear in the hearts of those he thought of as friends. Per history, even Curly Bill was wary of John Ringo.

If this were true, I wondered how one of my kind could evolve into such an antisocial monster? Kipp, relaxed his vigilance when he felt the other symbiont pull back from his aggressive examination of me. As the man spurred his horse in retreat, a thought came our way.

"I'll see you both in Tombstone," the man said.

Kipp finally allowed himself to relax and, after another comforting lick on the side of my cheek, returned to his side of the coach.

"Ma'am," the voice of Pete drifted down. "We'll go on now, I'm not sure why, but they weren't interested, and I think we can move on to Tombstone without further bother."

Kipp and I knew why, of course. One of the highwaymen was a symbiont, like us, and he chose to let us go…at least, for the moment. I looked to Kipp to explain the experience, since I still felt weakened.

"He is powerful, to be certain." Kipp folded his haunches and perched on the seat across from me. "But he lacks skills I have. He's just learned to do things that your group has decided are off limits. He has no social boundaries." Kipp smiled. "I am supposed to have social boundaries but choose to, uh, loosen them from time to time when it is convenient."

"Are you sure you can shut him down, Kipp?" I asked. I despised being this vulnerable, but the truth was that I was at the mercy of this unknown symbiont who may or may not be wearing the evil cloak of John Ringo.

Kipp glanced at me, and his amber eyes glowed softly in the small confines of the cabin.

"Petra, I don't mean to boast, but I can handle him. That is not the issue," he commented, shaking his massive head slightly. "I just think perhaps we need to turn around now that we know he's here. It's too dangerous, and there are other places we can go to experience the old West." He glanced out the window at the passing countryside. "Or we can go home," he added.

I, too, turned my view to gaze out the window. The landscape was beautiful, in a spare, minimalist way. The speed of the coach was pushing a pleasant breeze into the cabin, and with the setting of the sun, the temperature of the air transitioned to a pleasant coolness. We'd be in Tombstone shortly after nightfall. Now that the incident was behind me, I felt encouraged that I could handle John Ringo…or whoever he was. I'd never met another of my kind that inspired terror, even when there was strong dislike involved. A hallmark of my species was insatiable curiosity. And I'd spent many times hovering on the cusp of extreme danger due to my need to know the truth. That was the situation now.

"Kipp, I have to know. And just because he was overly aggressive back there, doesn't mean he will do so again. There is a possibility that he was reacting to the knowledge there was another symbiont close by."

Kipp completed his inspection of the land over which we were passing and curled his large body on the narrow bench seat. Casually, he licked at his forepaws in a gesture I recognized as one he used when delaying a response. The thoughts were progressing so rapidly in his head that I could scarce follow them or pluck out one particular notion.

"I don't mind going on to Tombstone," he finally answered with caution. "But you and I need to come to an understanding."

Across from my best friend and bonded partner, I felt my eyebrows rise to unusual heights. For a moment, my reaction was to chastise him for what appeared to be a tone he was taking with me, since I was the elder and experienced one of our team of two. Almost immediately, I dropped my head and began to examine the toes of my boots. There was no need for me to continue to feel as if I had to guide Kipp. He'd proven himself to be more than my equal, and he no longer required a teacher.

I looked up and met his clear, amber eyes. Wordlessly, we sat for at least a minute, our eyes locked, our minds curiously empty. Finally, I gave a deep sigh and nodded my head.

"And what is that understanding, Kipp?" I asked.

"I am unable to pretend as if I don't feel protective of you when you are threatened. Asking me to put that part of me aside is asking the impossible." He twisted his massive neck slightly from its cramped position in the small area in which we sat.

"And I'm intelligent enough to recognize the difference in impulsive reactivity and appropriate defensive and offensive posturing," Kipp remarked. "What I did at Lands

Point Colony was impulsive; what I did just a few moments ago was restrained and well thought out behavior." He smiled in his head. "Petra, you know the difference, too, despite what Juno and Philo try to tell us. We know ourselves and each other, and we must trust that knowledge."

I nodded my head in response. Now that we had reached the crest of the long grade that had slowed our momentum, the team picked up their former speed, and the coach regained its hypnotic rocking. The purple sky outside cloaked our tiny caravan in the desert in a veil of solitude. Occasionally, the voices of Pete and Dave would drift back to my ears, but they seemed content to say little to one another. I lifted my eyes.

"Kipp, I trust you completely. No symbiont has had the access to my mind that I've given you. I've been completely unguarded and undefended from you from the start, and that is not something I can say about Tula, Philo or even my husband." I stumbled in my words. "I've just felt responsible since I brought you to all this," I said, waving my hands.

Kipp tilted his head.

"Well, Mom, you can cut the apron string now. I'm a big boy, I'm all grown up and I can shift for myself."

I felt like we'd said enough on the subject. In my heart and mind, I would just allow Kipp to do what he needed to do; when I thought about it, there was no way to stop him anyway. And there was the distinct possibility that I would learn something along the way.

The coach moved relentlessly forward towards Tombstone where the unknown symbiont waited. I allowed my eyelids to drift shut, fatigued from the mental effort of the day. As I began to doze off, Kipp's mind reassuringly touched mine.

"I'll keep an eye on things," he promised.

And I knew he would.

CHAPTER 17

Tombstone was a dirty, aggressive, thriving town that had sprung up around the discovery of silver ore. The stage office was on Allen Street; the OK Corral could be found down the next block at Third Street and Fremont. I knew, from my inspections of maps of early Tombstone, that there were a number of hotels and boarding houses. The major players were all clustered on Allen, and these included the Cosmopolitan, Occidental and Grand Hotels. The saloons were many along this stretch of road, and there was high competition among all of them to pull in as many players as possible. The Earps, dealers in faro, worked at the Occidental Saloon from time to time. They, like so many others, had their ambitious fingers in multiple pies in order to make a serviceable living.

The coach began to slow, and I could hear Pete as he called out a soothing 'whoa' to the tired team of four. Outside my wooden box was C. W. Pinkham's stage office, which was the offloading point for all travelers to Tombstone.

It was now mid evening, and since we were still in late summer, the sun had just dropped below the far horizon. Desert chill crept into the coach where I sat, and I shivered in response. With envy, I looked across at Kipp who was enjoying his dense pelt of fur. He gazed back.

"Face it, Petra. We lupines are just better designed all round. We can hear, see and smell with more accuracy; we are definitely faster and our intuitions are keener. And I'm warm, and you're not."

I knew he was being playful with me as a way to continue to soothe me after the disturbing event in the desert. Feeling very adult, I stuck my tongue out at him and laughed as he tried to imitate my gesture. I peeked out of the coach; the town seemed to be bustling, even at this time of the evening.

Pete addressed a rude comment to a lanky young man who was seated in a rickety wooden chair on the porch of the stage office.

"Bud, get off your ass and get over here and get the lady's things from the boot." After a brief pause, Pete's voice drifted back to me. "Sorry, ma'am; didn't mean to use harsh language in your presence."

The aforementioned Bud rose, while muttering under his breath, and approached the coach, bringing with him a small hand truck. In a flash, he had my trunk—procured from Hill's store—and carpetbag stacked neatly and was waiting for me. Pete had dismounted, opened the door and extended a tough skinned hand that felt like a burlap sack as I left the coach.

"Thank you, Pete, for an uneventful journey." As I reached out, I placed an envelope with the extra payment I'd promised in his hand. He glanced up, and I was rewarded with a flash of the eyes; the bristles on his face moved a fraction in what I took to be a smile.

"Mrs. Totheroh, any time you need a driver, you just have them telegraph for Pete," he remarked before leaving me to see to his exhausted horses.

Kipp hopped down, and Bud almost lost his composure at the unexpected sight of the huge dog. When he saw Kipp was well behaved, the young man relaxed and turned towards me.

"Where to, ma'am?" Unlike most of the other men, he was wearing a rag cap; a thin hand with dirty, unkempt fingernails moved up to touch the narrow brim.

"I think we'll try the Cosmopolitan," I answered, trying to sound as if I were a confident steward over my existence.

"Why that one?" Kipp asked.

"It's next door to the Occidental Saloon, so I thought it would literally be in the middle of the action. And I think Doc stayed there at times. The Earps," I continued, "rented cottages on First and Fremont."

Kipp trotted along, mollified.

A large rumbling met our ears, and we hastily followed Bud's lead as he moved as far to the side of the hard packed street as possible. Up ahead, a heavily loaded wagon approached, pulled by the fabled twenty mule team that had stared back at me from a box of Borax. I knew, from my reading, that it must have come fresh from the stamp mill.

Kipp's eyes rounded. "Well, now that takes some skill," he commented in admiration of the driver who radiated confidence in his thoughts as well as his bearing. I, quite frankly, was relieved when they passed. The odor of twenty dirty, sweating mules lingered long after the last jangle of a harness bit had fallen silent.

On the opposite side of the street was the US Restaurant, and it was doing its best to overpower the mule stench. Lifting my head, I caught the aroma of some type of baking bread, and my mouth watered. Symbionts, with our peculiar metabolic needs, did not require food as frequently as humans. But we did experience hunger and were not immune to tasty foods. I glanced at Kipp and saw he was drooling.

"Let's get settled, first, if you don't mind," I requested, and he gave me a mental head nod in response.

We passed Hafford's Saloon and picked up the sounds of a piano which obviously was missing a few keys. But the pianist bravely managed to bang out 'Carry Me Back to Old Virginny'; I could hear more than one inebriated man lead off on another chorus. Kipp's head went up as he smelled what some might call ardent spirits—beer, whiskey and watered down bourbon. Kipp was asking me so many questions about everything that my head began to spin.

Bud finally stood back and gestured we should proceed him into the Cosmopolitan. The lobby, for this type of rapid growth town, was fairly spacious, and it seemed neatly kept. A thick woolen runner extended from the front door to the mahogany desk, behind which a rotund man wearing the popular leonine mustache resided. I glanced around the lobby and saw a few men sitting off in a parlor area; some were looking at what appeared to be newspapers, and a couple were playing checkers.

A lone woman checking in was enough to gather some interest; but a lone woman accompanied by a massive dog really caused the heads to swivel and the eyes to pop. From behind the desk, Mr. Big Mustache man folded his arms at his chest, preparing himself for the unknown.

Bud carefully unloaded the small burden he carried for me, and I placed a coin in his hand. Then I turned to the clerk and approached him, with my head up and shoulders back. It was time to reassume the part of wealthy widow, confident and pleasantly demanding.

"May I help you?" The clerk had a deep bass voice. Maybe in another time and place he could sing opera, I thought.

"I am Mrs. Totheroh," I replied. "I will be staying in Tombstone for the foreseeable future and require comfortable accommodations." I paused and glanced around the room in what I hoped was an appraising glance. "I was under the impression that the Cosmopolitan was superior to the Grand and the Occidental."

Of course, I had fed into his vanity and pride in the establishment where he worked. So, he nodded his dark head with enthusiasm. Behind me, the watching men in the room had the usual thoughts of curiosity and were raising eyebrows at one another behind my back. There were at least two who directed fairly lascivious thoughts aimed at me, and I had to counsel Kipp to drop his need to be my valiant cavalier.

"Chill out, Kipp," I mentally commanded, dropping my

hand down to his broad, auburn head.

The clerk, who introduced himself as Samuel Dent, cleared his throat.

"Mrs. Totheroh, we don't usually allow animals inside the Cosmopolitan."

I knew his mind was working on a way to capitalize on the situation. He'd sized me up as having money and wanted the cash as well as the cache of having me reside in his establishment.

"I think I can speak for the owner when I say that we will make an exception in your case, ma'am." His dark eyes glittered slightly, and he drew a large hand up to carefully brush the edges of his mustache into submission. "There will be extra charges to accommodate your dog."

"They ought to pay me to chase the rats out of this place," Kipp muttered.

"Quiet," I replied, trying not to laugh.

Mr. Dent pushed the large register to my side of the desk, and I dashed off my name with a casual flair, as if I'd written it ten thousand times. The clerk walked away for a moment, and I took the opportunity to turn the pages of the large book, scanning for any familiar name. There among the scribbled words, I found what I was looking for.

"Kipp, Doc Holliday registered here! He could be still a resident, unless he's moved to another place in town." The excitement of the trip finally hit me when I found the compact, neatly written signature. The idea of meeting iconic people from a lost time was growing on me, now that I was here in the midst of the action.

Dent returned with a young lad who nodded his head; though slight in build, he must have been deceptively strong, because he managed to pull my trunk up on his back and balanced the load with my carpetbag against his chest.

"The boy will show you to your room," Dent commented. It was obvious the young man was so insignificant that he didn't deserve to be addressed by a proper name.

With my skirts in hand, I followed the youth up the broad staircase; at the landing, we turned right and he led me to the end of the hall. I had the feeling that Mr. Dent had chosen the most expensive suite of rooms available in order to take advantage of the Kipp situation. But I was glad to be on the corner, since I would have more visual access. The young man carefully set down my trunk and bag and used a large brass key to unlock the door.

"Let me light the room for you, ma'am." The young man looked at me and added, "This is the presidential suite."

I smiled and asked, "Did the president stay here?"

The young man's face was open, and he nodded vigorously.

"Yes, ma'am. President Grant stayed here a couple of years ago. He and his wife, Julia," he added as an afterthought.

"What was he like?" I asked in genuine curiosity since I had a great interest in the American Civil War in terms of historical accuracy.

"He was very quiet and polite; I recall he didn't want a big fuss made or anything like that."

He walked ahead and lit the lantern on the wall and one on a marble topped mahogany table. The flickering oil fueled light was pleasantly muted. I caught a distinct fragrance of lavender as well as the scent of lemon polish that had been used to coax a luster from the dark wood furniture. It was obvious the Cosmopolitan was trying to appear upscale and combat the rawness of the wild territory in which it resided.

There was a small sitting room with a sofa covered in a deep red brocade fabric; the wood appeared to be mahogany, in a match for the little table. An upright, uncomfortable looking chair rested in the corner. A large window took up part of the wall and overlooked the expanse of Allen Street; directly across was the Occidental Hotel.

"What is your name, young man?" I asked.

He turned and hazarded a glance at me. His shyness was almost painful, but I caught beneath the mask a very keen mind. Here was yet another person who was limited by circumstances.

"You don't know that," Kipp commented. "He might get
fed up enough to leave this and go on to do great things."
Kipp knew I had a romantic streak a mile wide.

"They call me Eli, but my name is really Elijah," he
replied.

My Kipp's head snapped around. "Well, how's that for
karma and coincidence," he said. "Now, I'm feeling more
warmly towards the boy, too." He recalled, as did I, an old
story Fitzhugh had told of a lupine symbiont named Eli who
possessed many of the lost skills that Kipp retained.

I smiled. "Eli, it's nice to meet you. Would it be an
inconvenience to bring me some water?"

"Oh, no ma'am." He smiled; his teeth were white and all
intact, preserving what appeared to be a freshly handsome
face. "My job is to make sure that the customers are all
treated good."

"Eli, there are a few accommodations I require, and I will
pay you well to make certain my needs are met." I smiled
and gestured to Kipp. "As you can see, I have a large
traveling companion, who happens to be named Kipp."

Eli laughed softly. "I've always liked dogs." He bent down
and slapped his knee lightly, beckoning Kipp to approach.
Kipp, playing dog, wagged his tail and lolled his tongue out;
prancing slightly, he walked over and gave the boy a head
butt.

"I'll need fresh water daily, of course. And if you could
manage to get food delivered here at least some of the time, I
would be grateful, since I'm not fond of eating out. Kipp eats
chicken and beef with rice or noodles, and I'll need you to
help arrange something on a daily basis for him."

Eli nodded his head; he was bright, and I followed his
thoughts as he quickly problem solved how to best meet my
requests. He was of the sort he took things to be a challenge,
not a burden, and seemed happy to become my caretaker.
After lighting a lantern in the bedroom, which was of a good
size, he left, assuring me he would return with water, a light
snack for me, and a meal for Kipp.

I walked into the bedroom and over to the large double

window to the side of the hotel. It directly overlooked the Occidental Saloon. We were definitely in the position to view most of the comings and goings of the major players. I began to unpack my trunk and hung my dresses in the closet…at least there was a closet and not pegs on a wall. The garment I was wearing was just dusty, but not really soiled, and I thought a good airing out and a little water applied to a few spots would take care of the problem.

A discrete knock on the door announced Eli, who had brought water and assured me he had put in an order at the US Restaurant. After delivering the water, he discretely backed out of the room, leaving me to make as best attempt as I could to clean up. Kipp dropped on the floor to watch me.

After drawing the curtains shut, I unbuttoned my dress and pulled it from my shoulders; I hung it up on a hook by the door so that it could air. The removal of the corset and bustle almost made me shout with joy. I did my best to take a vigorous bird bath and felt better after having washed the dust and grime from my face and arms. Having enjoyed the luxury of the hip bath while in Tucson, I'd have to make an enquiry of Eli regarding that possibility. I'd just finished wrapping the robe about my body and cinching the belt when a soft tap alerted me to Eli.

"Hello, Mrs. Totheroh," he said. Despite his shyness, a pair of clear, gray eyes met mine beneath a forelock of blonde bangs that fell across his forehead. "I brought you a plate of vegetables, as you requested, and a dish of chopped beef and rice for Kipp."

I thanked him and gave him a generous tip. After he left Kipp, and I didn't think or speak for a few minutes as we satiated our hunger and thirst. I hadn't realized that I was, indeed, hungry and almost surprised myself by chasing the last stray pea around my plate with my fork. We both polished off every morsel.

Eli came by to pick up the plates, and I asked if he would accompany Kipp outside for a potty break—except, I didn't phrase it that casually. The boy, as before, was eager to serve, and I watched as he departed down a back staircase with Kipp at his side. Kipp's thoughts, however, were with me and I was somewhat envious when he went on high alert.

"Petra, guess who I just met? Doc Holliday just passed us on the staircase and when he stopped to talk to Eli, he reached down and patted my head. I just got patted by Doc Holliday; I can't believe it!"

Kipp was clearly intoxicated with the thought he'd met a celebrity.

"Gee, Kipp, did you get his autograph and a signed picture?" I needed him to calm down and tell me more about the encounter.

"Well, it was just fun and exciting to meet a notorious character from history." Kipp sounded a little deflated, and I regretted my sarcastic rejoinder.

"Oh, I'm just jealous, that's all," I commented, trying to soften the moment.

In but a minute, he was back at the door and a courteous Eli bade me good night and disappeared down the length of the hallway. Kipp dashed in and was still overcome with excitement. I went to the bed and lay down, exhausted; in a second, Kipp bounded up and nestled next to me, placing his head on my chest.

"Kipp, I know you are excited but try and turn off that brain for a while. I must get some sleep and your thoughts are pulling me." I rested my hand across the back of his neck and pulled him closer. My heart filled with love for my friend.

"Okay," he replied, stretching his mouth wide in a lupine yawn that slightly resembled a crocodile in action.

Sleep finally claimed us both, despite the ongoing noise from outside. It seemed that the people of Tombstone enjoyed playing faro, drinking and listening to music until late in the night. I drifted off to 'My Bonnie Lies Over the Ocean'. It would be a night of no dreams, despite the earlier encounter with the unnamed symbiont who seemed so threatening.

CHAPTER 18

I slept late the next morning, something that was uncharacteristic for me. When I awoke, Kipp was sitting on the floor by the large window, his head poked under the curtains as he gazed at the street below. He was clearly eager for us to perambulate the streets of Tombstone for the first time.

After taking care of my needs and washing my face as best I could with the water and pitcher and a scented bar of lavender soap, I chose a lightweight gown that was a rather pretty peach tone and a hat that was predominantly green. I know it was silly vanity, but I wanted to look as attractive as possible for my first promenade around town. As I managed to fasten the last button and smooth the fabric over my hips, Kipp turned to give me an appraising look.

"If I had the ability to wolf whistle, I would; but since I can't, I'll just say that you look beautiful."

I nodded my head and gave a little curtsey. My thoughts were that we would go to a café and perhaps get tea and a biscuit…something light. I was truly not hungry after last night's late feast. With Kipp at my side, I left the room, carefully pocketing the key in my reticule. We descended the main staircase, and I was crossing to the main entrance to the hotel, when a voice caught my attention.

"Excuse me, madam," a man's cultured voice with a

distinct southern accent called out from the sitting area on the far side of the lobby.

I turned and watched as a slender man approached. He was perhaps 5'10" tall, with thick blonde hair that appeared a little long to be in style. His face, with high cheekbones, was pale and a pair of vivid, intense blue eyes stared at me. He wore a mustache, which was in vogue for gentlemen at the present time.

"It's him, it's him!" Kipp almost shouted at me. So, it was John Holliday in the flesh. I had not thought I would meet one of the legends of the era this soon in my adventure.

"I don't mean to be impertinent, ma'am, but I met your companion last night and thought it would be polite to introduce myself." He was close and bowed slightly from the waist. Unexpectedly, he reached out and took my hand and gave a slight brush of his lips on the back of my hand. "I'm John Holliday," he added.

His thoughts towards me were ones filled with curiosity; he found me attractive, but more than that, he was just plain being nosey. Doc Holliday wasn't sure if I was a lady of the night or merely a lady.

Knowing his penchant for associating with at least one prostitute in the past in the figure of Big Nose Kate, I decided to clear things up immediately. It would not be a comfortable place for me to have Doc chasing me around town thinking I could become his next paramour.

"I am Petra Totheroh," I replied, tilting my head slightly. I knew the green in the bonnet I wore brought out the green in my hazel eyes. Doc thought so, too.

"What a charmingly unusual name," he drawled. "Petra! No doubt your mother was an aficionado of the ancient city." He was so close to the truth that I bit back a startled reply.

"Tombstone is a rather rough place that is filled with uncouth people," Doc continued in his measured tones. "If you don't have an escort for the morning, I would be honored if you would do me the pleasure and allow me to walk you to your destination."

I was hesitating but Kipp was yelling in my brain for me to "Do it!" In the end, I replied, "Thank you Mr. Holliday." He'd not introduced himself as Doc, and I would feign ignorance. "I am new to your town and will appreciate your guidance."

He was pleased but still curious as to my intent. And the massive presence of Kipp really threw him for a loop. John Holliday, decided, for the moment, to assume I was a lady, unescorted, and to treat me as if I were the queen of Sheba.

I glanced at the desk clerk, Mr. Dent, who was busy not watching us. His thoughts were one of fear and avoidance of Holliday. No doubt, he'd seen many instances where Doc displayed a vile temper and impatient bearing. Dent had learned to plead ignorance and look the other way.

From my reading, I knew that Doc was probably erratic when under the influence of alcohol, and was grateful he was currently sober. So I allowed him to tuck my hand up into the crook of his elbow, and we began our transit to the breakfast nook that occupied the far corner of the ground floor of the Grand Hotel. As we walked along, there were more than a few curious gazes at our odd trio, but people seemed as startled to see Doc out this early in the morning with a strange woman as they were to see an enormous wolf-like dog at my side. Kipp looked up and caught Doc's eyes on him; in return, Kipp lolled his mouth open in a passive, happy expression and wagged his tail.

Doc slightly cleared his throat. "May I learn of the origin of your most unusual traveling companion?"

I laughed. "His name is Kipp, and he was a gift from my late husband." I paused and let my hand drift along the soft dome of Kipp's large noggin. "So, he is very precious to me."

Doc had a silent 'aha' moment when a little piece of my puzzle fell into place for him. The fact I was a widow did not solve his curiosity over whether or not I was a prostitute, since it was not really unusual for women to be married and still be, uh, working. But his keen intuition led him to believe otherwise, and he relaxed. The role of gentleman was one he enjoyed, and for which he had scant opportunity to play in the roughness of the western frontier. We entered the Grand, and Doc confidently led me off to the side of the main lobby and through a doorway. There was a scattering of small tables. The woman who waited to greet us frowned upon seeing Kipp but just as quickly smiled when she saw the expression on Doc's face. We were seated in a moment, and Kipp took care to get between me and the wall so as to be unobtrusive. A young girl walked out and waited politely for our order.

"Mrs. Totheroh," Doc said, "is in pursuit of a nice pot of tea." He glanced up at the girl and smiled. "I happen to know you serve the best English Breakfast tea in Tombstone. So, perhaps you can bring a pot along with some of your sweet biscuits." He was being charming for my sake. As the girl disappeared, Doc turned towards me.

"So, Mr. Holliday, are you the social coordinator for Tombstone?" I decided to play with him and draw him out so Kipp could read his thoughts.

The morning light from the east gently highlighted the small table where we sat. The old-fashioned rippled glass windowpanes caused the scene outside to be slightly distorted. Doc was only about thirty years old but looked older; no doubt, the tuberculosis had taken a savage toll, and his skin looked fragile and paper thin. There were bluish stains beneath his eyes, a combination of late nights, too much liquor and poor health.

"No, ma'am," he answered. "But I decided to make an exception in your case since you are definitely a pleasant mystery that has come to visit our little hamlet." He paused while the tea and biscuits were delivered.

"Please," he commented, requesting I pour out.

I felt the sheen of perspiration on my forehead and wanted desperately to blot it but didn't want to appear conspicuous. I was clumsy to a fault and had visions of pouring tea in Doc Holliday's lap.

"Petra, settle down," Kipp said. "You are doing fine. Pour the stupid tea and draw him out more."

I darted a savage look at Kipp—the one without opposable thumbs was telling me to settle down and pour tea like I was a member of English gentry. I wasn't happy and tried to achieve calm. Reminding myself that I was playing a role, I feigned confidence when pouring and ignored the slightly raise eyebrow of John Holliday. If his thoughts were any measure—and they were—he was even more puzzled by me. An apparently cultured woman would be more adept and struggle less with something that should be second nature.

"Forgive my clumsiness," I said. "The long coach ride yesterday had me arriving late, and I didn't rest well."

"Good save," Kipp complimented me.

"Forgive my boorish insensitivity," Holliday replied. "I could have offered to take over this task."

"He really is enjoying this polite back and forth," Kipp observed. "It's something he doesn't get to do much anymore, and I am picking up very strong impulses of regret and sadness coming from some hidden room in his brain."

I took a sip of the tea, which was really quite good. "Well, get on it Kipp. You are supposed to be the major talent of our time, so get busy and see what you can find out." I was really joking, since our telepathic abilities were primarily focused on active thoughts. But Kipp, who never let the idea that we might be unable to do something, stop him. In his natural, unvarnished state, he never ceased to amaze me. He became quiet and focused to the point that I had to tune him out.

"And where is home, Mr. Holliday?" I nibbled delicately on one of the biscuits.

"I'm from the state of Georgia," he replied. "But I've not been there in more years than I can count."

I didn't require Kipp's skills to feel the rush of sadness pushed by anger that hit me full force. To gather myself, I took another sip of tea and offered to warm Doc's cup. His head went up suddenly and the predatory, calculating part of his nature went to the forefront. John Behan, the county sheriff, ambled in and was laying claim to a table across the room from us. Behan looked at Doc and gave a cool nod; then, he glanced at me in an appraising manner.

"He's a horn dog," Kipp commented, reflecting upon Behan's primitive thoughts.

"Where on earth did you hear that expression?" I asked, trying not to stare at Kipp.

He didn't answer and turned his mind towards Behan, instead.

"He's very confident but knows he is no match for Doc," Kipp shared. "He actually has a lot of hatred for Doc and recalls, with some amusement, the time he induced Kate Elder to lie about Doc and the Sandy stage murder."

I, of course, had telepathic skills, too, but it was nice to sit back and let Kipp give the blow by blow. My attention was focused on Doc, who became enraged at the very sight of Behan. Finally, Doc turned back to me.

"That handsome man over there is John Behan, the county sheriff." Doc said. "He and I don't typically see eye to eye on matters, and he has encouraged me to leave town more than once." He smiled, revealing straight, white teeth. No doubt he had benefited from having been a dentist and valuing the care of teeth. "Behan fancies himself as quite a ladies' man," Doc added, glancing at my face. I felt the rush of blood stain my cheeks.

"I'm quite comfortable here, thank you," I commented, staring into the amber depths of my tea.

Doc was quietly pleased with my reply, and I felt a little uncomfortable. This tableau was progressing more rapidly than I had planned, and I felt a couple of moves behind Holliday in this unexpected chess match. The scent of an expensive cologne drifted across the room, and I suspected the source to be Behan, who was impeccably groomed.

Kipp continued his intense focus on Doc, and I knew my curiosity would have to wait for another time. My skills allowed me to thrust and parry with my quarry but not to evaluate the man in the manner that Kipp might.

"So tell me about Georgia," I commented, hoping to draw

him out now that the ripple effect of Behan's presence had subsided.

Doc took a deep breath and seemed uneasy. He reached out thin fingers and carefully turned the bone china tea cup in his sensitive hands.

"I haven't been there in years. The war," he said, almost stuttering, "caused a disruption in my family, and I went to Baltimore to attend dental college."

I knew he was minimizing events, and that his comments to me were not exactly a lie but also did not ring completely true.

"Oh, and are you still a dentist?" I asked, trying to sound surprised.

"I don't practice anymore," he replied, and the disappointment over choices he'd made almost hovered over the table like a fog bank. Doc took a deep breath. "I have had to make changes in my life due to health concerns as well as others."

I wanted to push the issue and see if I could get him to reveal his life as a gambler and gunslinger but, after considering my options, came to the conclusion there was no appropriate way to pry the information loose. Any serious digging would blow my cover as a refined lady, so I would bide my time. Doc neatly shifted the attention to me.

"And what is your story, Mrs. Totheroh?" he asked. Sitting back in his chair, he crossed one leg over the other, careful to not crease his trousers.

As is true of my kind, I effortlessly spun a web of lies, beginning with my fictitious birth in Philadelphia up until I married and moved to Boston. Doc asked a couple of discrete questions about my mythical deceased spouse, and I answered that he had been in the banking business. After that comment, I dropped my head delicately, and this caused Doc to back away from further questions. Oddly, unlike many men, he was not afraid of a woman's tears; rather, Doc didn't want to cause me pain. He was, in a word, being kind and thoughtful. I glanced at Kipp whose head was slightly tilted; he was still immersed in his exploration of Doc's brain.

"Well, I don't want to occupy your entire morning with my nonsense," Doc finally said. "And quite honestly, I have an engagement and must be about some business."

I was relieved. Doc was an unusually intense man with a complicated, probably brilliant brain, and I felt a little tired just trying to deal with his thoughts. Kipp, as I knew by know, was stronger than I and was putting his abilities of concentration to the maximum test. I made to stand and Doc hopped up to extend a slender, cold hand to support my elbow. Once again, he bent from the waist to brush the back of my hand with his lips and then cut his vivid blue eyes up to my face.

"It has been a pleasure, ma'am." His thoughts darted ahead to how he could make an excuse to see me again. He cleared his throat. "Mrs. Totheroh, I would be honored if you would allow me to be your escort again, since you are without a guide to our fair city." He rushed on. "There's a small entertainment troupe who will be performing at the Vincent and Braden music hall, and I happen to know they will sing several popular Gilbert and Sullivan songs. There will be other recitations." He smiled. "It is about as close as you can get to culture in Tombstone."

Kipp interrupted my thoughts.

"He wants to introduce you to Wyatt Earp! Do it, say yes!" Kipp almost shouted into my brain.

"Why, thank you, Mr. Holliday." I smiled back at the notorious gun fighter and alleged killer of so many people. "That would be lovely." The moment felt surreal.

"Please, call me John," he replied. "I will collect you in the lobby of the Cosmopolitan Wednesday evening at seven o'clock."

Today was Monday, so I had a couple of days to recover from this encounter.

Doc discretely paid our debt for the tea and walked me to the doorway. Knowing he had an appointment, I excused him from escorting me back to the hotel with the excuse I wanted to exercise Kipp. With a tip of his broad brimmed gray hat, he nodded and walked away.

Kipp gave a slight sigh, and I turned to my partner.

"Are you okay?" I asked, looking down at him in concern.

He nodded and replied that he was just a little tired; the focus had been prolonged and unusually intense. We began to walk down Allen Street, away from the Cosmopolitan. There was supposed to be a cobbler's shop and I thought I would see about having a second pair of shoes made. Despite Suzanne's careful calculations, the ones supplied to me for this trip were just not very comfortable. We found the small building and met the proprietor, a pleasant middle-aged man named Adams. The shop was dark and unexpectedly cool, with the odor of leather and lanolin lurking in all corners of the room. While Mr. Adams fussed about trying to determine the shape of my foot and construct a boot to my needs (and I was impressed at the artistry of shoe making), I tried to pry information from Kipp.

"I don't want you to be mad at me," Kipp began, looking up at me, a crease of worry puckering the fur between his large, upright ears. I stayed silent and allowed him to say what he needed to tell me. "I know the Twelve tell us that we aren't supposed to dig too deeply in the minds of others, but I have abilities that make it difficult to not do so."

"Kipp, I think they don't want us doing it to each other without permission since we are telepathic, but for the purposes of understanding humans, I believe it is just part of the process."

Kipp looked up at me and his eyes rounded. "But I do more than that, Petra. I go into the places where old memories are stored, not just active thoughts."

I sat there, watching Mr. Adams measure my foot, feeling startled but not able to express that feeling in the darkness of the cobbler's shop. I knew Kipp was talented and had been surprised more than once over a skill that he, alone, seemed to possess. Either the rest of us had lost the ability genetically, or else we had socialized it out of ourselves.

"Kipp, how far back in a human's memories can you go?"
I wasn't sure I wanted to know this, since I'd have to decide
whether to share this new tidbit of forbidden activity or
keep it to myself.

Kipp's amber eyes took on a vacant look. "I picked out
pieces of his childhood."

I took a deep breath. "Kipp, do you have any more
secrets?"

He took a deep breath and exhaled slowly. "I don't know.
I just find things like this as we go along. I guess, since it's
natural to me, I don't think about it as something odd."

The cobbler's little girl, who was past a toddler but not
quite school age, ambled out and was delighted to see
Kipp, who in her mind was a big, fuzzy dog. I read the
concern in her father's mind and told him Kipp was very
gentle with children. Amused, I watched as the child
climbed upon Kipp as if he were a mountain top. Only once
did I caution her to not pull the doggie's ear, trying not to
laugh as I saw Kipp grimace.

The cobbler promised to deliver my new boots in two
days to the Cosmopolitan, and Kipp and I took our leave.
As we turned left down Allen, I saw a cluster of men who
were dressed in a manner that suggested they were
cowboys. All of them wore half length boots with high
heels; they had on long coats and brightly colored vests and
silk kerchiefs around their necks. Their broad brimmed hats
were more like sombreros than the hat type worn by Doc
and most of the other men in town.

As we passed them, a man's head went up, and I
recognized the symbiont from the stagecoach incident.
Kipp immediately went on guard, prepared to block the
telepathic connection if the humanoid symbiont tried to
push his way into my mind again. Instead, the thoughts of
the male were surprisingly meek.

"We really need to meet and talk." There was a sense of a
wistful smile in the way the telepathic entreaty was made.

After inquiring if I could handle a cart and horse—which
I could, unless the horse thought he was pulling a

charioteer from *Ben Hur*—he said that he would have one waiting for me the next morning at the front of the Cosmopolitan. I stumbled slightly on the hem of my skirt and bit back an exclamation. The symbiont stranger laughed out loud, the sound unexpectedly loud across the busy street.

"You take care now, hear," he said, drawling the words in my head. "I'll see you three miles out of town; just head north on Allen and go until you find me."

Kipp looked up at me, the revelations of his burrowing deeply into Doc's mind were no longer the topic of focus.

"Looks like we have a date," Kipp commented, his tail snapping in a wag of excitement.

CHAPTER 19

I confess to a restless night. The thought of meeting with the mysterious symbiont, who may or may not be the infamous Johnny Ringo, was weighing heavily on my mind. Having always been confident in my abilities to manage difficult situations, the encounter on the stage coach road had left me shaken, more so than I wished to admit.

Eli brought breakfast the next morning, but due to my nervous stomach, I had little appetite. Kipp finished his plate and then crunched away the crumbled pieces of my biscuit. I did enjoy some coffee, however, served in a fine silver pot. When Eli came to retrieve the plates, he mentioned there was a buggy and horse that had been brought to the front of the hotel by a man from the livery stable.

"Mrs. Totheroh, he says you ordered it for the day," Eli commented, looking at me through the forelock of blonde bangs that he effortlessly shifted to one side by a toss of his head. "Ma'am, no disrespect, but you shouldn't go off by yourself." He made a slight gesture. "There are more bandits around here than you can count, and there are Indians up in the Dragoon Mountains who still hold a grudge over losing their land."

I smiled and reached out to touch his arm lightly.

"Eli, I will be fine. Kipp will be with me, and I know what I'm doing."

The young man shook his head, muttering as he walked away, taking the tray of dirty dishes with him. I watched as he disappeared down the long hallway.

Kipp stared at me, weaving his thoughts with mine.

"Petra, we probably shouldn't do this. You are too nervous and unsure of yourself." He came over and gently head butted me. "There's nothing to prove here, you know. We are just on vacation and can ride out the days."

I scratched between his large, upright ears and then turned to walk over to the window overlooking the street. Below, a small buggy waited for me; the horse meant to pull it looked bored as it shifted from one hind foot to the other. A pleasant breeze cooled my face. I mentally did a slight calculation in my brain; today was September 8 and the climactic gun battle would take place on October 26 at about 3 o'clock in the afternoon. Most of my time would be spent in observation of the major players. But there was no way I could avoid contact with the yet unnamed symbiont for that long a period of time. I turned to look at Kipp.

"Kipp, you always tell me to trust you. So, I will ask the same of you. You need to trust me." I paused before adding, "I can handle it. I promise you."

I was wearing a dark blue dress, one more designed for traveling. I'd chosen it on purpose, not wanting in any remote way to give my male counterpart any cause to think I was dressing for him. The dark color made me appear more business-like than had the peach frock I wore to impress Doc Holliday.

The temperature outside was pleasant for a change, and I was grateful that I'd not have to be subjected to the seasonal hellacious heat level. Knowing my tendency to burn in the sun—hence the nose full of freckles—I pulled out the one hat I had that was equipped with a broader brim. To my surprise, Eli was waiting to assist me into the buggy. His mind was full of misgivings and general thoughts about the stupidity and wrongheadedness of women, but he, nevertheless, gave me a strong arm up. Kipp hopped up into the small cargo portion behind me. The horse looked calm enough, and with a confident 'giddyup', I slapped the reins lightly across the beast's back.

"I hope you know what you are doing," Kipp commented in reference to my driving skills, as he stuck his head over the bench seat to watch the unfolding scene.

I assured him this was not my first time behind the reins as we trotted past the storefronts and saloons. I kept my fingers crossed that we would not be seen by Doc and, fortunately, we managed to exit town without any encumbrances. After the first mile or so, Kipp managed to relax after he realized I had not been embellishing, and that I could actually handle a horse in harness. Off in the distance, I saw a gathering of cottonwood trees and deduced there must be a water supply that fell beneath my line of sight.

"He's up there, off to the left," Kipp commented, squinting his eyes in the bright glare of the sun. "And, no, I can't see him yet. I just hear his thoughts."

It was but a few seconds later that I did so, too. His mind was issuing a welcome to us, but there was a ring of unpleasantness to it that I could not quite quantify.

There was indeed a narrow stream of water that sparkled and danced in the blandness of the desert landscape. The trees, though small in stature, hovered around the source of life as if they were worried it might disappear in a moment. The area comprised a wash that could be transformed during a rain storm into a raging river-like torrent in mere seconds. But today, all was peaceful and quiet.

I pulled the horse to a stop under the shade of a tree, thinking he would enjoy the reprieve from the sun and heat. A tall, slender man walked towards me with a gait that was sinuous and graceful; he had removed his long coat and wore a clean white shirt that was neatly tucked into dark brown pants. He wore the unusual short boots with high heels that were preferred by his peers.

"I'm John Ringo," he said, obviously enjoying the flash

of historical recognition that played across my features.

Reaching up his hands to assist me, he smiled, and I was taken by his startlingly handsome face. Yes, in reading about him, the stories said he was well favored, of a tall build with auburn hair and blue eyes. But I hadn't been prepared for a close up of a male symbiont who had the looks of a professional model or movie star. Ringo smiled again, enjoying my thoughts. He knew he was handsome and enjoyed that fact.

His hands, well shaped with strong, tapered fingers, encircled my waist as he helped me from the buggy. As my feet hit the ground, I pushed immediately away from him as he made to linger longer than I liked. Kipp hopped down and took his place at my side. Ringo laughed softly.

"You can relax your guard," he commented to Kipp.

Kipp unexpectedly folded his haunches and sat while staring at Ringo. Somehow, he managed again to block all of his thoughts from Ringo, and in doing so, blocked them from me, too. I remembered that I'd just have to trust my knowledge of him and let him do what he needed to in these odd circumstances.

Ringo put his hands up in a mock surrender and said, "Okay, have it your way." He walked over to a large rock and sat down. "So, how did you two manage to find me?"

I frowned. "We weren't looking for you. We are just on vacation." I added, as an afterthought, "I am Petra Goodgame, and this is Kipp."

Ringo's eyes flicked towards Kipp again and then back to me.

"So, where is your symbiont?" I asked.

Ringo looked down at the sandy ground for a moment before turning his bright, blue eyes back on my face.

"I lost Ula some years back in Kansas City," he commented. The fact he was still disturbed and saddened by the event didn't take much energy to detect.

It was then it hit me; I'd heard that name before, and it had been told to me by Fitzhugh.

"You are John Gold, aren't you?" Before I allowed him to

respond, I added, "Fitzhugh's nephew."

His mouth jerked in a tight smile.

"You must have been the smartest kid in you class," he commented with sarcasm. "And the answer to your question is yes, but your Kipp already knew that. He is pushing me in ways I don't like," he commented, turning to stare at Kipp again.

I stepped forward, easily drawing his attention back towards me.

"I'm the one talking to you," I said.

His mouth widened in a smile that did not reach his lips. "Don't try good cop bad cop with me; I invented the game." Motioning with his hand, he invited me to join him on his granite perch. It was shady there with a mild breeze disturbing the top branches of the cottonwoods. Since there was no reason to stand around, I walked over and chose a relatively flat spot on the rocks, after checking carefully for scorpions and the like. Kipp padded after me, his footsteps soft on the sandy surface.

"So, what happened to you, John?" I asked.

He turned his head upwards for a moment, his blue eyes tracking a lone vulture that was circling ahead as it relaxed its large wings against an air pocket and glided, perfectly balanced.

"I didn't fit the mold, Petra." Gold shrugged his shoulders. "I wanted to travel to past conflicts, wars between great nations and societies. Those are the instances where the future of humanity is determined. The governing body didn't think I had the right temperament and refused my requests. So, one day Ula and I just left."

Kipp continued to keep his thoughts shuttered from me and Gold, but it was clear from his attitude that he was skeptical of Gold's simplistic telling of the tale.

"Your friend," Gold said, nodding at Kipp while speaking to me, "is unusual. He won't let me share thoughts with him but he obviously has a level of control that is way beyond the skill level of most symbionts." Gold smiled at me again and the blue eyes met mine. "Where did you find such a talented companion?"

I had decided to take Kipp's tactic and share little. "Kipp is unusual, but I don't really think that is any of your concern."

Gold started, in his typically aggressive way, to push into my thoughts and obtain the information anyway, and suddenly Kipp threw up a mental block that was startling in its effectiveness.

"See, that right there is what I'm talking about," Gold commented, shaking his head. "That's something you just don't run into every day." Laughing, he held up his hands in mock defense. "Kipp, I'm not going to hurt you or Petra."

Kipp, meanwhile, narrowed his eyes and stared back at Gold, his thoughts still hidden.

I continued my queries. "So, why did they think you were unsuitable for travel?" Reaching up, I pulled the hat from my head and placed it upon the rock. The wind hit the top of my head and teased my hair from the confining chignon.

Gold shrugged his shoulders. "I guess it doesn't hurt to tell you. Fitzhugh wouldn't have mentioned this, but he disapproved greatly of my father." Gold looked off into the desert, deep in thought. "My father was descended from a long line of symbionts who believed we were originally a warrior species. He and his clan visited all the great battles of history and were actively engaged in war." Gold turned back to me. "All this childish, simpering talk of peaceful noninterference was obscene in his eyes. He felt we are the superior species on earth, and that we should take a leadership role to these troglodytes that you call humans."

I darted a glance at Kipp, who remained like a stone statue. But in my heart, I felt sickened. I knew, from my history of our species, that there was a break off clan who rejected the passive role that the majority of us took in terms of our sharing the world with other species, most notably humans. I believed, as did most of my peers, that our abilities made us corruptible, and that we were compelled to follow our stance of supportive noninterference. Our ability to go back in time and manipulate history was eternally seductive and beckoned us to fall from grace.

"I know you disapprove, since you have been brainwashed to believe as you do. But I follow a different path." Gold's voice was flat and unemotional.

"That is why Ula left you, isn't it?" Kipp finally weighed in.

Gold stared at him and the smile left his face. "Yes, if you must know. She did not care for battle and death. One day, she disappeared into the night and left me adrift in this land." He stretched his hand. "But with my love of battle, I've managed to carve out a happy niche for myself."

"There's nothing happy about you," Kipp replied. "Most sociopaths are not happy people, and the same goes for symbionts."

Gold laughed softly, not willing to be drawn in by Kipp. "I'm not a sociopath; as I've made clear, I'm from a warrior class of symbionts. There is a difference since I'm vastly superior to humans, and there is no comparison."

"So, where have your travels taken you?" I asked, more curious than I wished to admit.

"I've been to most of the large battles of the American Civil War. I was with the Romans as they conquered much of what is now Europe. I even was with Genghis Khan and served as his advisor. There are countless others, but I doubt you would want to hear the details."

"And you've killed many people?" I looked off at the landscape, no longer willing to meet his eyes.

"Oh yes. Countless. I told you, I'm a warrior."

"No, you're just a murderer," Kipp injected. "A murderer who is trying to glamorize the thrill of power over life and death by posing as a warrior."

"And what is the difference?" Gold asked.

"A warrior fights for a cause; you fight for the enjoyment of fighting and having power over life and death." Kipp stared up at him. "You are beneath contempt."

Gold's expression changed to one of impatience. "I can see I'm surrounded by those who have been brainwashed with the typical symbiont message. I might have hoped to meet up with others who were able to think outside of the carefully prescribed box, but I see that it won't happen with you two."

Kipp stood and stretched fore and aft. The tiny wind hit his dense coat, brushing the auburn fur upright; he was strong, vital and confident and never more so than on that day did he communicate that message to Gold. He didn't need to tell Gold to not underestimate him, since the two had been sizing one another up since the moment they first made contact on that lonely road in the desert.

I didn't consider myself a lightweight in the world of my kind, but I also was realistic about my abilities. I was a very skilled time traveler. But in terms of the mental projective power that Kipp possessed that allowed him to dig into the depths of a human brain like an archeologist on a dig or the ability to block thought transmissions…those skills I lacked. After listening to Gold and observing Kipp, I did have cause to wonder if all of my kind possessed more expansive skills and had we been told otherwise in order to contain us and control us? But did it really matter?

"Yes, it does," Gold commented, answering my question for me. Kipp obviously had stopped blocking Gold from reading my thoughts for the moment.

"Why?" I asked, thinking Kipp allowed this back and forth for a reason.

"Because we are greater than you've been led to believe. We, as a species, do not have to exist to serve humans. We are the dominant and superior species on this planet."

Kipp sat quietly, waiting for me. I knew this sort of philosophical and ethical exchange was one where he would, despite his superior talents and skills, follow my lead. A tiny bead of sweat appeared on my forehead, but I stayed my hand to prevent its journey down the planes of my face.

"John," I said, my voice quiet, "history is full of humans who felt superior to others; it typically leads to war, subjugation and devastation." The quiet murmur of the nearby stream was soothing. "I am one of our kind who has made the choice to not follow that path to destruction. Just because you have the ability to do something doesn't mean you have to do it." I shrugged my shoulders. "So if that makes me weak, then so be it. My strength is in self-control and making a choice."

Gold looked away, his thoughts controlled as he looked off into the desert. When he turned back to gaze at me, his face was surprisingly passive.

"I hope you have a good time during your vacation here," he commented. "I might suggest you take care around Holliday." Gold's eyes dropped to meet Kipp's. "I realize that it's fascinating to meet all these characters, but Holliday is a magnet for trouble. I wouldn't want to see Petra get in the middle of something, uh, rough."

Kipp nodded his head and remained silent, but I felt a dart of irritation.

"What is this male protective talk?" I asked, putting my hands on my hips. "I don't need a male cavalier to keep me safe, thank you very much."

Gold laughed and said, "I wasn't addressing Kipp as your protector; I was speaking to him because he is more talented and has a greater skill set than do you, Petra. So unruffle your feathers and take a deep breath."

Feeling foolish, I walked to the buggy, Gold at my side. Gently, he took my elbow and assisted me to the seat. I looked down at him and again was struck by his features. A remarkably handsome face concealed an angry and aggressive interior. It was always easy to be drawn to the beautiful form and ignore all else of substance.

Kipp walked up and took one last glance at Gold, his eyes half narrowed. Gold smiled and nodded, giving Kipp a mock salute. Kipp hopped in the back of the buggy, and I clucked for the horse to move forward. As we departed from the shady reprieve of the stunted trees into the bright glare of sunlight, I realized my stomach was growling from hunger. Slapping the reins lightly on the back of the horse, I urged him into a slow trot.

"I'm hungry, too," Kipp commented, sticking his big head over the back of the seat and resting it on my shoulder. "I don't know about you, but that game of mental tag with Gold was tiring."

I took a deep breath. "Well, you had to expend a lot of energy to keep him off of me, and I'm sorry about that Kipp."

He was irritated at my words and let me know in no uncertain terms.

"No, I mean it Kipp. I'm not a baby and need to get stronger to deal with Gold. Maybe you can teach me some of the ways that you project outward and block."

Kipp considered my words. "So you think what Gold says is right…that all symbionts have some of the abilities that you've been told were lost over the centuries."

"Well, Kipp, he is only a couple of hundred years older than am I. Why would he have these skills and suddenly, after two hundred years, no other symbionts can do what he can? Philo is about his age or a little older. And then there is Fitzhugh."

Kipp nodded his head, and rested his jaw on my shoulder, the soft fur of his muzzle tickling the side of my face. I put a hand up and pulled him close.

"We'll begin today," Kipp promised.

CHAPTER 20

———◆———

I was relieved to return to my relatively spacious suite at the Cosmopolitan. Eli wordlessly took care of the horse and buggy and at my request was working on a hip bath with hot water. My plan was to clean the desert born dust off of my body and out of my hair; then, Kipp and I would cloister in the rooms until the following evening when I was scheduled to go out on a date with Doc Holliday. Yes, in any other time and place, I suppose it met the criteria of a date.

Eli poured the last bucket of water into the hip bath, which he had rolled from down the hallway on a little cart with wheels. A bucket stood by with clean water for rinsing. Unlike Emily, Eli didn't volunteer to stay and help me and beat a hasty retreat. After stripping off my sweat soaked dress, I stepped into the bath and almost collapsed with pleasure at feeling the warm water lap around my thighs. I perched on the little ledge of metal on the interior of the bath and scrubbed one foot and then the other with the lavender soap that seemed to be the rage of the day. Lacking shampoo, I bent forward and dunked my head; then, I used the bar of soap and vigorously coated the dark strands of hair with the soft milled soap.

Kipp had dropped to the floor on one of the woolen rugs and watched with interest. He was continually amused at the ablutions required by humans and humanoid symbionts and was happy to be of the lupine variety. His head rested on outstretched paws and the slanted, dark ringed eyes watched me; his thoughts were active and, as usual for Kipp, were moving with such alacrity that I scarce could keep up.

"I was thinking," Kipp finally commented, "of the skills or talents that I seem to possess that you do not." He shifted his weight and rolled on his side, thumping his tail as he watched me rinsing my hair. "I can implant thoughts into humans and animals—at least cats; we don't know if I can do it with symbionts, but recorded history might suggest that I can. And we know I can alter the outcomes of dreams in symbionts, since I did it with you; we must assume I have the same ability with humans." Kipp rolled on his back and stretched. "Apparently I can block the transmission of telepathic thoughts between symbionts, but so can John Gold."

I spoke up. "And we know that you can dig down into the human mind and recover suppressed memories, which is an unexpected step beyond working with active thoughts." I suppressed a shudder. "We know that Gold can do that also, to a certain degree, and he can do that with symbionts."

"Yes but not to the level I possess." Kipp was not bragging; he just stated facts.

I'd finished my bath and stepped out on a towel provided by Eli. After vigorously drying off, I wrapped a thick towel around my hair and pulled on my dressing gown. A soft tap on the door announced the return of Eli, who was there to remove the hip bath and towels. I also gave him two of my soiled gowns to take to the middle-aged widow who took in laundry from the Cosmopolitan. I'd managed to maintain clean undergarments by washing them in the basin in the room.

There was a little tub of hair dressing on the marble topped vanity, and I rubbed some into my hair before dragging a comb through the mass of dark tresses. I finished off the activity by braiding my hair and tying off the end with a ribbon.

"Okay, Kipp. We need to do some experimentation, and you are the only one with whom I'd trust my weary brain." I'd pulled the window covering closed and the room was actually rather pleasantly cool without the glare of sunlight. Walking to the bed, I lay down, my head resting lightly on the pillow. Kipp walked over and hopped up, resting his muzzle across my chest.

"We know you can get into the hidden memories of a human; we need to know if you can do the same with one of your own species. I trust you to see what you can learn from me."

Kipp gave me a gentle lick on the side of my face, and I began to relax, leaving my mind open and trying to focus on the picture on the far wall. It was my plan to not direct Kipp and just see what would happen. A human would not have been aware, but I felt Kipp as he began to merge his thoughts with mine in the manner of symbiont connectedness. He told me he loved me, and I smiled in response.

Then, I felt him push beyond the active thoughts and then it was as if he disappeared into my brain. I lost awareness of him as he began to ignore active thoughts and search for repressed and suppressed memories. From my perception, aside from the typical telepathic component, I was not aware what he was doing or where he traveled in his journey into my mind. So, a human would obviously have no awareness whatsoever. At some point, I actually dozed off.

"Petra, wake up," Kipp nuzzled me softly.

"What?" I replied, feeling confused momentarily. I looked toward the shuttered window and realized the day had drawn on towards early evening. From outside, I could hear the raucous cheers of a group of inebriated men from one of the numerous saloons that lined Allen Street.

"You were about to have a bad dream, so I thought I'd awaken you." Kipp stared at my face. "My journey into your memories may have jogged some things loose, and you were starting a dream based on what I was uncovering."

"And what was that, Kipp?" I managed to pull myself upright, and Kipp hopped off the bed. Uncharacteristically for my calm companion, he began to pace the small area.

"I'm not sure I should tell you," he commented.

"Kipp, you need to and the reason for this experiment is to see what skills our species possess. If you keep your thoughts to yourself, we'll never know." I knew he was worried about hurting me. I perceived his hesitation and knew I had to get aggressive with him. "And you don't have my permission to get into my brain and not tell me what you found."

Kipp took a deep sigh and finally allowed himself to sit, his haunches tucked neatly beneath the massive body.

"It has to do with baby George," he began, darting a glance at my face. I tried to control it but winced involuntarily.

"Go on," I said.

Kipp's thoughts were slow and halting. "After you got the call from the hospital, Philo drove you to Durham and walked with you to the emergency room at Duke."

"I remember all that, Kipp," I began.

"But you weren't actively thinking about it," he reminded me. "They are memories easily retrieved but not active thoughts." He took another deep breath. "It's odd and hard to describe, but it is as if I saw all of it from your eyes. You walked forward and a nurse took your arm and guided you through the emergency room. At some point, you passed a cubicle and glanced over to see a man lying on a bed with several staff surrounding him. You glanced down and looked at the nurse's hand on your arm; her nails were painted bright pink, and you thought that was odd."

Kipp stood and stretched and hopped back on the bed next to me. "You keep walking until you get to a far cubicle where all the drapes were drawn. The nurse stood back, and you walked forward to pull back the drape. A still form was on the bed; you realize it is your husband. The nurse's words finally reach your ears—he was killed in an automobile accident. His face looks relaxed and unscathed, as if he was just sleeping."

"Then you suddenly realized that your baby is missing." Kipp pushed closer and put his muzzle on my chest. "You asked the nurse where was baby George. The young woman takes your arm and guides you from the cubicle and you walk towards another one, where curtains are carefully pulled. You glance at Philo; his face is sad, the lines of age are deepened with grief." Kipp looked at me. "Philo was a good friend of your husband."

All of what Kipp was telling me was memories that I could access but avoided doing so. I took a deep breath and exhaled slowly through my mouth. I realized that I had no memories of what happened next. Obviously, I had repressed parts of what occurred.

"The nurse touches your arm again, and you walk forward." Kipp paused, and I knew he didn't want to continue. My hand found his broad head, and I gently caressed his ears.

"Go on," I said softly, my throat dry as the sandy Arizona desert.

"The nurse pulls back the curtain, and you see a small body on the bed. You realize it is George, but he is oddly not moving. You call out to him, and he is still." Kipp moved closer to me if that was possible.

I was horrified; the memory was one I'd managed to totally repress and now it was here, with me, once again. Swallowing hard, I nodded my head.

"You look down and see baby George; his body is covered, but his little face seems undamaged, as if he is just asleep."

The remainder of the memory had flooded back and the next thing I knew, Kipp was frantically licking the sides of my face, trying to dry my tears.

"Petra, I'm sorry," he said. He repeated it over and over again until I told him to stop.

I struggled to sit up, feeling trapped by the soft mattress. Finally I stood and pulled the sash of my dressing gown tighter around my waist. I understood why humans and symbionts suppressed and repressed memories of this sort. Dealing with them on a daily basis was immobilizing.

"I can make it go away again," Kipp commented softly.

I held up my hand. "No, Kipp. I'm not a child, and I've hidden out long enough. We'll let things be for now and see what happens."

Walking towards the window that overlooked the Occidental Saloon, I pulled back the curtain and peered outside. Darkness had fallen; a group of men had ridden up on horses and were in the act of entering the saloon. One of the figures stopped and glanced up at my window. With shock, I realized it was John Gold, otherwise known in this harsh land as Johnny Ringo.

"Hello, Petra," his thoughts easily made their way across the short distance. He immediately picked up on my agitated mind and made to politely inquire as to my state when Kipp, from behind me, stepped forward to push his large head to the window.

"Leave her be, Gold," Kipp commanded.

I otherwise might have stopped Kipp's involvement but was too agitated and fragile after the memory recovery of my deceased baby. My hand dropped down and I touched Kipp lightly. He glanced up and our eyes met. As much as I trusted Philo, Juno and my beloved Tula, I would not have allowed them, had they the skills, to enter my mind as I had Kipp. What if I were to lose him, as I had Tula, my husband, and dear George? Kipp nuzzled my hand.

"I'm not going anywhere, Petra," he commented with assuredness.

"You don't have control over fate," I replied.

"I plan on being very careful."

The loud commotions from the saloons on Allen Street stretched into the early morning hours, which was typical in

Tombstone. It was more pronounced on the weekends, when laborers from the silver mines and cowboys from outlying ranches could come to town to have a little fun. But even during the weekdays, the saloons appeared to stay consistently busy, opening late morning and staying active until after midnight. There was always gambling, and the prostitutes kept an active clientele. I think, looking back, that the trio of alcohol, gambling and prostitution was one of the mainstays of the local economy.

I felt refreshed when I awoke and my night had been curiously undisturbed by dreams. Glancing at Kipp, who lay next to me, his bright eyes on my face, I started to inquire if he had manipulated my dreams but chose not to. The memory recovery of the previous day had been traumatic enough, and I didn't have to act heroic and brave with my best friend. A whiff of the lavender soap with which I had washed my hair lightened my mood. Perhaps there was something to be said for aromatherapy.

A gentle tap on the door announced the arrival of Eli. I hopped up and, after making certain my dressing gown was discretely secured, made my way to the door.

"Good morning, Mrs. Totheroh," Eli said, his voice quiet and polite. His hands balanced a tray covered with a cloth towel. The aroma of fresh bread assailed my nostrils, and I realized I was hungry. The previous day, I'd eaten almost nothing. Kipp darted up, wagging his tail.

"Shall I take Kipp out for you?" Eli asked, peering at me through the fringe of blonde hair that fell across his forehead.

I nodded my head and watched as Kipp pranced at Eli's side down the hallway to the back staircase. While waiting for his return, I poured a cup of coffee from the silver plated coffee pot and inhaled the fragrance. Crumbling a biscuit, I nibbled at the corner. I'd never mastered the homemade biscuit and admired these cooks who could turn out such wonderful food with relatively primitive tools and wood burning stoves.

A tap on the door announced the return of Eli and Kipp,

who pushed past and began to attack his bowl of food with relish.

"Mrs. Totheroh, not to be rude or nothing, but Doc Holliday asked me to give you a message." Eli shifted from one foot to the other. The disapprobation with which he regarded Holliday was obvious. "He said to pay his respects, ma'am, and tell you that he will meet you in the lobby at seven this evening." Eli looked up at me; he wanted to say more but wasn't sure of himself due to what he perceived to be the vast differential in our mutual statuses.

"What is it, Eli?" I decided to prod him, knowing he needed scant encouragement.

"Mrs. Totheroh, it's none of my business, but Doc Holliday is a dangerous man. He, uh, brings problems wherever he goes. There's always someone gunning for him." Eli rubbed his hands together. "I just wanted you to know."

I smiled at the young man. "Thank you, Eli, for being concerned. I'm only going to be in Tombstone a short time." I made a slight gesture at Kipp. "And I don't go anywhere without Kipp, so I have a constant bodyguard."

Eli's thoughts betrayed his true sentiments. He thought that I was a typically naïve, ignorant woman who was overly confident and not willing to listen to male guidance. I expected this and took no offense.

He backed towards the door. "If you won't be needing anything else, ma'am," he said, nodding his head.

I intended on occupying my day learning more about Doc Holliday…from Kipp.

CHAPTER 21

"Kipp, you spent a lot of time the other day investigating Holliday's deeply imbedded memories. Tell me what you found out." I was sitting on the sofa in the sitting room. Kipp, having polished off the breakfast that Eli served, was relaxing on the floor, licking his paws.

"Do I have food on my whiskers?" he asked, as he tried to rub his face with a damp paw.

"No, Kipp. You are beautiful and shining clean. Now tell me about Holliday."

Kipp stretched out on his side, reflecting upon the fact he had eaten too much. Not only did he finish off his bowl of chicken and rice, he took care of my extra biscuit, uneaten eggs and skillet made white gravy.

"I could stay here, if only for the food and room service," he mused.

"You get food and room service at home, if I recall correctly," I commented, raising a dark eyebrow.

Outside, we heard a distant rumble of thunder. Dark clouds had gathered the day before, and now we were experiencing a rare and pleasant rain. I inhaled and felt the dampness enter my lungs. The Occidental Saloon next door had a tin roof, and the raindrops made high pitched noises as they plunked on the surface.

Kipp knew I would not be deterred. "Holliday is brilliant

and complex. I think he has a conscience and is capable of remorse, so you would probably not classify him as a total sociopath. But he has a way of turning around events to make them, uh, fit his way of looking at the world."

I pulled my feet up under me. The thin drapes blew inward as a gust of wind pushed into the room. The weather was beginning to change. We would be here a few more weeks, since Kipp was eager to be present for the OK Corral showdown.

"So, does he ever have regret when he kills someone?"

Kipp twisted his head up, stretching his neck. "Only once...so far. There was a gambler and Holliday attacked him with a knife." Kipp turned to me, his amber eyes almost appeared backlit in the dim room. "I think he needs a gun and distance; the up close knife attack left him sickened." Kipp paused and swallowed. "He calls it, uh, evisceration, when he thinks about it."

My mouth went dry. "I read about that one. And yes, I can imagine that would leave him with particularly bad memories."

"I saw it in my head like he did, and it made me feel bad," Kipp commented. "Anyway, he has a lot of sadness about his home in Georgia as well as intense bitterness about the American Civil War. He didn't feel passionate about the cause of the war, but he was angry over the outcome in terms of reconstruction. He, in his own mind, attributes his lung disease to the deprivation and starvation that he and his family faced.

"And I did get to dig into the mystery of his female cousin. He was in love with her and he, at least, thinks she loved him in return. His family did not approve and were the impetus behind his going to Baltimore to enter dental college. His cousin went to Atlanta and entered a, uh, nunnery. What is that?"

I took a few minutes to explain the concept of cloistered nuns. This led to a conversation about religion in general and Catholicism as well as other world beliefs. After a few minutes, I realized we had drifted from our original topic of conversation.

"So, Kipp, what is your conclusion about the man after your time inside his brain?"

Kipp sat quietly for a while, deep in thought. From outside, we heard a loud rumble as one of the 20 mule team drawn wagons rolled past the Cosmopolitan. The rain had tapered off, and the air from the window felt scrubbed and refreshed.

"I think he was raised to be a moral person. Overtime, bitterness and anger changed him. He does not fear death and almost feels, when he is drinking, that he is doing needed work by eliminating other people whom he feels are, uh, corrupt or evil." Kipp paused before adding, "But he has a sardonic view of himself as a total hypocrite." Kipp looked at me. "He's rather sad, in the end."

I decided to rest for the majority of the day. Wearing only my camisole with the attached drawers, I wandered back into the bedroom and lay on the bed. The room felt cool for daytime for a change, and I fell asleep despite the noise from outside the window. Kipp hopped up and nestled next to me. We both were preparing for the long evening ahead.

I was supposed to meet Doc in the lobby at 7 pm. With surprise, I awoke at 5 pm and realized I'd slept away most of the day. Although time travel and telepathy are part and parcel of being a symbiont, both were actually huge consumers of mental and physical resources, and the occasional bout of excessive sleep was helpful to a recovery of energy and alertness.

The impetus for my awakening was Eli, who had softly tapped on my door. Pulling my dressing gown around my body, I peered out into the hallway to greet the young man. Kipp was fairly dancing with need to go outside, so I asked Eli to take him downstairs and bring me back a pot of hot tea. Eli enjoyed taking care of us, but I always made certain he was well compensated for his time and trouble.

While they were gone, I splashed water into my face and

wondered how I could allow the day to go by in relative sloth. Recalling for the moment that I was actually on vacation, I took one of the embroidered hand towels from the ornate bronze washbasin stand and blotted the dampness from my skin. Looking up in the mirror, I saw my reflection staring back. For my age, which was greater than 400 years, I guess I was taking the weathering associated with travel relatively well. A human would think me in my late twenties, no older than mid thirties.

Kipp returned and plopped in the floor where he began to critique the various hair styles I tried in anticipation of the evening out with Doc Holliday. Styling hair was not one of my strengths, and I finally decided the most sophisticated hairdo that could be accomplished with only two hands would be a French braid that I twisted into a chignon in the back. It looked complex but in reality was simple. I'd found a couple of ornate combs at a shop in Tucson and used these to boost the appearance of the style.

While Kipp rattled on with observations of the town and some of the inhabitants, I pulled on the dreaded corset and pulled the laces tight enough that I could squeeze into a dress. Over that, I drew on the petticoat and tied the cord at the side. I'd selected a pale apricot gown which appeared to be the dressiest of my small wardrobe and would be more appropriate for evening wear.

"I like that color," Kipp commented. "Are you nervous?"

"Not really; how about you?" Carefully I pulled the gown over my head, being cautious to not disturb my coiffeur. The material of the dress cascaded to the floor; I took care to adjust the folds of fabric in the rear to correctly glide over the bank bustle. Even though I was in a hotel with a security vault, I had decided to keep my funds under my control and on my fanny. Kipp still wore his money collar, too. I'd not had to tap funds from his wearable bank.

"No, but I'm not sure how we will deal with John Gold."

"Maybe he won't be there tonight," I responded, feeling hopeful.

"He'll be there, Petra. Of that you can be sure." Kipp

rolled to his side.

I finally finished and executed a little pirouette in front of the mirror over the dresser.

"Doc will be excited to see you," Kipp commented, coming to his feet and stretching his jaws in a big yawn. Outside, we could hear the dueling pianos—one probably at the Occidental and the other up the street at Hafford's saloon.

"I'm excited to meet Wyatt Earp and some of the other notables," I replied, arching an eyebrow at Kipp. I reached for a crystal cut atomizer that contained some perfume.

"Please don't," Kipp requested. "It gives me a headache."

I stuck my tongue out and replaced the atomizer on the marble topped dresser.

"Are you ready?" I asked.

"Let me put on my bow tie," Kipp replied dryly.

With that, we exited the room; I locked the door and put the brass key into my reticule. With Kipp at my side, I walked down the hall, game face fully intact. It took a fair amount of coordination and concentration to not get my feet tangled in the long skirts, but I tried to appear competent and unruffled. I'm not sure what he would have done if I'd tripped on the stairs, but I think Kipp would have done his best to try and stop the calamitous roll to the ground floor.

The thoughts of a now familiar mind filtered into my brain, and I glanced up to see Doc Holliday waiting at the base of the stairs. He looked handsome, and the flickering, dim lights of the lobby served to camouflage the ravages of disease. He was wearing a crisp white shirt with the collar pressed into wings; a narrow black tie was neatly looped into a bow. The Norfolk tweed jacket fell to his hips, and his black trousers looked crisp as they draped to the top of a pair of polished boots.

At the desk, Dent, was wearing a smirk on his face until Doc turned towards him. Then, the clerk became an obsequious pile of protoplasm as he smiled and bobbed his head. I could not audibly hear the words exchanged but knew, from Doc's thoughts that he was advising the clerk that no one should disturb my room in my absence. It had not occurred to me that the reason my belongings seemed untouched was due to Doc having intervened. Obviously, Dent would have a passkey to go through my room whenever he wanted.

Doc turned back to me and smiled. Walking forward, he extended a thin hand and took my proffered hand, bending over it to bestow a light kiss on the back. He glanced at Kipp.

"I see you brought a body guard, although I can assure you my intentions are only those of a gentleman." He was amused but not really irritated at the presence of Kipp.

"I don't go anywhere without Kipp, Mr. Holliday. Do you think it will cause a disturbance at the music hall?" I tilted my head up and smiled.

Doc laughed softly. "Mrs. Totheroh, I can assure you that there will be no problem at all." His thoughts drifted towards darkness, since he recognized his intimidation factor and knew that no one at the hall would turn down Kipp since he was in the company of an infamous man.

"He's not proud of it, really," Kipp commented, "but he's not disingenuous and won't be dishonest about his influence over others."

Doc gently tucked my hand into the crook of his elbow, and with Kipp flanking me on the other side, our odd and improbable trio walked out of the Cosmopolitan and turned left up Allen Street. The Vincent and Braden's Music Hall was only a short distance ahead. We would be forced to pass by the entrances of a number of saloons, including the Occidental, the Alhambra and Campbell and Hatch saloon. The rain from earlier in the day had managed to subdue the restless dust and sand; it was actually becoming cool as the last flames of sunlight began to drop behind the far off Dragoon Mountains.

As we passed by the swinging doors to the Occidental, a man stepped out and directly into our path. It was John Gold in his locally familiar guise of Johnny Ringo. My memory of him as being almost physically perfect was unaltered now as he smiled down at me.

"Why, Mrs. Totheroh," he commented, "how nice to see you again."

The devil in him was coming out full force, since he was just trying to bait and antagonize Doc. But the real problem was that he was playing a dangerous game with an unpredictable force...or at least Doc would be unfathomable to another human. Ringo, of course, was one step ahead, telepathically speaking.

Kipp moved up to edge slightly in front of me and minimally bared his teeth. Gold's eyes flicked down as he stared at Kipp.

Before Doc could ask, I supplied the answer. "Mr. Ringo came to my assistance while I was struggling with some packages." I hoped Doc wouldn't ask for details. But he seemed mollified and nodded his head at Ringo.

"Why, then, I'm grateful to you, Johnny," Doc remarked, tipping the brim of his hat.

After we'd breezed past Ringo, Doc commented softly, "That man is very dangerous, and I'd advise caution."

Kipp paused and looked over his shoulder. Ringo was still standing where we'd left him, staring at our trio. "A truer statement I've never heard uttered," Kipp commented, before swinging around and trotting to keep up with us.

The saloons on Allen were loud and raucous, and we had to dodge more than one inebriated customer being summarily evicted for the evening. Just before we crossed Fifth, a man staggered out of the Golden Eagle Brewery and Saloon. Even if I had not been telepathic, I would have recognized Doc's expression of extreme dislike and hatred for the bandy legged man who staggered towards us. It was Ike Clanton, and putting him and Doc together was one of the more explosive combinations in Tombstone.

Ike probably had started the evening looking fairly neat, but after too many beers and whiskeys tossed back with an eager hand, his shirt tail was pulled loose from the confines of his belt; thick curly hair was completely on end, giving him an almost comical look of surprise.

Doc's hand pulled mine tighter into the crook of his supporting arm. I realized he did not want a confrontation with Ike since he felt responsible for safely conducting me to the music hall. But it was not in his nature to turn away, so he pushed forward and managed to edge past Ike, who finally quit weaving when he assumed a wide based stance.

"Doc, what's your hurry? I'd like to meet the pretty lady."

I'd always had a sensitive sense of smell, and the alcohol fumes billowing around Ike, both from his mouth as well as his skin pores, almost made me retch.

"Whew!" Kipp commented. I glanced down at him and suppressed a giggle as Kipp tried to cross his eyes.

Doc's temper began to flare at what he, with his code of gentility he'd adopted with me, took to be a potentially offensive comment by Ike.

The next thing I knew, Kipp took action to defuse the situation by allowing Doc to not have to deal with Ike. My friend and companion took a quick leap forward towards Clanton and gave a huge bark, showing almost every tooth in his head. Ike, startled, took a bad step back and tumbled off the wooden walkway and into the street. A chorus of raucous laughter came from the entrance of the saloon and a tall, dark man, followed by two nondescript companions, walked out to join our festive party.

"Curly Bill, I'd ask you to be respectful of the lady and make Ike behave, if that's possible," Doc's free hand was resting at the butt of his revolver, a fact not missed by Bill Brocious.

Curly Bill, from my brief read of him, was not characteristically vicious, as were many of those with whom he travelled. He was more amiable in general and saw relationships and enmities for what they were—either they facilitated business or they impeded it. He respected Doc's abilities and had no wish to push the moment into violence. Curly Bill was one of the more unattractive human males I'd seen, with heavy, brutish features and a thick body set on sturdy legs. His teeth, unlike Doc's, had not been cared for and were dark with stains and decay. His face peered at me from beneath the brim of a large sombrero. Grinning, he tipped his hat as he glanced at me.

"Very sorry, ma'am. Ike is usually well mannered, but he's had too much to drink tonight." Curly Bill glanced at his companions who had helped Ike to his feet. "Watching your dog scare him was the funniest thing I've seen all year."

Ike's thoughts towards me and Kipp were particularly dark, and I knew he didn't like being the butt of an unintended joke. The fact his friends were still laughing didn't help matters. I felt worried enough that I made a suggestion to Kipp, one that I'd sworn to avoid.

"Kipp, I want you to go into Ike's mind and manipulate his thoughts around what happened."

He looked startled since I was asking him to do the opposite of what we'd discussed previously. "Like what?" Kipp asked.

I took a deep breath and hazarded a look above; the night was clear and the constellations overhead were shining like chips of crystal suspended in the blue-black heavens.

"Make it into something funny, so that when his friends laugh, he is genuinely amused." After a brief pause, I added, "I don't want Ike provoked to change history." I was busy with Kipp and didn't notice the shadowy outline of John Gold, who had edged closer.

"Ike has a hair trigger temper and is easily forced into aggression because he has a low opinion of himself, when all is said and done." Gold's observation was made. It was also evident that he'd overheard my suggestion to Kipp and was fascinated and more than a little curious. There was no way now to exclude him from eavesdropping on our communication.

Kipp looked up at me and wagged his tail before directing his concentration at Ike Clanton. Somehow, and I'm not certain by what means, Kipp managed to block most of what he did from both me and Gold, much to the irritation of the latter. It was but a minute later that Ike laughed and slapped Curly Bill on the shoulder before disappearing back into the smoke filled depths of the saloon.

"That was a clever little parlor trick," Gold commented. "I'd like to find out just how you accomplished that, Kipp," he added, his thoughts filling our minds in a most unpleasant manner.

Meanwhile, Doc turned, and we continued towards the music hall. Gold was left to stand in the darkness, wondering as to what magic Kipp had woven.

"Mrs. Totheroh, how can I apologize adequately for that boorish scene?" Doc's honeyed tones made their way to my ears, and I was thankful for the distraction. The telepathic wars between Gold and Kipp as well as monitoring the thoughts of the humans and trying to prevent a gunfight were draining my energy.

"Oh, Mr. Holliday, please don't bother yourself," I replied, smiling at the man. He nodded in response. Kipp padded along softly, his thoughts guarded for the moment.

"I fully understand now why you have your Kipp in constant attendance. His size, bark and full set of teeth seem to be a deterrent," Doc remarked. "I hope to stay on his good side."

I laughed in response and decided to not say anything in reply. Maybe it was good to keep Doc Holliday a little off his game.

CHAPTER 22

The owners of the Vincent and Braden's Music Hall were making a brave attempt to infuse culture into the raw nerve that was Tombstone. There was a large area of floor seating; along the sides of the room were cordoned off boxes where people could pay more and escape the more rowdy element that congregated in the center of the floor. The furnishings were rather upscale, at least in the boxes, and waiters circulated to bring beverages and snacks ordered by patrons. It was simple to keep order since the Earp brothers were always in attendance as representatives of law enforcement. At that time, Virgil was the city marshal; Wyatt and Morgan were deputies.

At the door, a nervous attendant viewed Kipp but stopped short of saying anything since Doc Holliday was giving the young man his most icy, intimidating stare. So we waltzed past and Doc escorted me to one of the center boxes and ushered me inside. Two men were standing and were so close in resemblance to almost be startling. Wyatt and Virgil, the elder by some five years, were tall, slender men with light brown hair and blue eyes. Both were carefully and neatly groomed with thick leonine mustaches and crisp white collars. I wasn't certain how they managed to keep the ever present dust from marring the appearance of the long, black frock coats they both wore.

"Wyatt and Virgil, may I present Mrs. Totheroh," Doc announced, obviously using his best southern manners for the event. He was oddly proud of me and wanted to show me off.

Virgil, of the two, was more outgoing and smiled in response. His aura was one of comfortable self-assurance, and he introduced me to his wife, Allie, who smiled and extended her hand in greeting. Her unspoken thoughts betrayed her curiosity over my relationship with Doc; his track record with women was fairly well publicized.

On the other hand, Wyatt Earp was one of the most reserved, humorless human males I'd ever encountered. In retrospect, I don't think he lacked the ability to experience joy; simply, he was a very self-contained man who had learned to compartmentalize feelings with a mastery seldom seen. I decided to leave it to Kipp if he wanted to crack that particular nut. Personally, I just looked forward to a night of entertainment and relaxation. After all, symbionts need some downtime and aren't all about work.

Wyatt's pleasure at seeing Doc was evident, and it was obvious the two men had carved out an implicit trust and solid friendship. Wyatt was curious about me and my relationship with Doc; I thought it somewhat odd that the two men had not discussed it before realizing Doc wanted to surprise people and show me off as if I was a newly won prize. In short, he enjoyed escorting a lady.

Wyatt turned to introduce me to his common law wife, Mattie. She was an exceptionally plain featured woman and sadness hovered over her like a fog. Kipp, with his attraction towards the downtrodden, looked at her and felt compassion.

"What's wrong with her?" he asked, not fully understanding the dynamics of the human psyche.

I'd discerned the issue quickly. "She is emotionally needy and is, unfortunately for her, married to a man who is emotionally distant. Mattie will never get any closeness with him."

Kipp stared at me. "What's wrong with her mind? She is,

uh, all confused."

I knew this pattern in humans, too. "She is addicted to opium, Kipp. Humans, when they have feelings with which they can't cope, sometimes turn to drugs and alcohol to numb those feelings."

Kipp caught Mattie's eye and read in her mind that she liked dogs. Meekly, with his massive head down, he walked over to her and put his head in her lap. A smile crossed her face as she gently ran her hands over his ears and scratched the back of his head. For some reason, the moment irritated Wyatt. He couldn't make her happy and seemed aggravated that a dog could.

"Kind of unusual, isn't it Doc, to bring a dog to hear a reading from Hamlet?" Wyatt smiled but it didn't reach his blue eyes.

Doc laughed in an easy way. "Kipp is an unusual dog," he replied. "He just managed to warn off Johnny Ringo as well as scare Ike Clanton out of ten years growth."

Virgil nodded his head. "Maybe we need to deputize him, then." It was clear he was defusing the situation as he recognized Wyatt's disapproval.

"I like Mattie," Kipp commented to me. "She needs a friend." He knew, however, that he needed to minimize his presence and, after a brief circle, dropped to the floor at Mattie's feet, his warm back gently pressed against her legs.

It was all rather sad; I knew where the future lay. Wyatt would become involved with Josie and eventually leave Tombstone and abandon Mattie. With her drug addiction, she would resume supporting herself as a prostitute until she managed to overdose on laudanum and kill herself. I looked at her pain ravaged face and was glad Kipp could give her a little companionship for the moment.

Doc, with all the flash and flair of a gentleman, held my seat for me and carefully folded my shoulder wrap across the back of the chair. With all the merging humanity in the music hall, the multitude of bodies were fueling ample warmth. I noticed that most of the couples were using the side boxes, probably so that the women would not be overly subjected to the chaos and rude behaviors of some of the men who congregated in the center of the room. These included cowboys as well as other men who were interested in some entertainment.

The house manager, a round man wearing an aged formal suit and a top hat, finally came out and gestured for quiet. He knew, of course, that the Earp brothers were present and could serve as bouncers as needed.

The boxes where we sat were slightly elevated above the floor; I looked down and caught the eye of John Gold, who commenced a mental dialog with me. Of course, at the moment, I was listening to Doc, who was asking me questions about my having attending plays and shows while back east. It is a necessary skill of my kind that we can carry on telepathic conversations with other symbionts while simultaneously communicating with humans.

"So, Petra, where did Kipp get that amazing talent?" John asked. He finally averted his eyes and was staring ahead at the stage. Curly Bill sat next to him and bent his head towards John, laughing at something he found amusing.

I saw no reason to lie since it was obvious Kipp was different. "He comes from 70,000 years in the past, John." I paused to nod my head at Doc and comment on a play both he and I had seen before. "I was investigating a point in prehistory and my symbiont, Tula, was killed. Kipp and I stumbled upon one another, and he saved my life." There, I'd said it and now we could move on.

Gold was nothing if not brilliant. "Ah, that explains much. The rest of us have lost skills through time and inbreeding as well as being constantly told by our establishment that we can't do things." He paused, and I saw him run a well-shaped hand down his thigh to brush off a piece of lint that marred the crisp appearance of his trousers. "I, on the other hand, have spent my life pushing the envelope trying to maximize my potential." He turned and smiled up at me. "But I can't do what Kipp did."

I was tiring of this game. "John, I came here to watch this company perform songs from *H.M.S. Pinafore* as well listen to recitations from Shakespeare. So, please, leave me and Kipp alone for a few minutes." I took a deep breath, inhaling the scent of Doc's hair pomade as I did so. "And if it makes you feel better, I can't do it either."

To my surprise, Gold turned his attention forward and began focusing on the performances. Kipp, as would be appropriate in his role as dog, kept his head down and appeared to be asleep, but his mind was actively communicating with mine. He was clearly fascinated with the musings of Shakespeare and found the cadence of speech and use of language to be intriguing.

"I finally figured out what is compelling about humans," he commented. "It is their diversity and evolving nature. They are always full of surprises," he concluded.

"They are a bunch of primitive, violent animals," Gold weighed in from across the room.

"Delete the primitive and you are talking about yourself," Kipp replied. "And I know you are scheming to see if there is some way you can get rid of Petra and have me as your partner. So know this: I will never bond with you, ever. And if anything accidentally happens to Petra, I know who I'll hold responsible." Kipp's mind turned dark. "I come from a time that predates all the rules for symbiont behaviors; I can be both primitive and violent."

I sat up a notch straighter in my chair. Doc noticed and gently took my hand.

"Are you enjoying the songs?" he asked, dipping his blonde head closer so that he could speak softly and still be heard.

I partitioned off the back and forth between Kipp and Gold-Ringo that was both distracting and disturbing. "Why, yes, for a traveling company, the songs are quite well done. I especially think the young soprano singer is very talented."

Doc and I traded some polite conversation for a moment. Suddenly, a fight broke out on the main floor between one of the nameless cowboys and a well dressed citizen who apparently had taken exception to some verbal exchange relating to the citizen's sister and her, uh, physical attributes.

Wyatt stood up first, followed by Virgil, and swiftly left the box. I watched his tall body as he pushed through the crowd until he reached the two men. I knew his concern was that the fight would quickly envelope the other men as they took sides to support friends. And there were those who just enjoyed chaos and would fight for the sake of fighting. Kipp's head went up in interest.

"Reminds me of a wolf pack fighting over dominance, and who is gonna get the last scrap of elk."

Wyatt was physically a strong man, and when he reached the cowboy, he grabbed his shoulder and shoved him to the floor. Curly Bill was standing nearby and edged up, his dark, heavy features flushed with anger; this did not improve his appearance.

"Wyatt, you have no call to do that," Bill commented. He was flanked by Ringo, who darted a glance over at me in amusement.

"Heathens and brutes," Ringo remarked to me.

"Bill, you need to take your friend and move on out of here. The folks are wanting a nice pleasant evening and none of this nonsense." Virgil spoke up; his tactic was one of reasonable negotiation versus Wyatt's more direct approach.

"We paid money to see the show, too," Curly said. Then he smiled, exposing the set of horrible teeth. "But you know me, Marshal, I always want to help keep the peace."

I knew he was playing an angle. In the eyes of the citizens of Tombstone, Curly Bill wanted the people to view the Earp brothers as a source of malcontent and see the cowboy element as friendly to the town. So if he could bite back his agitation and look peaceful, then that furthered his goal. I was impressed with the calculating quality of his nature. John Behan, the county sheriff, was standing nearby but remained uninvolved. He, however, nodded his head a couple of times, in support of Curly Bill. Behan's neatly manicured hand reached up to smooth his pomade coated hair in a vain gesture. He was handsome and knew it.

Mattie, in her opium induced stupor, finally awakened enough to sit up, gazing in concern at Wyatt. Any intervention in these matters was inherently dangerous. Kipp, sat up, too, and placed his head on her knees to comfort her.

John Gold smirked. "Why you, Kipp, are bothering to mess with that old whore and drug addict is beyond me."

Kipp glanced at me, his amber eyes round; the expression in them was softened. "And that, John, is why you are who you are and can never understand us."

John Gold would never comprehend the unsullied nature of Kipp, who was inherently good, despite his earlier posturing of savagery.

Kipp's reply angered Gold, who retreated behind the departing bulk of Curly Bill and several cowboys. The house manager returned to wave the crowd back to peaceful civility, and the performers returned to the stage. The Earps reentered the box and took their seats. Wyatt was embarrassed by Mattie's comments of having been worried about him and brushed them away with the wave of his strong hand.

"He's interesting," Kipp remarked, glancing at me. "He has, for some reason, managed to push all of his emotions into the back of his mind. They are there, to be sure, but he intellectualizes everything and tamps down sentiment."

"If you want to go psyche exploring, Kipp, have at it," I replied. I, for one, wanted to listen to *H.M.S. Pinafore* without any further interruptions.

After the performances ended, Doc suggested to the others that we go to the tearoom at the Grand and have coffee. Virgil nodded his head enthusiastically as he was enjoying the evening out with Allie. Whereas Wyatt seemed to have little honest affection for Mattie, Virgil was the opposite and felt love towards Allie, who clung to his arm. Both Virgil and Wyatt were curious as to Doc's feelings towards me and had some cynical notion that perhaps he was after my rumored fortune. Maybe they didn't know Doc as well as they thought.

We exited the box as a group once the crowd on the floor had thinned. Doc took my arm, and we preceded the others by a couple of steps. Kipp followed me closely. As we stepped outside of the music hall, the cool evening air hit me, and I pulled my wrap closer about my shoulders. Kipp's head went up and a moment later, so did mine. There was something in the atmosphere, almost like the smell of acrid smoke; to a symbiont, it was a prelude of a dangerous series of thoughts.

Before I could sort out the thoughts and tweeze out the meaning, Kipp dashed forward and knocked me to the ground, his large body covering mine. Less than a second later, a bullet rang out and split the frigid air where my head had been before Kipp's physical take down. The lead projectile hit an oil lantern on the door facing of the music hall, splintering the glass globe into cascading shards. The moment was confusing: Wyatt, seeing Kipp charge me, pulled his gun, thinking for a second that my dog was attacking me. Fortunately, his controlled demeanor prevented any reactive behavior on his part, and he did not pull the trigger, since the barrel was pointed at Kipp. Kipp realized the danger he was in but did not move, putting my life ahead of his safety.

Doc saw the flash of the gun from across the street and pulled his nickel-plated revolver. Without hesitating, he dashed forward, his limp pronounced, flanked by Wyatt, and Virgil followed a step behind the other two men. There was a disturbance and then the sound of horse's hooves as the unknown shooter mounted his horse and was trying to escape. Wyatt took careful aim and pulled the trigger; the unknown man catapulted from his horse and hit the ground in a flurry of dirt and rock.

Kipp licked my face frantically. "Petra, I'm sorry!" He pulled away and waited while I sat up. Mattie, in her drug stupor, stood, mouth hanging open, watching the spectacle. Allie, who was more responsive, raced forward and took my arm, helping me to stand. I assured both her and Kipp that I was okay.

Kipp, knowing that I was unharmed, left my side and trotted to meet the trio of Doc, Wyatt and Virgil as they walked to the still body. Kipp's coat was bristled and a strip of raised hair went from his head to the base of his tail, which was brushed in agitation. He leaned forward and sniffed the man who lay on the cold ground. Wyatt, after carefully studying for any movement, used his foot to turn the body.

"It's Tim Martin," he commented. Turning, Wyatt looked back at me. "Why would Tim try to shoot Mrs. Totheroh?" The question was aimed at Doc, who was agitated; it was with restraint that Doc holstered his gun.

Kipp looked over his shoulder at where I stood in the dark street. "It was John Gold," he commented. "He wanted you and me to know that he can get to either one of us whenever he wants. He picked someone who was relatively incompetent since he was just trying to make a point."

I shivered and Allie put her arm around me. She, for a petite woman, was very strong and her arm held me like an iron band.

"Let's go get some tea," she said, thinking that the hot beverage would brace and comfort me. I allowed her to pull me towards the Grand, followed by a silent Mattie. Kipp trotted up, not willing to be away from my side lest Gold concoct some other fun activity for the evening.

"I'll straighten things out with him," Kipp commented grimly.

"No, you will not, Kipp," I replied. "He is trying to manipulate you into acting. The best thing you can do is keep him off his guard."

"Then, it's time we go home," Kipp replied, upping his pace to keep up with Allie, who was motivated to get us off the dark street.

"No, it's not. I will not let some worthless sociopath drive me to behave one way or another, Kipp. We will complete our time here; the last time we talked, we planned on staying until the OK Corral shootout. So, we have a few more weeks." I glanced at Kipp, who met my eyes. "Either you believe we are a strong enough team that we can overcome evil and adversity or you don't." I threw down the challenge to my partner.

Kipp stayed silent and closely guarded his thoughts as he followed us into the Grand. Allie, in a commanding voice, ordered a pot of tea. The staff in the tearoom had witnessed the shooting and were happy to accommodate the Earp party. We were joined in a few moments by Doc, who had regained his composure and was focused on my wellbeing.

"Petra, my dear," he began, using my given name for the first time, "Are you unharmed?"

I nodded and smiled. "Yes, thanks to Kipp."

Doc patted his knee, and Kipp played happy dog for him, moving up to get his large ears scratched.

"He is a marvel, no doubt about it. Dogs have such keen instincts. He must have known you were in danger and moved to protect you." Doc turned his blue eyes on me and took a moment to search my face. "I see why you don't want to be separated from him." Doc was being pleasant and solicitous, but his thoughts were dark. He knew, as well as did Wyatt and Virgil, that Tim Marin would have no reason to try to assassinate me. However, neither of them considered the true puppet master might be Johnny Ringo, the man I knew to be John Gold. Doc was burning inside with anger, and he would not stop until he found the man responsible.

By the time the tea was delivered, Wyatt had rejoined our party. Virgil, as town marshal, was seeing to the disposition of the body of Tim Martin. The waitress, knowing Wyatt's preferences, brought a cup of coffee and set it before him.

"Mrs. Totheroh," Wyatt began, turning his expressionless face to mine, "Do you have any idea who might want to have you harmed?"

I shook my head, keeping my eyes wide, as if I were still in some sort of shock following the shooting.

Allie patted my arm. "Wyatt, this is not the time to

interrogate her," she commented.

He looked at her; the two of them clearly did not like one another. She thought he was an unforgivably cold, detached man, and he thought her to be a drag on his brother. In the end, the brothers' influence with one another would surpass the machinations of any woman.

Doc, reading the table as usual, smoothly intervened.

"I will accompany Mrs. Totheroh back to her hotel. I think the evening has been a bit more than perhaps she wished for."

Wyatt stood. "I will walk with you, Doc, just in case there is another person who wants to make a name for himself tonight." Doc nodded his head in gratitude. There was no one he trusted more to protect his back than Wyatt Earp. In that way, their relationship was more than a little like mine and Kipp's.

With my protective wedge of Doc, Wyatt Earp and Kipp, I returned to the Cosmopolitan. The activities of the evening had left me exhausted; I fell onto the bed, partially clothed, and too tired to remove all the layers of garments. Kipp moved next to me, his head on my shoulder. Together, we fell asleep; our usually active brains were inert for a change.

CHAPTER 23

A soft tap on the door to my room caused me to sit up suddenly; obviously, the previous night's activities had left me somewhat hyper vigilant. My sleep had been deep and dreamless, and I felt almost as if I had a hangover, but without the causative factor of alcohol in the mix. Kipp was on the floor by the window, stretched out in a small pool of sunlight that was filtering past the thin curtains. Stretching his head back, he yawned and thumped his tail.

"I thought you'd never get up," he commented. "And I hope that's Eli because I really need to go out."

I was still partially clothed but not decent for entertaining, so I pulled my dressing gown on and managed to push my tangled mass of hair away from my face. I opened the door to find Eli waiting patiently, his head down, eyes partially hidden beneath the heavy fringe of blonde bangs. He peeked through them, and his thoughts confirmed my fears. The fact I looked rough was no surprise.

"I heard what happened," he began before I waved him off.

"Eli, I appreciate your concern, but I really don't feel like talking about it. But if you would please take Kipp out, I would be grateful."

While the young man and Kipp disappeared down the

back staircase, I went back to the bedroom and stripped off
the remainder of last night's clothes. The dress would have
to be cleaned since there was a large dirt stain on the front,
marring the soft apricot fabric; Kipp had saved my life but
the dress had not fared so well. I decided to give up my
petticoat, the dress, and a few other items for Eli to take to
the woman who did laundry for guests at the hotel. I had
not told Kipp, but I was physically sore from his rough
tackle the night before and just wanted to stay in the room
for a couple of days and recover.

When Eli returned, I knew he was irritated at me and
wanted to tell me he was concerned for me and how I
needed to leave Tombstone now that I had been marked by
some rogue element for injury or death. But instead, he bit
back his commentary and asked what I would like to eat.
The weather outside was decidedly cooler, and that was
fueling my appetite. I'd not eaten much lately and asked Eli
to bring a nice cross sample of anything that looked good;
any meat would go to Kipp. I also inquired if he could
manage the hip bath again, thinking the hot water would
help with my sore body; in any case, my hair was dirty and
needed a good scrub. That would be my day, I thought with
pleased satisfaction: eat, bathe, wash hair, and try to divert
Kipp from his brooding mental state.

Walking over to the window, I stared out at the street.
There was an impressive bustle of humanity; a familiar
mind was nearby, like a wisp of wood smoke in the air, and
I watched as an inebriated Doc Holliday walked from the
doorway of the Occidental Saloon. He leaned on a cane,
although he seemed to leave this crutch behind when
escorting me. His gait and behavior did not betray his
alcohol use, but rather it was the content of his thoughts
that revealed all. I was surprised to find myself a prominent
figure in the musings of his addled mind. Doc obviously
felt responsible for what had happened to me the previous
night and consequently spent a night at the Occidental
drinking and gambling to soothe his angst.

The slender figure that was clothed in the garments worn

to the music hall the previous evening, paused in the bright glare of the sun and tilted his pale head up to my window. I pulled back so as not to be seen. He wondered if he could visit me later, in my sitting room, once he was adequately sober. Doc saw someone he obviously knew and raised a hand in a salutation. His thoughts were diverted elsewhere, and I decided to preempt his visit to me by asking Eli to give him a note.

Quickly, and before Eli returned, I sat at the small desk and used the house stationary to pen a quick missive. In it, I complemented Doc on the previous evening and commented on the quality of the performers at the music hall. Then, I inquired if he would be free for luncheon two days hence. This, I hoped, would reassure him that I was unharmed and also that I did not hold him responsible for what had happened.

There was a tap on the door; Eli had returned with Kipp and informed me he was off to fetch breakfast. I handed him the note and asked him to make certain that Doc received it. A frown gathered on the normally smooth brow of the young man, but he nodded his head. Clearly, he thought I was in a social class way above the usually drunk Doc. It was rather sweet in that Eli felt mildly protective of me.

After breakfast, Eli brought the much desired hip bath which was partially filled with hot water; once it was in place, Eli topped it off with a steaming bucket. With a nod he disappeared, and I hastened to divest myself of clothing and stepped gingerly into the liquid warmth.

Kipp curled up on the wool rug in a little patch of sunlight and fixed his gaze on me. Suddenly, he sat up and darted over to me.

"Petra, there is a huge blue mark on your back, going down to your backside and thighs!" His observations took on a slightly hysterical tone. I managed to crane my head around and could see part of what he mentioned.

"Kipp, it's just a big bruise. And it's really not very sore," I added, smiling at my friend.

"It's due to me, isn't it?" Kipp's head dropped. "I hit you

too hard when I pushed you down last night."

"Kipp, all things considered, I'd rather have a bruise than have been shot." I stared at him until he returned my gaze. "You did the right thing, believe me."

I made a conscious effort to change the dialog to something pleasant, and we began to discuss the music from the Gilbert and Sullivan operetta as well as some readings from Shakespeare. Kipp was mildly confused by some of the phrasing and archaic words, so I did my best to explain. He was clearly fascinated by Shakespeare and was clever enough to appreciate the inherent beauty and poetry in the language.

I perched on the little ledge in the hip bath; the lavender soap had fallen from my fingers, and I was chasing it around the bottom of the tub with my toes. My hair, now clean, smelled of the freshness of the soap. Sighing with pleasure I began to rinse with the extra pail of water Eli had left.

"I just don't understand why that feels so good," Kipp commented. "When I get wet, I smell funny and dirt sticks to my fur."

Finished, I stepped out of the bath and wrapped my hair in a towel. I put on a clean chemise and had buttoned the drawers to the top garment when there was a tap on the door; thinking it was Eli, I, with my dressing gown pulled snugly around my body, stepped forward without giving thought. Kipp was distracted by a loud dialog filtering up to the bedroom window from the street; two men were rudely and aggressively challenging one another over the outcome of a faro game. It had the edginess of a violent escalation.

It was not Eli, however. I opened the door and was face to face with John Gold. He must have carefully guarded his thoughts since he had to know I would not have answered if I'd realized he stood on the other side of the oak barrier. Kipp was at my side in a flash, teeth bared, with a rumbling growl escalating in intensity.

"I want to talk," Gold said. "I give you my word I didn't cause that shooting last night."

I may not possess the skills of Kipp or even John Gold, but

my intuition as well as my telepathic read told me that Gold was telling the truth. Kipp must have realized it, too, since both his teeth and the growling disappeared.

"I'd rather people not know you are here," I commented. "Doc Holliday, in particular, would take offense, and I don't want to influence history any more than possible."

Gold nodded his head in agreement. "I came up the back staircase and waited until it was clear."

Even though I was decently covered, I felt a little self-conscious; Gold might be of the same species as I, but in most respects he was a virtual stranger to me. Reading my thoughts in his unrestricted manner, Gold flashed a smile.

"Sorry to have caught you unawares. But I bet that bath felt good."

I nodded. "I've lived through this before in terms of not having running water, adequate toilet facilities and no electricity. Of all, I think I miss the hot water the most."

"You are a little younger than I, aren't you?" Gold took a seat in the upright chair in the small sitting room that preceded the bedroom area. I sat on the sofa; Kipp lay directly between us, in his Sphinx pose, with a rigid posture, ears upright, swiveled towards Gold.

I saw no reason to be guarded. "Yes; as far as I know, we've never met, but Fitzhugh spoke of you to me."

"Do you have family, other than Kipp?"

"No; both of my parents are dead; I was married, once, and had a baby. My husband and baby are dead, too." My voice sounded flat and neutral to my ears.

Gold nodded his head and avoided murmuring any words of sympathy that might sound false or contrived.

"So what do you want, Gold?" Kipp asked, clearly exasperated with the polite back and forth. From outside the window, we heard the creak of wood and the rumble of wheels as a wagon passed on Allen Street. The weight of the team caused the floor of the Cosmopolitan to vibrate. A whiff of hot, sweaty mules in mass wafted through the sitting room.

"Well, Kipp, for the moment, I wanted to reconnect with

my own kind." Gold raised his eyebrows; he was strikingly handsome and knew it, of course. "And, yes, I had some thoughts that you and I might make a splendid traveling team with our skills." Gold looked at me. "I don't mean to be rude, but my talents are more advanced than are yours."

I laughed lightly. "Did you consider perhaps the only reason is that you have failed to observe the traditional restrictions we symbionts place upon ourselves. How do you know I'm not as skilled as you?"

He tipped his head. "Point taken; but you never would, since you lack the ruthless quality that I embrace." Gold glanced at Kipp, who was still rigid as a statue, his thoughts closed. "But I think Kipp could be as ruthless as I under the right circumstances." Kipp wisely did not take the bait and remained silent.

"In any case, I wanted to tell you that it was Frank Stillwell that caused that shooting. He told Tim Martin that I wanted you killed. Frank also told Tim that he'd be paid a large sum of money if he shot you."

"And why would he do that?" I asked.

"Frank thinks you are carrying a wad of money and have it stashed somewhere. He thought he could manage to steal some from the hotel vault, since he has blackmail information he can use to influence the clerk. Frank, being a coward, told Tim I was the one behind it and that I'd kill Tim if he didn't comply."

Gold glanced at Kipp. "You know I'm telling the truth. The reason you thought I was the instigator was because Tim's last thoughts before he died were about me."

Kipp remained silent but his posture relaxed and the tenseness of his muscular body diminished. Gold seemed ready to move on.

"I never really studied this part of history, except for hearing about the OK Corral, as did everyone else. What specifically happens to me?" Gold relaxed back in the chair and rested his hands on his thighs.

Kipp's ears swiveled back to me, and I shuttered my thoughts. Gold was waiting and was not attempting to read my mind; I knew if he did, Kipp would through up a block like a 350 pound lineman for the Chicago Bears. I, for one, would not disclose the future since there would be a risk of Gold reacting in such a manner to change the outcome. History revealed that Gold was found dead under mysterious circumstances two years hence, either a suicide or a murder/execution. I dipped my head down.

"Ah, you know but won't tell me." Gold shrugged his shoulders. "You can't blame me for trying." Leaning forward, he raised one eyebrow and smiled. "You can appreciate my self-control in that I didn't go exploring to find the answer to my question."

Kipp stood and yawned, exposing most of his impressive set of ivory teeth. Then he deliberately stretched, the movement displaying his muscular physique. None of this obvious posturing was lost on Gold, who smiled in response.

Gold stood and glanced around the small room. "If you will take a look in the hallway and see if it is clear, I'll leave now." Smiling down at me, his face took on a wistful appearance before he resumed the hard mask he normally wore. "It was good to reconnect with my own kind for a moment."

After he left, I went back into the bedroom and sat before the vanity, looking at myself in the mirror. The minor imperfections and ripples in the glass caused a subtle distortion to my face, and I think I looked sadder than I actually felt. But the meeting with Gold had been bittersweet, to say the least. I'd made the decision to never mention any of this to Fitzhugh, since there was no need to have him worry about the nephew he once loved.

"I still don't trust him and am glad he's gone," Kipp commented. He sat behind me, and I met his eyes in the mirror. "He's gone rogue, and I don't think he's coming back to our side any time soon." Kipp's large ears flicked. "Gold can say all the right things, but in his heart he's manipulative and self-serving."

"Okay, Kipp, I hear what you're saying. I didn't invite

him here, and I'm glad he's gone, too," I replied, feeling defensive for some odd reason.

"Yes, but you were feeling sorry for him," Kipp said. "That is a trap, Petra."

I put down the hairbrush and turned around on the small stool to look at Kipp. His large, beautiful amber eyes ringed with dark fur stared at my face. The scent of the lavender soap I'd used on my hair was subtle and pleasant in the confines of the room.

"Kipp, you were left alone after your mother died. Until I appeared, you faced a future of isolation. I guess when I look at Gold, I see the same situation. So no matter how corrupt he's become, it is sad."

Kipp cocked his head slightly. "There's one big difference: I didn't create my situation…Gold did."

I spent most of my time cloistered in the room, since my back was sore after Kipp's magnificent tackle during the assassination attempt on my life. Eli provided me with another hot hip bath, and the heat of the water seemed to relieve the pain of the bruised muscles. Thankfully, the October weather was cooling in a pleasant trajectory, and both Kipp and I were happy that the summer heat had passed. I'd received a carefully penned missive from Doc, which informed me he was delighted to have luncheon with me on Friday, and the day had arrived.

Kipp, who had neglected his reading, asked me to put the note from Doc on the floor and struggled to decipher the cursive handwriting, since his experiences to date were with printed type.

"This is pretty and artistic," he commented, tilting his head to the side.

I leaned forward and helped him navigate through the loops and curves and a few archaic phrasings. The sound of the tinny piano at the Oriental drifted up to my loft, and I found myself softly singing along to "My Bonnie Lies Over the Ocean."

"That's something I've never tried," Kipp said, looking up at me from the note, which rested on his paws. I thought if only he had a pair of reading glasses perched upon his nose that the moment would be complete.

"What?" I asked.

"Singing."

"Kipp, you continually surprise me with new talents and skills that no lupine symbiont possesses. I'd really like to keep one thing that I can do that you can't, and that will be singing, if you don't mind." He laughed good naturedly in response.

Eli had brought, at my request, copies of the local papers—the *Tombstone Nugget* and the *Tombstone Epitaph*. I filtered through them and was somewhat amused at the stories of locals, including the horror of one woman who went to retrieve her laundry from the line stretched across her back porch only to find that her knickers with the lace edging had gone missing.

"The *Nugget* was edited by Harry Woods, if I recall correctly," Kipp commented.

I placed it on the floor so that he could peruse the front page.

"Yes, and it took a pro Democratic stance in support of John Behan and the cowboy element. The *Epitaph*, edited by John Clum," I said, holding up the page, "supported the Earps and the vigilantes. Clum was staunchly Republican."

"So, humans don't really evolve, do they?" Kipp continued without waiting for a reply from me. "They are tribal, to a fault, and band together…and not necessarily for the good of the whole."

I considered Kipp's thoughts. Humans were tribal, but that probably was a result of having lived in dangerous times when people gathered together for reasons of survival. Maybe that was still the instinctive motivator.

I knew, from my studies, that the struggles in Arizona had to do with political posturing in terms of how counties were carved out, and who controlled what. It had not been pretty, and the stewardship of John Fremont as governor was filled with conflict and political maneuvering. In other words, for humans, nothing seemed to have changed from the 1880's to the present day in terms of the sleazy nature of politics. It all was about power and control, dual issues that never seemed to leave the human species.

Kipp rolled over and tilted his head back to look at me. "So how do you feel about lunch with Doc today?"

I dropped onto the bed and stared up at the ceiling. "I'm not sure, Kipp. I feel conflicted in some ways; usually, I take things more in stride and don't worry so much."

Kipp rose and came over to hop up on the bed next to me. He rested his muzzle across my chest, and my hand draped over his back, my fingers finding their way through his dense pelt to lightly scratch his skin.

"It bothers you that Doc obviously has developed some affection for you," Kipp commented.

"Yes, but I'm not sure why. I've had this happen before and usually it rolls off my back." I took a deep breath and exhaled slowly as I tried to will the tension from my body. Stress was not a welcome visitor for a symbiont since focus and concentration was necessary for the telepathic part of our nature. From the window overlooking the Oriental, I heard the rolling wheels of a wagon as it made its way down Allen Street. A braying mule protested the enthusiastic application of a whip across his back.

Kipp, as usual, was more perceptive than I. "Petra, you feel sorry for him."

Maybe I did, but I wasn't really aware of it until that moment. "And why would that be?" I asked. The lavender scent in my hair drifted up and hung over my face in a gentle, soft cloud of fragrance. Doc would smell it, too, I thought.

Kipp focused on me for a few minutes while I remained silent. "You know his time on earth is short, and after we leave here he will continue to decline until he dies, alone, in a sanitarium in Colorado. He's estranged from his family and chose to follow a life of extreme violence." Kipp turned slightly so that I could reach further down his back to continue my scratching. "You think there is more to him than that, but it's too late for him."

I laughed softly. "And how do you come to that conclusion?"

Kipp pressed his jaw down on my breastbone until it hurt. "Don't be obtuse," he commented. "It was when I told you he felt remorse about the man he eviscerated. And it was even more than that, Petra. Doc talks to God about his actions, but he thinks he cannot be forgiven. You must hear his thoughts, and it makes you sad."

Kipp, as usual, hit the nail squarely on the head; his honesty was bracing.

"Kipp, I was brought up to believe that everyone can be forgiven. Humans and symbionts alike are sinners, and we have to strive for redemption." I took a deep, sighing breath. "It does make me sad Doc no longer believes that, and he carries pain inside." I flexed my right leg, which was threatening to go numb. "But none of that causes me to overlook the fact that Doc is a killer...but maybe not a cold blooded one." I gently moved Kipp aside and sat up; the bruise on my back was bothering me, and I needed to change positions.

"I've lied to humans about who I am for four hundred years, and there have been a few times that fact left me feeling uncomfortable. One was with Purdy; I felt close to her in many ways and didn't like deceiving her."

Kipp nodded his head. "Me, too. I still miss her and Alice. One is left wondering what happened to them and how they felt about our disappearance."

"Maybe I hate to do that to Doc, since I know he has, in a short time, developed some affection for me."

Kipp decided to give me the equivalent of a slap. "This is what you do, Petra...what we do. We, for some reason, have abilities that humans lack. And as you so carefully tell me, we cannot allow ourselves to do anything to change history. So you are playing a role, much like an actor." He took his paw and placed it on my arm. "It is your nature, Petra."

He was right, of course, and I had absolutely no business groveling in the depths of this morose mood that had overtaken me.

"I need to start getting ready," I commented as I left the softness of the bed; my bare feet found the woolen rug on the floor, and I scrunched my toes up in the soft, warm fibers. Winter here was probably unpleasant, and I looked forward to going home soon.

CHAPTER 24

I chose the medium blue dress in my small wardrobe, since I'd not worn it yet. With only a few garments, I tried to mentally keep note of a circulation pattern, so that I didn't wear the same thing daily. This one was a pretty shade that was flattering to my coloring. Lupine symbionts had a full range of color discrimination in their vision, and Kipp favored me in blue more than most other colors.

Sitting at the marble topped dresser, I made a valiant effort at dressing my hair in something that looked ornate. With a mild level of frustration, I thought that I would probably never find all of the hairpins that were buried in my dark tresses as I coiled another loop and secured it at the nape of my neck.

"That's interesting," Kipp remarked, as he craned his head slightly to follow the movements of my arms and hands.

"Is that your polite way of telling me it looks horrible?" I raised my eyebrows at his reflection in the mirror.

He looked shocked and assured me that the back of my head looked nice. Since I didn't have a hand mirror and couldn't see my efforts, I had to take his assurances as true.

Finally, I stood and turned around. "Is my bustle straight?" I asked. It felt slightly catawampus, and I had no desire to provoke the other women in town to fits of humor at my expense.

"You look beautiful, as usual. Doc will be entranced," he added.

A short time later, I was descending the main staircase to the lobby of the Cosmopolitan. Kipp, with his head up, stuck by my side as he canvassed the minds of the few men who were seated in the main lobby. After the attempt on my life, he would be on guard and more so than usual. Doc was waiting at the bottom of the staircase, his gray hat captured in his hands in a courteous gesture.

"Why, Petra, my dear," he began. "You look lovely," he added, his eyes making a polite survey of my attire, careful to not linger too long in any one location.

"Good afternoon, Mr. Holliday," I replied, extending my hand for him to gently grasp.

His flesh was cool, and I felt the fragility of his diseased body through the thin covering of skin over bone; my eyes met his. He was dying, even now, and his time on earth was ticking to zero. Was that fact what motivated him to be fearless in the face of danger that might make another man flinch?

"Hello, Kipp," he said, bending down to ruffle Kipp's ears. His affection for Kipp was genuine.

"Did you have a dog when you were a boy?" I asked, smiling. "You seem to like Kipp."

He shrugged his shoulders in response. "I once had a dog, but that was a long time ago." He obviously discounted any connection with his past to the present. "Kipp saved your life and that makes him precious to me."

I was taken off guard by his very personal response and, since I had no good reply, kept my mouth shut. He replaced his hat, settling it carefully on his head and reached out to tuck my hand in the crook of his elbow.

"I thought, unless you have a preference, that we might dine at the U.S. Restaurant. They have a rather good luncheon menu," he added quickly, as he glanced at my face for approval. I merely nodded my head as we left the lobby and turned right up Allen Street. Kipp flanked my other side, and our trio began to walk down the wooden sidewalk. The air was decidedly cool on that day, and I was grateful for my wrap. It seemed many years had passed when I had shivered from the extreme cold of the prehistoric tundra where I met Kipp. Due to the miracle of time travel, the episode had elapsed over a rather insignificant amount of time. I'd never liked the cold again after that particular adventure.

"Petra, I want to make a slight detour, if you don't object," Doc commented. I knew he was excited and had a surprise for me.

We turned right on Fourth Street and then left on Fremont. There was less traffic on this street than on Allen, but even so, we had to time our crossing as a couple of men on horseback were driving a small herd of horses down the street. The dust that was stirring due to their passage quickly settled, and we stepped off the sidewalk. Overhead, a bright sun did little to warm the air.

"This is the street that the OK Corral is on," Kipp remarked with excitement. The gunfight was looming on the calendar, and I could only hope that our presence had not disturbed the flow of energy that would form the future. The men driving the horses pushed them forward, and then they turned in to an area to the left that was probably the corral. I looked up and saw a man, short, middle aged with a shock of gray hair, staring back at me from the doorway of a building we approached.

"Hello, John," Doc called out. "Petra, my dear, may I present John Clum."

I met the man's direct gaze; his eyes were dark blue and fringed with thick lashes that would inspire envy in most women. Knowing it was expected, I held out my hand with a dainty gesture. Kipp, meanwhile, was restraining himself from dancing in place with excitement.

John Clum tilted his head in response and smiled. "I've heard about you, Mrs. Totheroh," he commented. "Something about a shooting the other night that made the crime column of the paper managed by my competitor." He cleared his throat. "I chose to not publish the tale since I thought it would only embolden gossips and the criminal element."

That wasn't the real reason, of course, but he was telling me what he wanted me to think. It seems that Doc had paid him a little visit and asked him to not give publicity to the episode so as to minimize my discomfort over the matter. Since Clum and the Earps were friends, it made sense he would do a favor for Doc.

"John has the distinction of publishing a fine paper that illustrates law and order and supports the vigilantes who oppose the lawless behaviors of the cowboys," Doc managed to say in one sentence.

For a moment, I thought it odd that Clum would not be interested in talking with me since allegedly I was from back east and might have some interesting viewpoints of the western theater. But I realized that he viewed me as totally off limits due to Doc—whose territorial attitude towards me was a bit uncomfortable—but there was really no way around it.

"Doc thinks he is keeping you safe," Kipp commented. "It's a rough town, and you've been shot at once." I tried not to shrug my shoulders at Kipp's telepathic remarks.

After another moment of polite exchange with the editor, Doc resumed our perambulation. Just past the Epitaph's office was the millinery shop of Mrs. Addie Bourland. A little bell tinkled as Doc opened the door and ushered me inside. Kipp, as always, was by my side but immediately lay down at the door so that he would be as unobtrusive as possible. A tall, thin woman with a topknot of dark hair laced with gray walked into the large room; a pair of wire rimmed spectacles were perched upon her nose. She obviously knew Doc on sight, and the expression of disapproval almost crossed her small face before she mastered the reaction. Business was business, after all, and it had been slow as of late.

"May I help you?" she asked, directing the query at us both. She tried to keep her eyes on us, but they inadvertently darted to the large form of Kipp, who was as still as a marble statue.

The small shop was filled with sample garments; many were finished and could be purchased as readymade with some minor alterations. Along the wall was an inset ledge where multiple rolls of fabric rested for the discriminating lady who wished to choose a particular bolt. On a large cutting table were books of styles and patterns. I turned back to Mrs. Borland and noted the pin cushion on her wrist that was bristling like a porcupine.

Doc had removed his hat again. "You have a lovely blue bonnet in the window there," he said, pointing with a slender finger. "I was hoping that my friend Mrs. Totheroh could try on that hat since it seems to match the blue in her garment."

I darted a glance at Kipp, who slowly winked back. So, Doc wanted to buy me a hat. I almost giggled since it seemed sweet and funny all at once. Doc Holliday, notorious killer, wanted to buy me, Petra Goodgame, a little blue bonnet. Of course, I didn't want to become more beholden to him, but there was no way to avoid this and not seem peevish.

Mrs. Bourland walked to the window and retrieved the scrap of blue from the head form and brought it to me, as she carefully straightened the ribbons and some lace netting.

"I'm rather fond of this one," she commented. "It will be serviceable now that anything with straw is put away for next spring."

Did the old rule about no straw from the first of September until Easter go back this far, I wondered? Kipp took a deep sigh and exhaled as his thoughts followed mine. Human mores were inexplicable and unfathomable.

"They'll shoot each other in a second but then worry about whether it's too late in the season to wear a straw hat. Amazing," Kipp commented wryly.

He wanted to get up and poke around the fascinating shop but realized Mrs. Bourland's passive tolerance would only stretch so far. She already was quietly miffed at my moxie at having brought him inside her place without her consent. But she planned on adding a little extra to the price of the hat to compensate and soothe her soul.

I allowed Mrs. Bourland to set the hat on my coiled hair, angling it a little before she tied the ribbon beneath my chin. I knew, from her thoughts, that the hat was complimentary to my features. Doc almost beamed as he discreetly took Mrs. Bourland aside to settle the bill.

"Don't protest," Kipp said. "Let him do it. He's enjoying taking care of you in this little manner, and it is really an innocent gesture of kindness. He doesn't want anything…and I mean anything…in return."

Accompanied by a self satisfied Doc Holliday, I walked back the way we'd come. The U.S. Restaurant was on Allen, and we retraced our steps.

"Mr. Holliday," I began before he corrected me.

"John…please call me John," he entreated, as he took my arm when I stepped up on the wooden sidewalk.

I felt a blush stain my cheeks, which were already slightly colored from the cool temperature. Kipp chuckled to himself and irritated me in the process.

"It's easy for you, Kipp," I grumbled. "I'm not sure what to do with him."

"Petra, you were saying," Holliday prompted me.

"I was going to say that you really shouldn't buy me gifts." I smiled at him. "It is very kind of you, but I feel like we don't really know each other well enough."

Doc didn't miss a beat. "Well, then, I will take your comments to suggest that we must get to know one another better." He was nothing if not confident and sublimely suave.

"You just couldn't leave it alone, could you?" Kipp asked. "He just wanted to buy you a silly hat, and you make a big deal out of it."

I took a deep breath. "Kipp, it feels wrong to take things from him when I know I can't return any sort of affection for him."

"It makes the man feel good; he enjoys squiring you around town like a knight protecting a lady. He's dying, Petra. What's the harm?" Kipp unobtrusively pushed against my leg to get my attention. "Your problem is you think too much."

I was getting more than a little irritated. "Thank you, Professor Plum. And next you'll tell me that it was Colonel Mustard in the conservatory with the candlestick." Kipp missed my frame of reference and was puzzled. I stubbornly avoided giving him any information and decided that it was good to have a few things that belonged to just me, even if it was the game of Clue.

Our little party entered the U.S. Restaurant after Doc quietly paid the man at the door a little bribe to allow Kipp to accompany us to a table up front near a large street facing window. Doc courteously held my chair and then gently removed my wrap and folded it over an unused chair. Kipp squeezed in so as to be unobtrusive. A young girl appeared and, at Doc's request, just as quickly disappeared to bring us a pot of tea. I started to look for a printed menu and realized they probably didn't furnish such.

"So, my dear, how do you find Tombstone so far?" Doc asked, smiling as he relaxed back in his chair. He'd removed his hat upon entry to the building, and his golden hair lay smoothly on his head as neatly as if it had just been combed.

I knew he was hoping I'd make some comment of a positive nature. He wanted me to stay here, at least for now.

"Oh, it's very interesting," I replied.

"That's what people say to be polite," he rejoined with a soft laugh.

"Well, it is different from home," I commented, dipping my head slightly.

Doc's head went up and before I could read his thoughts, I knew he'd gone on high alert. One could almost smell the alarm that came from him like smoke off of a fire. I followed his gaze. Ike Clanton, Bill Brocious, John Ringo and Billy Clanton ambled in as a tight group, their heads swiveling as befit men who had reputations and enemies. The sunlight chased them into the room, dust particles dancing in the filtered rays. Someone dropped a plate, and the shattering sound caused all four men's head to jerk in unison, looking for danger, as always.

Ike Clanton inadvertently caught sight of our little party sitting quietly in the front. The server was delivering a pot of tea which steamed comfortingly as she placed it on our table. Ike, unable to stop himself, swaggered over to us, leaving his friends to stare after him. I knew, from their thoughts, that they were uninterested in a confrontation today. Curly Bill, if anything, was simply hungry. Ringo, or John Gold as I knew him, caught my eyes briefly. Doc, at my side, began to bristle with the arrival of Ike.

"So, Doc, I see you are still in the company of that mangy dog," Ike commented with a sneer. Of course, his comment was double edged. He could have been talking about me or Kipp. The words were obviously meant as an insult to me, too.

Kipp began to rise before I cautioned him not to. His intent was to get in front of me in a protective manner.

"Don't move," I ordered Kipp. "You'll provoke him and that's what he wants." My hand drifted down to touch the soft dome of Kipp's head.

Doc, despite his illness, stood with ease. I knew I'd seen him rely upon a cane from time to time, but he left it behind when in my company.

"Ike, I'm ready for you anytime you want," Doc said with a low voice, his drawl pronounced. He was unafraid and completely certain that he could effortlessly take Ike. In the back of his mind, he realized that one of the remaining three cowboys would probably do the same to him before he could fire the next shot.

Kipp's mind reached across the room to connect with John Gold. "This is not the time, Gold. These men must survive for the OK Corral shootout or else history might change." Kipp's head peered up over the edge of the table.

"Do something."

The corner of Gold's mouth twitched, but he walked forward, making certain that he kept his hand away from his gun lest he provoke Doc to pull.

"Ike, come on. I'm hungry, and if you start shooting, I'll miss dinner."

Ike, fixated on Doc in a stare down, ignored the comment, his hand hovering perilously close to the holster.

"I mean it, Ike," Gold said, his voice slightly more emphatic. "If you don't come over here and sit down, I'm gonna shoot you myself." Gold's tone changed, and somehow he conveyed he was not joking.

Ike's blue eyes blinked a couple of times, but he allowed Gold to clasp his shoulder and pull him away. Doc was ready and more than willing and able to have a gunfight but really was not motivated to do so with me sitting there. He did have fear that I might be caught in the crossfire.

Kipp moved slightly so that his big skull rested on the top of my right foot. "That was close. I'm glad Gold decided to do the right thing."

Doc's soft drawl caught my ear. "I'm so sorry, my dear. There are those in this town who lack manners and are boorish in behavior. Mr. Clanton and his ilk are a menace to the peace here." His voice changed tone slightly. "And the county sheriff, Behan, does all he can to cover up and protect them. They basically are thieves, rustlers and robbers who manage to float above the law due to Behan and other political alliances."

"Doc doesn't see that that he does anything wrong, does he?" Kipp commented. "He's a bad guy, too, but thinks since he is aligned with who he sees as being representative of law and order that he is somehow relieved of his own crimes."

"No, Kipp. He does know his actions are wrong...at least in the terms of moral right and wrong. I think this particular day and age forces people to choose sides for survival. He, as it happens, chose the side of the Earps, and he does think they are on the side of good, despite any later historical musings to the contrary." I jiggled Kipp's head slightly with my toe in an affectionate manner.

The girl who was serving us returned when the minor confrontation ended. She was visibly nervous, however, and peeked cautiously over her shoulder a few times at the table across the floor where Brocious, Ringo, and the Clanton brothers sat. Doc ordered a steak for himself, and I requested whatever vegetables they might have simmering in the back. This was one time Kipp would have to wait his turn.

I managed my barely adequate pour out of the tea, and Doc and I had just enjoyed our first sips when the restaurant door swung back and Wyatt and Virgil Earp walked in. Immaculate, as usual, their long black coats were devoid of the ever present dust. As they drew closer, I noticed the white collars that were buttoned tightly up against the tan skin of their throats. Virgil, followed by Wyatt, swept off his hat when he saw me.

"Good afternoon, Mrs. Totheroh," Virgil addressed me with a pleasant smile. Wyatt merely nodded his head and kept his facial expression neutral. He was the most controlled man I'd ever met.

Doc murmured a greeting in response and made a polite invitation for the two men to join us. He really hoped they wouldn't and was quietly relieved when they both declined.

"Dinner's waiting at home but thanks, Doc," Virgil remarked. "We heard there was a little trouble here and wondered if you need us to clear out the, uh, problem element?"

Doc turned his head slightly and gazed at the table where his four enemies sat. The waitress had brought a pitcher of water to their table and was bent forward to take their orders.

"No, Virgil. I think the issue is settled for the moment. It was peculiar, but Johnny Ringo didn't want a throw down and managed to pull Ike back to reason."

Wyatt turned and appraised the men with his cool gaze. He knew the true danger would come from Ringo and then

Brocious. Ike Clanton, for the most part, was a big talker and his brother, Billy, would not act without Ike's consent.

Virgil began to back off. "Well, if you're sure, Doc." He nodded at me and left the room, with Wyatt carefully guarding Virgil's exit.

"Have you noticed, Petra, there is always the need here to have someone watch your back?" Kipp commented. "That wouldn't be a pleasant way to live."

No, indeed, I thought. Doc began to engage me in pleasant, petty dialog. I was glad Kipp and I had made this trip but was equally glad that I could choose another time and place in which to reside.

CHAPTER 25

I awoke early the next morning due to the fact Kipp's busy mind had interrupted my rest. I suppose that is the down side of telepathy, especially when one is paired with a very gifted and strong minded partner.

It was bracingly cool in the room, but I benefited from the heavy weight of Kipp and his auburn coat as he rested his chin upon my chest. He nuzzled my face with his damp nose once he realized I was awake.

"Sorry," he commented. "I tried to keep my thoughts to myself, but I guess I lost focus for a moment."

"So, what's up?" I asked, biting back a yawn.

"I was thinking about something that was rolling around deep inside Doc's mind when he was confronted by Ike today." Kipp turned his massive head and was lost in profile from the ambient light easing into the bedroom from outside.

"I didn't hear anything unusual," I replied with a frown.

"It was underneath the anger and agitation." Kipp paused as he tried to accurately recall the thoughts. "It was something about 'Hail Mary, with grace, you are blessed.'"

I knew what he was trying to say, even though his words were incorrect and incomplete.

"Hail, Mary, full of grace, the Lord is with you; blessed are you among women and blessed is the fruit of your womb, Jesus. Holy Mary, Mother of

*God, pray for us sinners, now and at the hour of our
death. Amen."*

"That's it, Petra." Kipp's head went up. "What does it
mean, and why would Doc be thinking it?"

I considered my reply. "Well, it is a preliminary prayer for
praying the Rosary, which is something that Catholics do."
Since I was not a theologian, my explanations about
Catholicism were probably full of fault. More to the point
would be to understand why Doc was making a stab at a
preliminary Rosary prayer while in the midst of a challenge.
It was then I recalled a factoid.

"Kipp, when Doc leaves Tombstone after all the legal dust
clears from the vengeance ride which follows the OK Corral,
he finally ends up in a sanitarium in Colorado. The story
goes that he converted to Catholicism shortly before his
death."

"Why would he do that?" Kipp asked. "I mean, after a
lifetime of having taken the evil path, isn't it a little late to
turn over one's life at the last minute?"

"I'm not a priest or a minister, so don't take my word as
gospel," I replied, enjoying my clever play on words.
"Christians believe they can be forgiven of sins, even if the
sins were heinous."

"So, are you saying Doc could be contrite at the end of his
life and be sincere?"

"It is not for me to know, Kipp. You've been inside his
head, and you might have a better sense of him than do I."

Kipp became quiet as I threaded my fingers through the
fur on the crest of his head. He was a cerebral one, always
questioning, forever seeking. I wished I were smarter and
more adept at providing the intellectual challenges he
needed.

"So, you're not the sharpest knife in the drawer, but I love
you anyway," Kipp remarked in response to my self-
deprecating thoughts.

I had to laugh out loud, my voice echoing in the stillness of
the darkened bedroom.

* * *

I never fully fell asleep again after the recitation of the preliminary Rosary prayer. My body tossed and turned as I attempted to get comfortable, and the more vigorously I pursued sleep, the more adroitly it eluded me. As dawn began to break, I could hear the town beginning to rustle in preparation for a new day. The gambling halls and saloons were beginning to empty as men wobbled from smoke filled rooms to the chilled dimness that waited outside.

One familiar pattern of thoughts circling in the miasma revealed an inebriated Doc Holliday, who had finished a semi successful night of playing faro. Although he'd taken great pains for me to not seem him drunk, it was obvious that he still was tossing back the whiskey on a regular basis. I suppose he'd have to or else he would have gone into delirium tremens. I heard his voice increase in volume; even when drunk, he kept his cultured drawl and didn't slur his words, although he did mobilize a stream of profanity that he managed to suppress while serving as my squire. The object of his agitation was Ike Clanton, who'd happened to exit Haffords just as Doc left the Oriental.

I left my bed and walked over to the window, where I could cautiously peer out without being seen. The tall figure of Wyatt Earp approached Doc; he encouraged Doc to go to his room at the Cosmopolitan and sleep it off. Wyatt was probably the only human being on earth who held any persuasive sway over the emotionally labile Doc. Wyatt was definitely the yin to Doc's yang. Ike, lacking any common sense because he, too, was drunk, began to weave up Allen Street toward the two men.

"I swear I'll kill you the next time I see you, Holliday," Ike called out.

I saw Doc's hand move down to his holster, only to be stopped by Wyatt. Fortunately, Virgil appeared on the run and approached Ike. I didn't bother to telepathically eavesdrop, since I knew Virgil was probably threatening Ike with a bash in the head or jail if he didn't shut his mouth. Doc turned his head towards my window, but I knew I was not visible to him. His head dropped before his hands relaxed, and he began to walk towards the front entrance of the Cosmopolitan. Wyatt joined Virgil, and Ike, confronted by the brothers as a tag team, began to back away. The Earps finally turned and began to walk towards the Crystal Palace saloon, where they maintained an upstairs office. Ike's brother, Billy, who appeared sober, walked over from the front of Haffords and began to lead Ike from the conflict. Another threat was put on hold, at least for the moment.

Kipp had not left the soft bed and monitored all that was going on in the street below with an ease that was to be envied. I tippy toed across the cold, wooden planks, and crawled back in the bed. Reaching down, I pulled the quilt up to my chin.

"This will escalate again," Kipp commented. "Ike and Doc will have a severe confrontation the day before the gunfight." His head turned towards the window, where the purplish light of early morning teased the small gap of exposed window along the edges of the curtain. "What is the date, Petra?"

My eyes turned up slightly as I tried to recall. "It is October 22," I replied after counting on my fingers a couple of times. Kipp's brushy tail hit me in the face as he turned around a couple of times before settling with a grunt.

"Why do you do that?" I asked, referring to the circling behavior.

"I just feel like doing it," Kipp replied.

I knew, from his thoughts, that he was thinking of what history told us in terms of what would happen next.

"Well," I said, "today is October 22. The gunfight at the OK Corral will take place at about 3 pm on October 26. On October 25, Ike Clanton will ride into town with his brother, Billy, the McLaury brothers, and Billy Claiborne." I turned slightly in the bed. My back was still slightly sore and staying in one position too long was not well advised. "Frank McLaury, who hates Doc, has a verbal confrontation with him that could escalate but doesn't due to the intervention of Ike. Ike has his own issues with Doc but wants to control what happens and when.

"Later that night and early into the next morning, Ike will go to the Oriental where he begins to gamble and drink— and I mean drink large amounts of alcohol. Doc, unfortunately, is doing the same thing, and it is not a good mix of alcohol, losing money at faro and becoming increasingly agitated."

"Why do humans drink alcohol until they become silly and irrational?" Kipp asked.

I laughed. "If you can answer that one, you will become rich and famous, my son. Humans drink because they enjoy the feeling, but unfortunately they also get uninhibited, and then chaos ensues."

At some point, I fell asleep again and only awakened when Kipp gently nuzzled the side of my face.

"Petra, someone is knocking on the door," he said. "It's Eli," he added, since my brain was thick with sleep.

I managed to sit up, and my feet hit the still cold floor. Daylight illuminated the frame of the window, and I was unsure how long I'd napped. After grabbing my dressing gown, I walked hurriedly to the door. Opening it a little, I peeked out and smiled at the characteristically understated Eli.

"Good morning, ma'am," he said. His clear gray eyes met mine, and he nodded his head. "I was on my way over to the diner and thought I'd see if you had a preference."

Kipp was behind me in a flash, asking to go out. Eli, at my request, disappeared down the hallway with Kipp at his side. I watched them depart and closed the door softly. My own chamber pot awaited me after a long night. Yes, an asset of modern days, at least to my way of thinking, was indoor plumbing.

While Kipp was gone, I poured water into the basin and washed the sleep from my face. Looking up, my slightly distorted reflection stared back at me. To humans, I was a young woman and definitely not the 400 plus year old symbiont that I was in reality.

After Kipp returned, I finished dressing while Eli went to retrieve food. The layers of garments provided an ongoing challenge, and I'd just fastened the last button when a soft tap sounded on the door. Eli brought a tray of food but also a sealed envelope. His disapproval was obvious, but he knew his place in the scheme of things and just laid it carefully on the tray. With a nod, he disappeared. A kind natured and bright young man, I thought. For a second I wondered what he might have achieved in contemporary times.

Kipp's head was buried in the bowl of chopped chicken and rice. "Who's the note from?" he asked between gulps.

I did not have his level of hunger and was sipping a cup of coffee. After looking at the unfamiliar handwriting on the envelope, I opened the small missive, using my butter knife.

"It's from John Gold," I answered, moving past the neat cursive handwriting to the signature. Kipp's head swiveled around so quickly that a piece of chicken flew across the room.

"What does he want?"

I plopped down on the sofa and began to read. The note was short and to the point. "It seems he wants to meet with us once again; he asks that we take the buggy, as we did before, and meet him in the same place."

"When?" Kipp asked, no longer interested in his food.

"October 24, which is tomorrow and two days before the gunfight."

Our interactions with Gold, to date, had been varied. And despite our last meeting where he reassured me that he had no evil designs on me or Kipp, I still did not trust him. But, as was typical of my kind, I couldn't just turn my head away and ignore the compelling drive within me to find out what Gold wanted. I looked up at Kipp, who took a deep breath as his eyes met mine.

"Well, we both know we shouldn't meet with him, but I want to go, too," Kipp said. His attention returned to the bowl of food, and he began to eat again, but with less enthusiasm.

The note indicated Gold would arrange a buggy for the morning. All I knew was that with the increasingly cold temperatures, I would need a woolen wrap if I were to go riding out in the desert. A trip to Mrs. Bourland's shop would be on my itinerary for today.

The sun was bright in a turquoise sky but did little to tamp down the brisk cold air that caused my exhaled breath to create little visible puffs of condensation. Eli, with his usual intense thoughts directed at my wrongheadedness, assisted me into a small buggy; Kipp hopped aboard, and I gave the horse some encouragement to move forward.

"He's hoping you won't use the whip," Kipp supplied helpfully.

I gave Kipp a dose of stink eye and suggested he not tell me how to drive. The horse seemed motivated by the cool air and darted forward. The streets were busy as usual, despite the early hour; ranchers typically made their runs to town at daybreak for supplies and such. And the stamp mill was already moving out ore; we had to dodge one twenty mule team and wagon that felt ambitious enough to occupy the majority of Allen Street. Fortunately, Doc was not up and about yet, since he stayed out gambling and drinking late the previous night.

It didn't take us long to reach the meeting place of before, and I saw John's tethered horse before he came into view. I pulled up my horse and the buggy creaked to a stop. John's tall figure, clad in the typical cowboy garb, approached from a grove of stunted trees that hovered near the rock filled wash. He'd left his hat hanging on the pommel of his saddle, and the mild breeze ruffled his auburn hair. Smiling, he reached up to help me down. His thoughts were neutral; Kipp stood in the back of the buggy, focused as he dug into Gold's brain for any hidden agendas.

John looked at Kipp and grinned. "Satisfied?" he asked.

Kipp huffed and hopped down to the sandy soil. "Not really," he finally answered.

John was still holding my hand from having helped me dismount, and I pulled it free.

"We're here," I commented. "So what do you want?"

"I don't remember the exact date of the gunfight between the Earps and the Clantons, but I think it was late October. So, it should be coming up soon. And I figure you will be leaving after that." He paused and looked searchingly at my face. I was guarding my thoughts and would know if he tried to pry his way inside my skull.

"I wanted a last meeting with you and Kipp since you are like me." His voice was soft and unexpectedly plaintive in tone. But it rang true.

I could have argued that I was not remotely like him but chose not to. Making the point would be unnecessary and probably cruel. We might have been of the same species, but we were in no way similar in terms of values or temperament.

"Are you going to tell Fitzhugh that you saw me?" Gold's eyes flicked towards Kipp as he posed the question.

"No," Kipp answered. "Why would we make him sad? He would be disappointed that you have taken a corrupt path."

Gold smiled, but the expression did not make it to his eyes. "Ah, Kipp. Are you always this direct? I think Petra might have tried to lie to me to make me feel good, but you are the blunt one, aren't you?"

Kipp narrowed his eyes. "I just remember what you did to Petra during the stagecoach ride; I don't trust you, nor do I like you."

Gold tipped his handsome head down and stared at his feet for a moment. When he looked back up, there was a trace of wistful sadness.

"I've led a bad life; there is no doubt about it. And I was the cause of my own symbiont deserting me. But I did want a last moment with two of my own kind. Believe it or not, I get lonely here." He was holding a small brown twig in his hands which he was busy twisting into nothingness. "When will you leave?"

A burst of cool wind hit me, and I pulled the woolen cape that I'd bought from Addie Bourland a little closer. John reached out and gently pulled the collar up so that it protected my vulnerable neck.

Kipp spoke up. "We will stay for the gunfight and probably leave when there is an opportune moment afterwards."

"And how will you explain your departure to Doc? He is more than just a little smitten," John asked, still looking at me.

I took a deep breath. "I will make up some lie." My voice sounded bitter. "That's what we do, isn't it?"

Kipp, responding to the tone of my voice, moved to my side and gently nuzzled my hand.

"Let's go, Petra," he said, dropping his head down so that my hand rested on top of his skull.

Gold, knowing our interview was at an end, wordlessly took my elbow and escorted me back to the buggy. I gathered my skirts carefully to make the ascent; it was more difficult to do than was apparent from modern day movies, where women scampered unimpeded up and down from wagons while their voluminous skirts flowed gracefully.

Suddenly, we heard the sound of a horse's hooves pattering out the gentle cadence of a mild lope. It was too late for Gold to disappear, and I was loathe to be found here in his company. But there was nothing to do about it, and I gathered the reins in my hand and encouraged my horse to move forward. The buggy gave a mild lurch and Kipp, in the back, scrambled with his four feet to keep purchase on the boards. Gold had hurried over to his horse and mounted. Just as he did so, the figure of John Holliday appeared, his horse slowing to a walk.

"Good morning, Petra," he called out. His eyes darted to the form of Gold. "Ringo," he said, his face expressionless. His thoughts, however, were dark. I knew I needed to supply an explanation.

"Thank goodness you are here, John," I said, purposely using Doc's given name since it lent a familiarity that I hoped would defuse him. "Kipp and I had taken a ride to enjoy this lovely weather, and I was having a little trouble with my horse. Mr. Ringo was kind enough to stop and assist me. But I was concerned over the trip back to Tombstone."

Doc believed me but never trusted Ringo to perform any act from a motivation of goodness. "What was the problem?" he asked, his blue eyes staring unblinkingly at Gold.

"Oh, he picked up a stone in his hoof, but I managed to dig it out easy enough." Gold lied as easily as did I.

Doc looked at me and noticed I was wearing the blue bonnet he'd bought me. He thought I looked pretty with the hat perched on my dark hair along with the new cape for warmth.

"Well, then, Johnny," he said, addressing the being he thought to be a human named Ringo, "I am in your debt. The safety of Mrs. Totheroh is of utmost concern to me." He then went a bit further. "I'd be under obligation to you if you'd accompany us back to Tombstone so that I can see to her safe return."

Gold tried to control the expression of amazement on his face.

"Why of course, Doc, I'll be glad to do that. I have some business in town, anyway."

History will not record the strange journey as three symbionts and one human rode in company along the dusty road to Tombstone, two days before the infamous gunfight at the OK Corral would take place.

CHAPTER 26

October 26th finally arrived. Bad luck, if you believe in such, had touched me…and in an unpleasant manner. I was escorting Kipp down the back staircase so that he could take care of his elimination needs, when I managed to get tangled up in the long skirt I was wearing. In many ways, this was a date on my calendar that had been waiting for my arrival. I grabbed at the handrail but failed to get a good grip and descended the last few steps in a rolling, acrobatic tumble. Fortunately, Kipp was a little behind me, so that I didn't take him out like a bowling ball striking a hapless pin. Naturally, he was horrified and frantically licked my face in an attempt to reassure himself that I hadn't broken my silly neck. To make a long story short, I managed to twist my ankle, severely enough to cause considerable pain. Kipp ran, in the fashion of Lassie, to bring Eli. Once I was back in my room, the local physician paid a visit and placed a menthol wrap on the afflicted joint.

I'd been conflicted over whether or not I wanted to view the gunfight. After years of traveling back and forth in time and experiencing all aspects of humanity, violence and death had no appeal for me, whatsoever. But Kipp was determined to view the events, if for no other reason than to weed through the various conflicting stories that had been handed down over the years.

I had misgivings about letting him go without me but knew his telepathic talents were so profound that he could look after himself. After all, I was his partner, not his mother, and in the end, I couldn't tell him what to do regardless.

During the early part of the day, we gleaned information from Eli as well as from our telepathic intrusion into the minds of the various townspeople who began to mill in small groups along the margins of Allen Street. It seemed that the brouhaha began at midnight when Ike Clanton and Doc Holliday had a confrontation at the Occidental Saloon. The building tension had fomented for days, with various members of the cowboy coalition making overt threats towards Doc as well as the Earp brothers. Frank McLaury had openly expressed his desire to kill Wyatt, while Ike Clanton made various levels of threats towards everyone he regarded to be part of the opposition. Wyatt had persuaded Doc to go to his room and cool down after the last challenge was made. In a town seething with hot emotion, it probably was beneficial to have the cool, controlled presence of Wyatt Earp.

The groundwork for the ultimate showdown was being set as morning stretched into early afternoon. Virgil caught Ike, with rifle in hand, sneaking down an alleyway and bashed him over the head with the barrel of his pistol. Virgil and Morgan dragged the senseless Ike to Judge Wallace's courtroom. When Ike finally recovered, he continued with his verbal threats against the Earps and was sufficiently rude and disrespectful to annoy the judge, who fined him for breach of the peace.

The citizens of Tombstone were divided in their loyalties: either one supported the cowboy element or was on the side of the vigilantes and the Earp brothers. Kipp and I, from our vantage point in the Cosmopolitan Hotel, continued our canvassing of opinions and musings.

"Petra, I really want to go out there and be a part of this moment in history," Kipp remarked. "I know you can't go and don't want to, even if your ankle was okay." He left the window and came over to join me where I lay on the bed with my bandaged foot propped up. I could feel the anxiety crawl up my back and willed my shoulders to relax. This was dangerous business.

"But why, Kipp?"

"If part of what we do is to see if recorded history and actual history are one in the same, I must see what happens." He nuzzled my hand. "I know it will be violent, aggressive and horrifying." Kipp looked up at me. "I'm ready for that."

I looked up at the ceiling and sighed deeply. "Okay, Kipp." With a grimace, I stood and hobbled over to the door, which I reluctantly opened. "I don't know where Eli is. You can probably go down the staircase and bark; sometimes the door is left ajar, and you can just push it open." I didn't look at him as he brushed past me.

"I'll be back," he promised, not glancing back as he trotted to the end of the hallway.

Since I was up, I hastily dressed for no particular reason other than it seemed to be the thing to do. My ankle was throbbing, and I sat down in the little anteroom to my suite. Kipp's thoughts, clear and vivid, filled my mind, and I saw everything as did he, just as if I were there.

Wyatt Earp and his brothers Virgil and Morgan formed a determined phalanx of tall men dressed in black as they walked with purpose down Allen Street. Doc Holliday, wearing a long, gray overcoat, met them in the street; his limp was forcing him to lean heavily on his walking stick. He expressed agitation at Wyatt, who told him the upcoming gun battle did not concern him.

"That's a hell of thing for you to say to me," Doc retorted. From the corner of his eye, Doc caught sight of Kipp and turned his head. His blue eyes searched for me, since I was usually inseparable from Kipp, and was relieved that I was absent since violence was about to erupt.

Virgil handed Doc a sawed off shotgun he'd procured from the Wells Fargo office and took Doc's walking stick. Doc was already armed with his nickel-plated Colt, but he wordlessly took the shotgun and concealed it up under the flap of his long coat. The quartet continued the walk down Allen; Doc was whistling some made up tune as he limped along. Pockets of people lined the street, knowing that a confrontation was inevitable. Most, if not all, had taken sides and there was more than one monetary wager on the outcome.

Doc's head went up as he saw an outlaw, Wes Fuller, dart up an alleyway. Glaring at Virgil, Doc remarked, "You ought to have cut him down."

Virgil, in his role of city marshal, wasn't about the business of shooting a retreating man, however, and the walk continued. Kipp weaved in and out of the collected spectators before he crossed Allen. Doc smiled at the other three men.

"We have a body guard," he laughed, gesturing at Kipp. The Earp brothers did not reply since they did not share Doc's fondness for the dog or his owner, in the form of one Petra Totheroh.

The four men, trailed by Kipp, were met in the street by an agitated Johnny Behan. He assured Virgil that he had disarmed the McLaurys, Billy Claiborne and the Clanton brothers. Wyatt's attitude was one of disbelief; none of the men present believed that Behan would escort the cowboys to jail, as he had promised, for a breach of the peace charge.

Kipp's impressions filtered back to me. "I think Behan really didn't want this to become violent. He thinks he temporarily defused the situation and at least partially disarmed some of the cowboys. But at the same time, he hates the Earps and resents their challenges to him and his authority."

Behan, meanwhile, failed to convince the Earps of his lawful intentions and turned to run ahead where he took refuge at Fly's studio on Fremont, directly across from the OK Corral. The Earps and Doc reached the corral yard; Doc dropped back from the group of brothers to block any flanking maneuver on the part of the cowboys, who were strung out in a line in front of an adobe wall at the west end of the corral lot.

Despite Behan's feeble intervention, both Billy and Ike Clanton wore holsters with one revolver apiece. Billy Claiborne, with the mind of a wannabe gunslinger, had a double holster rig with two guns. Frank McLaury was visibly armed, but his brother, Tom, was not. Their horses were tied, and the butts of rifles jutted up from the saddle boards.

Kipp crossed over and sat down on the boardwalk in front of Fly's. Turning his head slightly, he could see the outline of Behan behind the windowpanes; the man's thoughts were agitated and conflicted. Behan possessed a visceral hatred for Wyatt, which had intensified when Behan's lady love, Josie, left him and made it widely known around Tombstone that she was interested in Wyatt. Kipp's ears swiveled forward as he heard Virgil tell the assembled cowboys that they were under arrest.

I, of course, had been following the activities from my room. Normally, the distance and quantity of milling human thoughts would impair my telepathic accuracy, but my connection with Kipp was so intense, that the images were as clear as if I'd been present. Never having believed in intuition, I was unexpectedly overwhelmed with a sense that Kipp was in danger. As I sat there in the now familiar suite in the Cosmopolitan, the feeling grew in intensity. I was dressed, except for my shoes. Standing, I ignored the pain in my foot and shoved my feet into my boots. With as much speed as I could muster, I made for the rear staircase.

From the back alley behind the hotel, I headed towards Fremont and the corral. The gunfight was already over, having taken less than a minute from beginning to end. From Kipp's thoughts, I knew that Frank and his brother Tom both lay dead on the dusty floor of the corral. Billy Clanton had been killed, too. Morgan and Virgil were both seriously wounded, while Doc had suffered a minor bullet wound, when a shot fired by Frank McLaury scored a raw trough along the flesh of his back.

I drew within sight of the spectacle; a crowd was

gathering and voices were loud. The wisps of smoke from the fired guns hovered in the air like a thin fog, while the acrid smell of gun powder filled the air. It was then, on the far right side, hovering in the entry to an alley, I saw the shadowy figure of Ike Clanton. I might not have recognized him except for the quality and content of his noxious thoughts. His hand drifted down towards his holster, and I knew his plans: as a last evil gesture, he meant to shoot Kipp, who was busy watching the chaos from the front of Fly's studio. Kipp normally would have detected such a thing, but with the active and agitated thoughts of so many humans in a small area, Ike's toxic mental stew was passing unnoticed.

I started forward but was stopped short by a strong hand on my shoulder. Looking around, I saw the hand belonged to John Gold—or Johnny Ringo, the character he played so well in these violent times. Giving my shoulder a slight squeeze, John started forward at a rapid pace. He was within a few feet of Ike, who had drawn his gun and was targeting Kipp.

"If you don't put away that gun, Ike, I'm gonna shoot you where you stand." Gold had not pulled but his well-manicured finger tips were touching the butt of his revolver.

Ike was not sure of himself, but he was quite certain of Johnny Ringo. And he knew the man did not make idle threats. Kipp's head snapped around now that he heard the dialog, and his amber eyes widened. With a nod, he acknowledged Gold and the fact that his fellow symbiont, who had become a notorious and enthusiastic killer of men, saved his life. Ike turned and fled down the alley and was lost to sight in a few seconds.

I rushed forward into the melee while trying to minimize my limp. Doc was seated on the wooden boardwalk that helped to frame the entrance to Fly's. His head went up when he saw me.

"Petra, this is no place for you," he began.

Ignoring him, I said, "Let me help you up," and I slipped

my hand beneath his thin elbow.

An open ended buckboard rolled forward, and a group of men carefully loaded Morgan and then Virgil in the back.

"Take 'em to Morgan's house," Wyatt shouted. Then he turned to Behan, who had finally left Fly's studio and was staring ruefully at the bodies that lay sprawled in the dirt.

Behan began to tell Wyatt that he was under arrest, but Wyatt just turned and walked away. I saw the harsh, rigid expression on Wyatt's face and considered the fact Behan was probably lucky Wyatt didn't shoot him dead right there.

"Are you okay?" Wyatt asked, a small smile pulling at his lips, which were almost hidden beneath the thick mustache, as he looked at Doc.

"You know me, Wyatt. It will take more than a cowboy to put me away."

Doc, lacking his cane, allowed me to gently support his arm. Wyatt looked at me, his face composed and controlled in the midst of chaos, and lightly touched the brim of his hat.

"Obliged, ma'am," he said before walking away.

Kipp joined Doc and me and took a protective stance on the other side of the wounded gunslinger. As we made our way back towards the Cosmopolitan, I noticed that the streets cleared in front of our party.

"Well, Kipp, was it what you thought it would be?" I slowed my steps a little to accommodate Doc. His wound was not life threatening, but I knew it had to be painful.

"The courage of humans is remarkable," Kipp responded. "I'm not sure why anyone would want to face another armed person and try and dodge flying bullets." Kipp took a deep breath and nuzzled Doc's hand. "It is a cautionary tale for all of us to try and find reasonable ways to solve problems."

At the door of the Cosmopolitan, Eli darted out and relieved me of my burden. With as little dialog as possible, Kipp and I returned to our room. My ankle throbbed and my nerves were on edge after having witnessed the near shooting of Kipp, so I bypassed the sofa and collapsed on the bed. I'm not an overly emotional sort, but I began to cry.

Kipp hopped up and nestled next to me; somehow he managed to wedge his large skull under my arm so that my hand was on his neck.

"It's alright, Petra. Nothing bad happened to me."

I finally managed to sit up and pushed my tousled hair from my face.

"Kipp, once again you put yourself in danger. It's just not something I can deal with and stay calm and collected."

Kipp was wise enough to refrain from debating the subject and snuggled closer. Outside, the shadows were lengthening as the day began to make its journey towards evening and night. We stayed like that, quiet, in the dark room. There was an ongoing cacophony of voices as groups of citizens on the street continued to debate and process the shootout. Anger and agitation floated up to where I lay. A soft tap on my door disturbed my repose; I hesitated but a moment as I recognized the familiar thoughts of Eli and finally rose.

"Mrs. Totheroh," Eli greeted me, his gray eyes sober. "Doc Holliday is asking, ma'am, if you would meet him downstairs in the lobby. He said I should tell you he won't take up much of your time, but he desires to speak to you."

I didn't want to see Doc or anyone else associated with Tombstone, with the exception of John Gold. I owed him my gratitude for having saved Kipp. With a sigh, I told Eli to advise Doc I'd be down in fifteen minutes. The mirror betrayed my reddened, swollen face, and I dashed a little water from the basin and gently dabbed my skin with the towel. A gunshot rang out somewhere in town, and I dropped the towel to the floor. Kipp darted forward and picked up the cloth in his jaws.

"Here," he said, handing it to me.

In less than fifteen minutes, I descended the staircase and was directed by the clerk, who was someone other than Dent, to a small sitting room off of the main floor. The room was dimly lit, and the flickering light cast from the oil lantern caused shadows to dance on the walls. For a brief moment, I caught the pale profile of John Holiday, cast in relief. It was easy to see the handsome man he'd once been before the ravages of disease and evil deeds consumed him. Kipp followed my thoughts and the subsequent descent into sadness.

"He once knew joy," Kipp reminded me. And he would know, considering his telepathic journey inside the man's mind.

As I approached, the spare, lone figure of John Holliday stood. He had no hat to remove and merely bowed his head.

"Petra, my dear." A faint smile curved his lips. "I'm so sorry to disturb you in this rude manner, but I must speak to you before I leave to go to see to Morgan and Virgil." He gave a slight wince as he beckoned me to take a seat across from him. His eyes dropped to gaze briefly at Kipp.

"Things are about to escalate here, and I would feel relieved if you would leave Tombstone. I fear that anyone associated with me or the Earps will be a target, and I can't keep myself and the Earp brothers safe if I am worried about you."

I almost sighed with relief. Doc was giving me permission to leave and even encouraged that action.

I nodded my head. "I understand," I said, trying to meet the intense gaze of his eyes. Kipp came close and pressed against my knees. My fingers, which felt suddenly cold, found comfort as they combed their way through his dense pelt. "I will ask Eli to have a telegram sent to Tucson for the driver, Pete, who told me he would drive me anywhere at any time." I smiled, but it was a faint, shadowy expression.

"I would say that after all this is over, perhaps we could meet again. But, both you and I know that is not possible." Doc's eyes were bright. "You are a fine woman and deserve happiness." His face tilted down as he regarded his polished boots. "I think only death and tragedy follow me."

Kipp stood and walked over to Doc and placed his head

on the man's knees. Kipp's flag-like tail waved gently back and forth. Doc's eyes met his, and the two locked gazes for a long moment.

"Petra, I sometimes get the feeling that Kipp understands everything I think and feel," Doc commented.

"I know, John. I feel that way, too."

The stage jerked around a turn in the road from Tombstone to Tucson. Kipp and I were retracing the path that had brought us here what seemed to be years ago. I felt safe since Pete and Dave were at the helm, as before.

"Kipp, I was so preoccupied with your safety, that I lost track of your thoughts and impressions during the gunfight. What did you observe that might validate popular history or negate it?" I tried to stretch and change positions on the unforgiving bench seat. Across from me, Kipp was laying the length of his seat, gazing out the window at the passing vista.

"First of all, Behan wasn't entirely honest. He did confiscate weapons from the cowboys, but they had more pistols in their saddlebags. Behan, knowing them, couldn't have thought they would be unprepared." Kipp turned his head to look at me. "However, Tom McLaury wasn't armed initially; Morgan saw him move his hands towards his waist and honestly thought he was pulling a gun. After everything started, Tom tried to get a rifle from his saddle board, but it was too late by then."

"Why did Doc ask me to leave?" I asked, dropping my head back and staring at the ceiling of the rocking coach. We'd left at dawn, and I was enjoying the cooler ride than the one we'd experienced a few months earlier.

Kipp almost snorted. "You know why, Petra. He was trying to protect you. And the reason he didn't offer to meet you later, is because he thinks he will be dead shortly…either from a gunfight or the disease. He genuinely developed caring feelings for you."

It all made me sad. In my job, one had to learn how to

keep involvements at a distance, and I'd failed miserably. And on top of that, everything had been built on a collapsible pyramid of lies.

"It wasn't your fault, Petra, and you didn't encourage him. Doc, at this point in his life, needed to feel hopeful and inspired about something…and that something was you. He's a bad man who's led a desperate life, and you gave him a few weeks of happiness. I think he felt he made a difference in your life—and a positive one, too."

I knew I lacked Kipp's skills but also recognized the truth of what he said about Doc. My telepathic reading of John Holliday had revealed much to me. I would probably be thinking about these days and the events that had transpired for a long time.

CHAPTER 27

The trip home was uneventful. Upon our arrival in Tucson, I located a small, discrete boarding house where Kipp and I could withdraw from the view of the curious. My trunk, which had been courteously delivered by Pete and Dave, contained the garments I'd collected during the trip. I pushed a few things into my carpet bag/shoulder sling that Suzanne had created and left the other items in the trunk with a note that it should be delivered to dear Emily in the hope she could use some of the items to enrich her humble existence. Even though it was a violation of symbiont rules, I included several pieces of currency that would seem like a windfall to the girl.

I donned one of the dresses made for me in Tombstone, with the thought Suzanne would find the authentic garment fascinating, and began mental preparations for the time shift. Kipp, meanwhile, was busy relaxing and conserving energy. Looking at the small pile of belongings, I pulled out the blue hat given to me by one John Holliday, gunslinger and notorious killer of men. With a glance at Kipp, I placed the bonnet on my head and secured the ribbons beneath my chin. After placing what I chose in the shoulder sling and wrapping it tightly about my body, I took my place on the narrow single bed. Kipp hopped up next to me and began to focus.

* * *

Time travel, and the experiences one has during the journey, always changes the symbiont. Often, the change is positive and enriching—but, occasionally it's not. Even in the case of a vacation trip, we were always debriefed to a certain degree. I was lackluster and unmotivated, and the group who tried to glean information from me finally threw up their hands in despair. Kipp was much more accommodating than was I, and they finally left me alone and turned their inquisition on him. Suzanne, however, was delighted to get the few things I'd brought back and was fascinated with my blue bonnet, the one thing I told her she could not have. And I didn't bother to explain myself, either.

Part of my hesitancy to share had to do with the issues with Doc Holliday and my brief, but conflicted, association with him. But more to the point was the surprise of finding Fitzhugh's long lost nephew, John Gold, living the corrupted persona of Johnny Ringo. Even though I recognized he'd made his life choices, the symbiont in me despaired for one of my kind who was abandoned and unable to return home. I, too, had almost shared his fate, had it not been for the miracle of Kipp. And in the end, John saved my Kipp, so I would be forever grateful to him. What a shame such brilliance and potential would be wasted. And as history revealed, Johnny Ringo would be found dead, two years hence, under mysterious circumstances. So even though I just saw him and felt the touch of his hand on my shoulder, he was long since dead.

I'd even half wondered if John Gold would try to contact us again on our lonely trip from Tombstone to Tucson, but he didn't. I suppose there was nothing to discuss had he trailed our coach on that lonely stretch of hard packed road and pulled us over for a chat. Kipp knew the wanderings of my mind, of course, and monitored as I occasionally stared out the window of the coach, wondering and waiting for something that did not happen.

* * *

Time travel being what it is—an imperfect endeavor—I'd returned home during my favorite time of year, and that is mid fall. The leaves that year were breathtaking, and I spent every moment of my down time outside—either walking in my neighborhood or out in Duke Forest. So one brisk, bright Saturday morning, Philo called me.

"I'll be there in half an hour; we're going for a ride," he barked, in his typically bossy manner. Before I could accept or decline, he rung off.

Kipp looked at me from where he was sprawled on the kitchen floor. He'd eaten earlier and was licking his paws as a part of his morning ablutions.

"So, what does Philo want?" he asked. Kipp had been remarkably restrained since our return. Maybe, since he knew me best, he had decided to just let me percolate on my own without interference. A few times, he tried to enter and sooth the boiling cauldron of my mind but decided that it was not, uh, soup yet, and departed with alacrity.

"He wants to take a ride," I commented.

I put on my sweatpants and an old sweatshirt that had a stain on the front from where I'd made lasagna a couple of years ago. No matter what the commercials advertise, there are just a few food stains that won't be budged. It looked sloppy and horrible, but I didn't care. Kipp followed me into my room.

"I'm ready," he announced, executing a funny little half bow, knowing he sounded silly as he said it.

"Bravo," I replied, arching a dark eyebrow.

My brain tingled, and I knew Philo pulled up outside; there was no need, of course, to honk the horn. In less than a minute, Kipp and I squeezed into his tiny Honda, and he jerked away from the curb like a racehorse leaving the starting gate.

To my surprise, he didn't launch into an accusatory interrogation. Instead, he shared some funny and odd stories of things that had happened while I was gone.

"They're still trying to convince someone to take Andrea's place on the Twelve, since she was, uh, relocated." Philo darted a glance at me.

"Why don't you do it?" I asked. "You have the knowledge base and temperament," I added.

Philo shrugged his shoulders. "They want young blood. But in any case, I want less of that sort of thing and more of something else. I'm actually thinking of joining Fitzhugh in the library and helping with his research." He paused for a second. "Peter is helping on a clerical basis but really can't do what Fitzhugh needs."

Philo yanked the wheel of his car to avoid a pothole, and Kipp went flying across the back seat.

"Hey, watch it," Kipp cautioned. "Not all of us in the car are using a seat belt."

"Sorry," Philo muttered, looking in the rear view mirror at Kipp's face. As an effort to mend bad feelings, Philo partially lowered his window so that Kipp could enjoy the breeze in his dog-like way.

We chatted on about things having to do with Technicorps, and Philo even casually mentioned some things about his family. I knew his wife and two sons, one of whom was my age and a fellow traveler. Finally, we arrived at Duke Forest and parked at one of the entrance points. Within a minute, we disappeared into its colorful depths.

Kipp, enjoying his freedom, darted ahead. There were some low lying bushes that were tipped with autumnal flame. As Kipp stood in front of them, his auburn coat caught a ray of sunlight that was filtering through the trees and he looked as if he was on fire.

I glanced at Philo. "Thanks, I needed this."

He reached over and squeezed my shoulder. We trudged along the trails, picking, as was my preference, the less taken pathways. Kipp would run ahead and then rejoin us, his tail wagging with joy.

We finally reached my favorite spot—the copse of trees that seemed backlit with an odd, silvery glow. I sat on a fallen oak; Philo, after checking for spiders and other creepy crawlies, sat, too.

"I appreciate the fact you've not pushed me since I've been back," I commented.

Philo held up his hands. "I didn't bring you here for that."

I smiled at him and reached out to lightly touch his arm. "I know. But I think it's time to talk about it."

Kipp finished his ramblings and returned to us; after a brief inspection of the ground, he circled and plopped on a bed of crisp ferns. His bright amber eyes stared at my face.

"Kipp is an amazing traveler," I remarked. "I thought I was good in partnership with Tula, in terms of our accuracy, but Kipp is spot on." I gazed down at my lupine partner. "He's truly remarkable and a gift—and in more ways than one." I took a deep breath. "We discovered he can go into repressed memory banks of humans—as well as symbionts—and retrieve thoughts that are not active."

Philo's eyebrows raised, but he said nothing.

"And he can block thoughts of a symbiont if there is an unwelcomed telepathic intrusion into the mind of another." I reached down to brush some clinging debris from my sweats. Looking up, I half closed my eyes in response to the almost painful brightness of the fall canopy of leaves overhead. A pleasant breeze caressed my face and caused the leaves to rustle energetically. The forest had the smell of fall; one could detect the impending death of the foliage.

"And how would you know that, Petra?" Philo asked.

I didn't answer immediately, so Kipp took over.

"We ran into a symbiont in Tombstone, someone who should not have been there." Kipp licked his paw, a gesture I'd come to recognize as a pause while he was gathering his thoughts. "It was John Gold, the nephew of Fitzhugh."

Philo wore a look of amazement and curiosity. "He disappeared a long time ago." Then Philo frowned. "I hate to say it, but he was a loose cannon…brilliant and talented but completely out of control."

Kipp commented wryly, "Well, then, nothing has changed. He assumed the life of an outlaw."

"And Ula?" Philo asked. "I know she would not have cooperated with such goings on."

"No, she abandoned him," I replied, finding my voice. Briefly, I shared the sad tale of John Gold. "But in the end, he saved Kipp from being shot, so I am in his debt."

"Is that what has left you so disturbed?" Philo asked.

I sat so long without replying that he finally started to stand; I held out my hand and stayed him.

"I don't know, exactly. Our main contacts were with two individuals and both were tragic and sad, given to a life of evil and despair. John Gold, as Johnny Ringo, was one. And, yes, leaving him behind was difficult. I keep thinking that if the story is true, he killed himself two years after we left."

"Or someone else did the job," Kipp commented. Rising, he came forward to rest his big noggin on my knees. I leaned forward and pressed my cheek against the top of his head. "He had an impressive list of enemies," Kipp added.

"And for whatever reason, Doc Holliday was drawn to me and became my confidant and protector. It was as if I symbolized the parts of him that could be good, kind and patient, while the other side of him was a killer." I sighed deeply.

"Doc already was conflicted but was too deeply imbedded in his role of gunfighter to make any changes," Kipp explained. "Petra's presence made him think about his choices instead of losing himself in an alcoholic stupor all the time." Kipp looked up at Philo. "It was sad."

"You returned everything to Suzanne, as is customary, since things go to the archives or vault," Philo commented. "She complained you had a blue bonnet that you refused to give up. Suzanne talked with me and started to file a formal request for it but I told her not to." His dark eyes found mine. "Did Doc give you the hat?"

Wordlessly, I nodded.

"And she looked real pretty in it, too," Kipp chimed in.

"Oh, shut up, Kipp," I said, a trifle crossly. I didn't care for being embarrassed.

He opened his jaws and gave me a brief, but impressive love bite on my wrist.

Philo stood and, after brushing away the debris and crushed leaves on his pants, held out a hand to me.

"Travelling is not for the faint of heart," he said, his voice mild. "It takes a toll, every time you go, and that is why it is a game for the young." His face was relaxed. "I will block all thoughts of John Gold. There is no reason for Fitzhugh to know anything about it."

I relaxed my shoulders; unexpectedly, they had scooted upwards with tension. Rolling my head from right to left, I took a deep breath and exhaled.

"Thanks."

"Petra, are you finished with that translation yet?"

The voice of Fitzhugh disturbed my concentration, and it was with effort that I refrained from replying that if he would leave me alone, I could spend my time working instead of answering him. I heard his familiar steps as he approached me from the rear of the library. Oddly, I was learning to like this place. The dark green walls, that were painted the color of some Victorian mausoleum, combined with the musty smells of old manuscripts to create a coziness that could not be found elsewhere in Technicorps.

Lily, having awakened from her feline slumber, darted between my ankles and tried to sharpen her claws on my kneecap.

"Ouch, you little devil," I cried, reaching down to peel her off. Behind, me, Fitzhugh chuckled.

"Hurts when she does that," he commented.

I turned and looked at his face. We'd unexpectedly become close, and I felt a growing fondness for him. I knew he would not go searching my brain in violation of symbiont rules, but nonetheless, I kept my thoughts of his nephew, John Gold, deeply hidden.

"I brought you some tea," Fitzhugh added, setting down the dainty china cup. The mild fragrance of bergamot floated from the vessel, hidden in a whiff of steamy vapor. I took note that Fitzhugh no longer chided me to take care and not spill a beverage on his precious parchments. Maybe his trust was growing.

Before I could thank him, the door to the library pushed open and Kipp stepped inside. Lily abandoned me and went over to arch her body against his long legs.

"How's your day?" I asked.

Kipp came over and propped his head on my table where I was working.

"Well, I actually am enjoying the in-house job they gave me. It's fun, interesting and challenging. And I like thinking that I make a difference."

Philo convinced the Twelve that Kipp's gifts made him the perfect tutor for the next generation of young lupines who would eventually become travelers.

"Juno and I are working together to teach them how to read English," he added. Kipp crossed his eyes. "Not easy, let me tell you."

I laughed softly.

"Can I expect any written information from you two about your trip to Tombstone?" Fitzhugh asked. "You know, we always need to update our historical records, even if it is merely a vacation trip."

I took a deep breath and looked at Kipp. My hand reached out to tug gently on his upright ears.

"No, Fitzhugh, I don't think so. We didn't find anything unexpected, and there were no mysteries to uncover."

The old symbiont nodded.

"Let me know if you want some more tea," he said, his voice trailing off as he disappeared into the stacks.

I looked at Kipp and he nodded.

"Tombstone is closed." His eyes brightened. "Where are we going next?"

*Turn the page for an
excerpt from*

WHITECHAPEL,
1888

The Symbiont Time Travel
Adventures Series

Book Three

❖

T.L.B. Wood

With Kipp and Vashti secured in the four wheeler, we made the short trip to Regent's Park. Unhurried, we toured the flower walk as well as spending some time listening to the band. There were many people who had shared our notion; a couple of children propelling hoops with sticks raced by. To the left, a large field of thick green grass expanded to cover a small hillock. Kipp and Vashti decided to play dog and chased one another in circles as well as trying to engage some true canines in play. The dogs knew the lupines for what they were but appeared to decide that a game was a game, after all, and most of them entered into the robust activity. Harrow led me to a vacant bench as we sat to watch. I was laughing when I became aware that Harrow was watching me intently. Turning my head, I boldly met his eyes.

"Yes?" I asked.

"I think I just enjoy watching you when you are happy," he replied.

It was an intimate reply, and I turned my head away in confusion. Maybe going on an outing was not a good idea. But as Kipp had said, whether I did so or not, Harrow's attraction to me was indisputable. Purposefully, I had limited my telepathy when with him, not liking the unfair advantage it gave me over him. I was left as unguarded as any human female might be when navigating the uncertain waters of the human heart.

Harrow cleared his throat. "I must make a brief trip to my family's home," he said. I noticed he took care to not call it "my" home. "I thought it might be a pleasant trip for you and Silas—and Kipp and Vashti, too—so that you could see more of England than just London." Obviously the fact that we were peculiar Americans who were strangely attached to our dogs had settled in with the man.

"That sounds nice, if you're certain we would not be a burden," I responded. "I will leave it to you to discuss it with Silas and make the plans, if he is in agreement." There, I thought, feeling very self-satisfied. If I left the decision making to Silas, then I could not question my own motives.

Unexpectedly, I became aware of some disturbed thoughts emanating from someone in close proximity to our location—sufficient in their intensity that my attention was grabbed despite the fact my telepathy was aimless and unfocused. The anger and unquenchable lust for violence almost left me breathless as I struggled to control my emotional response. Without being obvious, I turned my head and scanned the nearby crowd of people. The thoughts were decidedly male, and it only took me less than a minute to recognize the familiarity to what I'd learned about Jack the Ripper by reading his letters to the police and media. What I heard, echoing in the back of my head, were the early musings of the man who would one day be called Jack the Ripper. He was walking through the dense cluster of people, much like a wolf among sheep, thinking of how he would like to target some of them for his particular style of torture and murder. My heart rate began to accelerate as well as my breathing.

"Petra, are you well?" Harrow asked, as he peered at my face with worry. "You are very pale and your hands are shaking." He reached out and took my hands in his as if to steady me.

I tried to smile at him. "Perhaps I am a little overheated…maybe some lemonade?"

He was off in a flash, and I took the opportunity to get Kipp's attention focused on the thoughts of the unidentified man who was circling nearby. Turning my head again, I tried to unobtrusively locate the man but was unable to connect a face to the agitation swirling in the air. Kipp darted up at that moment.

"I hear him, too, Petra," Kipp said. His fur bristled in an automatic response to a threat. Vashti followed close behind; her head went up as her nostrils flared. It was with great effort that both lupines controlled showing their teeth in an aggressive reaction. A moment later, the thoughts began to dissipate; the man must be leaving. Stalking prey like he did in the park was just a preamble to an escalation of what was to come later. I could follow the sick, sexual perversion of his mind and recognize that as with all such budding serial killers, the mere act of walking and thinking about killing people would eventually fail to satisfy his urges. He would, and much too soon, have to act on the thoughts in order to meet the demands of his twisted mind.

——————◆——————

WHITECHAPEL, 1888
available in print and ebook

THE SYMBIONT
TIME TRAVEL ADVENTURES
SERIES

T.L.B. Wood began her appreciation of literature at an early age, encouraged by her mother who was an English teacher. T.L. is a certified adult behavioral health clinical nurse specialist and works as a case manager as well as a clinical instructor at a school of nursing. She and her husband share a love of nature, and more than one rescued dog or cat in need of a caring family has found a forever home with the Wood Family. When not feeding and caring for her menagerie, T.L. can be found at her desk, writing, or taking long walks as she envisions new stories to be told.

You can contact T.L. through her publisher at
TLBWood@epublishingworks.com